a *Deal* with the *Earl*

D1738990

SADIE BOSQUE

First edition

Editing by Tracy Liebchen
Cover art by The Brazen Wallflower Designs

This book was professionally typeset on Reedsy.
Find out more at reedsy.com

Prologue

Julie Weston's diary

June 5th, 1808

It was love at first sight.

He was five, and I was four. He fell into the lake while fetching my hat, then he climbed out with a grin on his face and my hat in one hand. "Is this yours?" he asked me, waving it all the way to the shore. I giggled. He was the handsomest boy I had ever seen. And that was the moment I realized he was going to be my husband. Now, thirteen years later, it is finally going to come true. We are eloping at dawn.

1

J ulie sat on the bed, fidgeting fiercely. It was the day John had finally come back from school, the day would change the direction of the rest of her life. Finally, they would elope and start their happily ever after, just like in the fairytales. She would get Mary back, and they would be out of her father's reach.

Julie closed her eyes, imagining the merry scene: John waiting for her at the end of the aisle, his handsome face lit with his boyish smile.

As the third son of a local baron, John had little in the way of capital. He had always promised he would get a job in a solicitor firm in London after finishing school. As a general clerk or assistant, he'd be able to support their little family.

She cared not about any of that. As the daughter of a marquess, she had never lacked luxuries, but none of those luxuries mattered to her more than a life with John. He was her lifelong neighbor and friend. Her hero, her confidante, and soon, he would be her husband. She would give all the world's wealth to finally be with him.

A knock on her balcony doors made her jump. She looked up to find John's beloved figure standing on the other side. He had gotten taller since she saw him last. He had always been a couple of inches shorter than her, which she found endearing.

Now, as she walked to the doors and opened them, she had to tilt her head back slightly to look into his beautiful hazel eyes. She held his gaze for an enchanted moment before falling straight into his arms. She snuggled closer to him and ran her hands up his back. He was still lean and well-muscled, and he smelled like clover leaves and horses.

"How happy I am to see you," she said against his shirt.

2

Acknowledgement

To my fabulous Beta readers:
  Nicole Yost
  Jes Ekker
  and Michelle Lokeigh

Special thanks to my critique partner, and an amazing author, Diana Bold

The story would not be the same without you. Thank you for making my experience in publishing a novel unforgettable.

Author's note

This work of fiction contains adult content, strong language, violence, off-page death, bullying, nightmares, pregnancy, and miscarriage.

Reader discretion is advised.

To my elder sister, Aida. I wouldn't be here if not for you.
Thank you, for supporting me in every endeavor.

Contents

He cuddled her close to his heart, then gently nudged her chin up, placing a soft kiss on her lips. Taking her by the hand, he led her to sit on the edge of her bed.

"How are you, sweetheart?" he asked.

Julie laid her head on his shoulder. "Better now," she half-whispered.

They sat in companionable silence, a silence she didn't want to break. Yet she had to.

John laced his fingers with hers and squeezed her hand as if he sensed she needed his courage and strength.

"Father is planning to take me to London in three weeks to prepare for my debut," she finally said.

"We can't let that happen." His arms tightened around her, hugging her closer. "I am not letting you go," he whispered into her hair.

"Good." She sat up abruptly, twisting to look at him. "Let's elope on the morrow."

"We can't leave tomorrow." He looked at her with those serious hazel eyes of his. "We haven't got enough funds. Where are we to live?"

"We'll rent a place, something small and cheap."

"I've saved up my allowance," he explained with furrowed brows. "But it's not enough, Julie. Maybe for the first month or so, but then what?"

"We'll work," she reasoned, looking up at him pleadingly.

"I shall." He brushed his knuckles over the apple of her cheek. "But you—you are not used to labor. I can't ask that of you."

She frowned at him. "I can teach. I can sew. I am not useless."

"I didn't say you were." John looked at her with nothing but adoration reflected in his eyes. "I just want the best life for you."

"The best life for me is with you," she said earnestly, her eyes filling with tears. "I'll do anything to stay with you!"

John looked into her sad eyes, then down at her lips. He lowered his head slowly, giving her the sweetest kiss. He brushed his lips over hers several times until she started copying his movements and kissing him back.

He had never kissed her like this before. The kiss was warm, wet, and confusing. It felt urgent, yet somehow gentle. He suckled her lower lip between his and snaked his arm around her waist before moving it lower.

A knock sounded at the door, startling them apart. "Julie, it's your father. Open the door!" called the threatening male voice from the other side.

"I-I am already in bed," she called with a stammer.

"Open the door this moment, or I'll break it down!" her father shouted through the door.

"Fine," she said, trembling. "I'll get dressed."

"Now!" he roared.

John stood and hurried to the balcony doors with Julie. He turned to her as he reached the threshold.

"Let me make all the preparations on the morrow, and we can elope the next morning. What do you think?" he asked, brushing his palm over her cheek.

"Very well," she murmured and stood on tiptoes to give him a kiss.

He lowered his head to meet her lips and brushed them softly with his.

"I love you." With these words, he turned and climbed over the balcony railing.

"I love you," she whispered into nothingness.

"This moment, Julie!" her father bellowed again from behind her door.

Julie put on her dressing gown and hurried to open it.

"Why did it take you so long to open the damned door?" Norfolk demanded, charging into her room, looking around.

"I was sleeping," she lied.

He looked up at her. "I know for a fact that you are lying," he snarled.

"I am not!"

"Then the boy who climbed up to your balcony was not here just now?" he yelled at her, getting red in the face.

Julie blanched. "There was no one here!" she cried in desperation.

"You lying little whore!" He grabbed her painfully by the arm. "If you think I would let that mongrel anywhere near you, think again!" he snarled in her face. "Do you want to live like a pauper? Or do you want a child like Mary?" He said the last with disgust twisting his face.

"There is nothing wrong with Mary!" she yelled back at him. "And I'd rather be poor than living with someone like you!"

"You ungrateful bitch." He threw her toward the bed, and she fell heavily, hitting her head on the bedpost. Sharp pain originating in her skull radiated through her entire body. "We are leaving for London tomorrow."

"No!" she yelled.

"And if you are carrying that mongrel's child, I promise you I shall find a way to get rid of it!" With these ominous words, he stormed from her room, shutting the door behind him with a slam that made Julie flinch.

She scrambled to sit against the bed, tears streaming down her cheeks. She hugged her knees, tucking her forehead against them. Julie sat crying for several minutes before her tears dried and simple reason started penetrating the thick fog of despair.

She was wasting her time crouching on the floor, feeling sorry for herself. What she needed was a plan. Yes, she was going to collect her most necessary belongings and run away at dawn.

John always took his morning rides early, before anyone else awoke. She would meet him in the field, and they would run away before her father figured out that she was missing. Julie stood gingerly and went to the washbasin to clean the blood from the injury at the back of her head.

She packed her unmentionables, a couple of gowns, a cloak, shoes into her valise. Then collected all the coins she had into a single purse before placing it all next to the bed. She dressed hastily into her simplest, sturdiest gown and lay down under the covers, waiting for the dawn to come.

Julie tossed and turned, unable to shut her eyes from the excitement of the night. Instead, she stood and walked over to the writing desk, flipping through her diary. The diary she'd started writing after the worst year of her life. To deal with her grief and loneliness, she'd written down all her childhood memories, so she would never forget that at one time, she'd been happy.

She flipped the pages absentmindedly, reading silly anecdotes of her and John climbing trees, jumping into the lake, and chasing the dragonflies. Playing with Mary, reading to her...

Her eyes filled with tears, and she blinked them back. There was no use crying now. She needed to act. Julie picked up a quill, dipped it into an inkwell, opened the diary to a fresh page, and started scribbling.

Her brief entry finished with the decisive words: *We are eloping at dawn.*

* * *

Julie dozed on and off several times during the night. She couldn't let herself fall fully asleep and lose her moment of opportunity. As soon as the first light of dawn touched the sky, she scrambled out of bed, threw her valise out the window, climbed over her balcony railing and down the trellis outlining the wall.

When she hit the ground, she looked around for a moment before running with all her might toward the field where she knew she would find John. She couldn't risk being detected if she took a horse from the stables. So, she ran, panting, the valise dangling in her hand.

She was sweaty and out of breath when she finally saw the outline of John riding his horse. Her depleted strength suddenly found new wings, and she ran to him as fast as her legs would carry her, screaming for him to turn around. Her hair tumbled from the knot at her nape and was getting in her face as she ran. Her gown wove between her legs, almost making her trip. She probably looked a fright, but she didn't care.

At that moment, John turned and spotted her. He turned his horse toward her, and a few short moments later, they were reunited.

"What happened?" he asked, jumping off the horse before

it even slowed its pace.

"My father," she said, breathing heavily and shaking. "He-he saw you last night."

"What?"

Julie was still catching her breath, so she just nodded, gulping for air. "He's taking me to London today. In a few hours," she said, frantically clutching at his arms. "Unless you take me instead. Right now."

"Don't fret, Julie." He took her gently by the arms and ran soothing hands over her upper arms. "It's going to be fine. We'll leave," he said in a gentle voice.

"Now," Julie begged, her heart clenching in fright.

"Now," he repeated quietly.

Julie closed her eyes in relief, but before she could express her joy, they heard horse's hooves coming upon them quickly.

John hugged her to him and whispered in her ear, "Climb up on the horse and leave. Now. Gallop as fast as you can. I'll catch up to you."

"But—" Julie's eyes widened in horror, then filled with tears.

"Don't argue, sweet. Go, now!" He nudged her toward the horse again as he stepped between her and the rider.

Julie scrambled to do as he commanded.

"Don't you dare mount that horse, Julie!" her father sneered as she was about to grab the horse's reins.

Julie froze with her hand mid-air, too frightened to turn around and face him.

"She's old enough. She doesn't want to live with you," John said in a loud, autocratic voice she hadn't heard him use before.

"The law says she's not. And who do you think you are to dictate to me?" The marquess's voice grated on Julie's nerves.

She turned around to say a few choice words to him herself, but what she saw made her heart stick in her throat. Lord Norfolk had a pistol trained on John. "Yes," he continued, seeing her fear-stricken face. "I'll kill him before you make a single step."

"You wouldn't!" she yelled.

"Oh, trust me, I would!" Norfolk sneered back. "And no judge will prosecute me for killing my daughter's kidnapper and rapist."

"He is not—" she began fiercely.

"Who are they going to believe? You? Him?" He didn't even attempt to hide his disgust while indicating John with a tilt of his head. "Or me, the marquess?"

Julie's nostrils flared in anger, but she couldn't do or say anything. She felt paralyzed.

"Be a good girl now and climb my mount." Norfolk indicated the horse with a wave of his pistol. "And we'll leave with everyone's limbs intact."

"I shan't let you!" John took a step forward.

"Careful, youth. Who's going to protect her if you're dead?" Her father smiled menacingly. "Now, Julie! Climb the horse. You don't want your brave knight dead now, do you?"

Julie swallowed hard and walked forward to her father's horse.

"Julie, no!" John's voice was hoarse with emotion.

Julie turned to him and regarded him with sorrow-filled eyes. Then she silently shook her head and climbed atop the horse. Several moments later, she and the marquess were galloping toward their house, with John still standing there staring after them.

Her father dragged her by her hair inside the house, up the

stairs, and into the late marchioness's room.

"You will stay here," he sneered at her. "Until I nail those balcony doors of yours shut!" He turned to leave the room, pausing at the threshold. "Then, I want you to pack your bags properly. I am going to marry you off to someone as quickly as possible."

Julie couldn't even gather a gasp of air to respond before he left the room and shut the door with a loud thump. A minute later, she was aware of two footmen being stationed outside the door.

She knew that the marquess himself slept in the next room, adjoined by the dressing room. She was trapped.

Julie looked around silently, her gaze falling to the bed. She shook her head from the assailing memories. She was indeed trapped in the most horrifying room of the house.

* * *

Contrary to the marquess's threats of leaving for London immediately, Julie stayed in the marchioness's room for the next three days. She was afraid to breathe or make any extra noise, not daring to draw any attention to herself. She prayed he would forget about her and start acting as if she didn't exist, as he had before. She studied the room carefully for exits, but there were none. There wasn't even a balcony. Both the windows led to a twelve-foot drop directly into the willowy bushes.

The housekeeper brought her food, but otherwise, no one spoke to her. Everyone else was prohibited from entering her room—or cell was more like it. The footmen changed guard every few hours, but two were always stationed outside her door. The valise Julie had tried to escape with was not given back to her, so she didn't even have her diary to pass the time. She wasn't allowed books or any other entertainment or occupation.

Julie was sure she would slowly lose her mind. The imprisonment itself might not have much impact, besides skull-numbing boredom, but *where* she was imprisoned played tricks with her conscious mind. The nights were the worst. She could practically hear her mother's screams—see all that blood again, her ashen, fear-stricken face. She couldn't possibly sleep in that bed.

Instead, she dragged the coverlet over and lay on the floor by the bed, facing the door for the few meager hours she managed to sleep. Mostly she sat curled up on the floor, singing to herself, like she used to sing to Mary when her little sister was distressed. She cried herself to sleep every night, praying for angels to save her, for John to find a way to break her free, for her father to forget her existence.

No angels seemed to be interested in her plight, however. Three days after her imprisonment, she was sent back to her room. Her bags had been packed, and all her belongings were missing from the drawers. She frantically searched for the letters John had sent her throughout his Eton years, but she only found one charred corner of a letter by the hearth.

Norfolk had burned them all. *How dare he?* She took the charred piece of paper and stared at it for a long while until it blurred in front of her eyes, and tears started falling on her hands.

She was still sitting, crying by the hearth, when she heard a soft knock on the French doors leading to the balcony.

Julie spun and saw John. For a moment, she couldn't believe

her eyes. She froze, thinking she was hallucinating. But he knocked again and smiled sadly. Julie leaped from her seat and nearly crashed through the balcony doors. Only they were nailed shut.

"John," she whispered, frantically touching the glass doors.

John put his fingers against the frosty glass on the other side from where she was touching them.

"John," she repeated with a shaking voice, "I thought I'd never see you again."

John lowered his head as if in guilt. Worry creased her forehead, and she stepped even closer to the doors.

"What is it?" She shoved the words past the growing lump in her throat.

"I'm leaving tomorrow," he said, his voice hoarse.

"What?" Her voice grew frantic. "Where?"

"The army." A pause. "Your father—he helped buy me a commission."

"He is sending you to the army. Because of me?"

"Julie—" John closed his eyes in agony. "I wish there was something I could do. But my father regards this as a gift from heaven. Many dream of buying a commission to the queen's army."

"But not you." A lone tear streaked down her face. "Please, not you." Her last plea was almost inaudible.

He looked at her, his eyes glinting with unshed tears.

She stared back, tears falling down her cheeks. "He's going to marry me to someone else."

"He can't force you." His voice cracked.

"Like he can't force you?" She laughed bitterly. Then she sobered and shook her head, taking a step back from the doors. "Come back to me," she pleaded. "Come back safe, so

12

we can be together again."

"I shall," he vowed. "Maybe in a year or two, but I'll come back. Promise you will wait for me?"

As if he even has to ask.

"I promise." She swallowed the lump in her throat and lowered her forehead to the door. John mirrored the action. They stood like that for a long while, praying to see each other again. Praying to be together again.

"I promise." The words echoed between them.

Chapter 1

December 15th, 1811.

Robert woke up surrounded by red satin sheets. He rubbed his eyes and turned his head to see a beautiful brunette sitting at the vanity, brushing out her hair. Her red silk dressing gown gaped open to reveal her enticing décolletage.

"Good morning," she murmured, noticing his intense stare.

"Good morning, beautiful," Robert said in a rugged voice. "Why are you up?"

"Because it's mid-morning and I am hungry," she answered, still staring at her reflection.

Vanessa loved her reflection more than she loved anything else. She could spend hours staring into it.

"Well, maybe I am hungry too." Robert stood from the bed and sauntered toward her. He stopped just behind her, his hips at her eye level in the mirror. "But not for food."

Vanessa glanced at his reflection and licked her lips, clearly aware of what he was hungry for.

"Well?" he asked, placing his hand on her hair and rubbing it slightly.

She turned to him and stared at his raging erection. She licked her lips again. "I suppose I could overlook breakfast for this," she said in a sultry whisper, still staring at his crotch.

"Indeed, you could." Robert started directing her head to where he wanted her when a knock sounded at her door.

She drew away, irritated, and stalked toward the exit. "What's wrong?" she asked the invisible entity just beyond the room.

Robert sat on the edge of the bed, staring at his mistress's curvy, inviting form. Her bottom was swaying, asking for his hands to touch her and for his—

She closed the door with a decisive click. "It's for you," she said, confusion wrinkling her brows.

Robert took an envelope with his father's seal on it and groaned inwardly. The Duke of Rutland rarely sent his summons, and when he did, he expected a prompt response. Robert tore into the envelope and read a few lines of the text he knew he'd find there. His father almost always used the same wording when he wrote to him.

Come to my study at once. There is an urgent matter to discuss.

That was all. No introduction, no goodbyes, no loving words. Just a cold and efficient summons. Robert stood and walked toward the chair with his clothes draped over it and started drawing on his shirt.

"You are leaving?" Vanessa pouted prettily. "What about my breakfast?" She looked mournfully at his deflating erection.

"We'll have to reschedule." Robert drew on his pants. "The

duke is expecting me."

"How long will you continue jumping at his every word?"

"As long as I depend on him financially. Which means, as long as he is the duke." Robert put on the rest of his clothes efficiently. When he was done, he walked up to Vanessa and placed a chaste kiss on her forehead. "I'll come when I can." With these parting words, he walked through the door.

He hadn't lied to Vanessa when he said that he depended on the duke as long as he lived. Most of his assets were from his father's estates, though Robert was the one who ran most of them. He also had several business ventures of his own. He loved the land, and he loved a challenge, so he always looked for ways to enhance their financial situation, even if it didn't need enhancing.

But Rutland was his father. As distant and cold as he was, Robert truly admired him. Rutland had a one-track mind. If he did something, he did it with his full concentration, without wavering. He stuck to his routine and never broke it. He was a truly remarkable person. Unfortunately, he never concentrated on his son and only looked for him when he needed something. Which meant that he needed his son now. And although Robert would never admit it aloud to anyone, he looked forward to these moments.

Robert reached his father's townhouse in half an hour and immediately walked to the study. He knocked three times and entered without waiting for an answer, just like he had been instructed to do since childhood. His father claimed he had no need for distractions and meaningless pleasantries.

The duke was sitting behind his grand mahogany table, dictating something to his secretary. Robert waited for him to finish. Finally, the duke let his secretary leave and gestured for his son to take his place.

"Clydesdale, you are right on time." Rutland had always called his son by his title, never his name. Not even when Robert was a child. "So, I gather my note reached you at your mistress's." He paused for emphasis. "Again."

"What do you want me to do? Be celibate?" Robert raised his eyebrow.

"No." The duke looked at his son thoughtfully. "I want you to get married."

Robert's eyes widened. It was the last thing he expected to be discussing today. He was seven and twenty. Much too young to marry by many gentlemen's standards. Of course, he had been willing to marry much earlier when he had fancied himself in love. Now, however, that was not the case.

"Why?" he asked.

"Because I am not getting any younger. I am not getting healthier, either. The doctor says my heart problem is back." He spread his hands in a nonchalant shrug. "And I want to see that you have an heir before I die." A pause. "Not just that, of course. You are already running most of the estates and doing all the work, and I want you to assume my place in Parliament as well."

"You don't look very ill to me," Robert protested.

"No, not yet. But I want to see how you handle yourself before I *am* too sick to do anything about it. I'll share the responsibilities in Parliament with you this year until you settle down. But next year, I want to retire to Hampshire for good." At Robert's raised brow, he continued, "It's warmer there. I don't want to spend winters in London anymore; the smoke isn't doing me any good. Or at least that's what the doctor says."

"What will you be doing there alone?" Robert frowned.

"Walk, fish, rest." He shrugged. "What do old people do with their time?"

"You're not that old."

"I am old enough. And you are old enough to get a wife. I was much younger than you when I took your mother as a wife." Seeing that Robert was about to protest, he put up a staying hand. "That is not the only reason. You cannot possibly take on all the burdens of the estate alone. Someone has to run the household, act as a hostess at your balls and soirees. You need a good and gently bred young wife who will help establish your weight in society. I know your peers respect you, but you need to win the respect of my peers for me to rest easily in my retirement."

Robert cleared his throat. "Your Grace, you know that after the last time—" The unpleasant memories of his last betrothal assailed him suddenly.

Rutland waved his hands impatiently. "I know, you don't want to get duped again. And I sympathize. In fact, I agree with you. You know how I feel about unnecessary emotions."

Robert scoffed. He didn't think the duke possessed said 'unnecessary' emotions.

"I think what you need is a marriage of convenience."

Robert narrowed his eyes in suspicion. The old duke had something up his sleeve.

"You know your mother and I married for that purpose. And, well, we had a pleasant life." The duke's eyes softened at the memory of his wife. The memory of her was the only thing able to soften the older man. For some reason, the duke was born without the ability for deep emotion. Still, Robert's soft and beautiful mother had coaxed even that out of him.

18

However, after she passed away, she seemed to have taken all his warmth and love with her. "That's exactly what you need."

"As you said," Robert started carefully. "With all the responsibilities of the estates, and since you want me to assume the seat in Parliament, I shan't have much time for scouring the balls for perfectly mannered young ladies. Besides, I'd rather not go through the courting."

"I agree," the duke said evenly. "Going through the season, then the courting and betrothal, all of it is a long and drawn-out process you don't have time to bother with. What you need is a marquess's or a duke's daughter, who is of an age and ready to marry a future duke."

Robert scoffed. *As easy as that, is it?* "Where am I supposed to find these ready-made brides, pray tell? Especially if I am to avoid the social whirl?"

"That's the best part. You don't have to," the duke announced almost cheerfully.

Robert stared at him. Rutland looked much too satisfied with himself. Which meant only one thing. He had found an extremely efficient way to solve his problem.

"One of the peers wants to marry off his daughter suitably. He reached out himself, offering his daughter for you," the duke said.

"Suitably," Robert drawled. "You mean into a good title and money?"

Rutland nodded. "You are a soon-to-be duke with a fortune. She is beautiful, young, and appropriately raised. Everything necessary for producing an heir." Rutland stated it in such a matter-of-fact tone that Robert almost chuckled.

Indeed, a beautiful woman and a rich man made the best heirs together. He supposed he was a walking example of that.

"Fine," he conceded.

Robert didn't want a wife. He didn't think he needed one either. He was happy going through his life as he was, with Vanessa available for his immediate needs whenever it suited him. But looking at the duke's self-satisfied smirk, he couldn't refuse. He probably still had that deep-seated need to please his father, to make him proud, to coax some sort of positive emotion out of him.

To be loved by him.

Besides, it wasn't like he was saving himself for some great love. If the duke had everything arranged, he needn't bother going through courting or otherwise applying himself. So he relented.

"I suppose I need to get married eventually in this lifetime. Why not now?" He shrugged. "Who is she?"

* * *

Julie was sitting in the library, curled up in a chair, a book on her lap. The library was vast, with little in the way of comfortable furniture. Aside from row upon row of books, there was a hearth at one end and the single leather chair she currently occupied. This and her bedroom were her two favorite rooms in the house, where she could hide away from reality. At the moment, however, reality weaved around her and seeped through her, inescapable.

She'd sat motionless, staring at the pages of the book without comprehension, ever since she received the letter from John. As an unmarried lady, she could not officially correspond with a gentleman unless they were betrothed.

Still, she'd bribed one of her maids to send the letters on her behalf. John's replies came in the same fashion, through the same maid. In the latest, he'd written that he was injured during his last battle and had spent several nights in the hospital, feverish, dreaming of her.

Her eyes glazed over with tears, but they wouldn't fall. What if he died? What if he never returned from the war? She couldn't let those thoughts get to her, but she couldn't chase them away either. When was the last time anything good had happened to her? She swallowed the lump in her throat. She couldn't think like that. He'd be back; he'd promised.

He would have been back several months before, but just as the time came for him to return, the war with Napoleon broke out, and the Crown called all the officers to the front lines. She couldn't help but be angry at fate for keeping him away from her. Keeping her away from happiness. She had managed to stave off her father's and chaperone's attempts at getting her married so far, but she knew it wouldn't last forever. Her father's patience would run thin, eventually.

She heard the doorknob turn, and then confident steps entering the room. Julie raised her head and saw her father a few feet from the doorway.

A frown creased Julie's forehead. Norfolk rarely sought her out. Despite his threats to marry her off as soon as John had left for the army, the moment Norfolk arrived in London, he had forgotten her existence. Or at least she had hoped that was the case.

Instead, he'd hired her a chaperone, Mrs. Darling, the most stuffy and stern woman he could find. He ordered her to guard Julie and not let her marry anyone below her station or a certain standard of wealth. The woman took the order to heart, not letting Julie dance—much less go for a ride with—a gentleman she didn't deem worthy of her charge.

Mrs. Darling's ambition was to marry her to a duke, a marquess, or an earl. With Julie's bloodline and upbringing, Mrs. Darling said these were the only titles that would do for her. Julie didn't protest; the woman was doing her a favor. Julie would not marry in any case. Not while she was waiting for John to return.

Now, as Norfolk was standing there in the doorway, wearing his bright red waistcoat and cream suit, unpleasant chills moved down her spine.

The season had yet to start. She'd thought she was free of her father's attention for at least another month.

She knew he wasn't happy with her lack of progress on the marriage mart, even if that wasn't entirely her fault. Ladies in their fourth season were almost certainly doomed to spinsterhood. But there was still a full month before the season. There was still hope that John would come back, and she wouldn't have to go through this season at all.

"There you are," Norfolk said in a jovial voice, breaking into her thoughts. "I requested your maids to pack. We are leaving for a house party in Hampshire in two days."

A house party, right before the start of the season? A sense of foreboding assailed Julie, and she licked her dry lips. "May I be excused from the party?" she asked, although she knew the answer.

"No, *my dear.*" Norfolk snarled the endearment. "I think I've been patient enough with you. I've given you three damned seasons to find a husband, and you've proven useless even in that. How difficult can it be to ensnare a husband? No matter," he answered his own question in a calmer tone, which only made Julie shiver even more. "Now, I am taking things into my own hands." He turned back toward the door and threw over his shoulder, "You are going to the house party. And you will be betrothed by the end." He paused at the door before turning the handle and walking out, leaving a horrified Julie staring after him.

Chapter 2

Travel to Hampshire was dreadful. Julie's father hadn't spoken a word to her, ignoring her as always. However, she had an eerie feeling he was studying her from across the carriage the entire time. She shielded herself with a book and refused to acknowledge him.

Her chaperone, on the other hand, was chattering all the way, just as she always did. Occasionally, she would mutter something under her breath when the carriage hit a hole in the road and her embroidery either slipped from her fingers or she messed up a loop.

Julie spent her time thinking and calculating ways she could leave the house party unattached. Throughout the years, she had come up with elaborate ruses to discourage the most eager of gentlemen who passed her chaperone's stern standards.

She learned rather quickly what put her in gentlemen's bad graces. Gentlemen disliked young ladies who had opinions of their own, who weren't afraid to be outspoken, and who pointed out gentlemen's flaws, as Julie did. Gentlemen, she noted, as a rule, liked their egos flattered. But even that wasn't always enough.

Lord Lansdowne, an old marquess, was most adamant to marry Julie, and she could not shake him off no matter what she tried.

He was fascinated with everything about her. Lansdowne was at least thrice her age, twice her girth, and generally smelled of rotting fish. He pawed her and slobbered all over her during dances, raked her with his lecherous gaze across the ballroom, and aspired to sit by her during every dinner. He had the rank and the influence to fit the bill for her father, and he was in need of a young heiress to bear his children. Out of desperation, she used the last card she had up her sleeve.

She unleashed a rumor about Mary.

She told the *ton* everything about her little sister. How she was born different, how their father sent her off to the asylum. Julie felt shame for using the innocent angel in such an atrocious way, but she had no choice. In order to fight for her future, she had to use everything at her disposal and all her wiles.

Unfortunately, the old marquess wasn't even dissuaded by it. She'd alienated every single person except for him. While the rest of the *ton* snickered behind her back, shunned her, and otherwise ignored her existence, he only pressed his suit. In fact, now that it was apparent she would not have another contender for her hand, he was most eager to marry her.

Where her earthly means had failed her, providence had intervened. Before any papers could be drawn for the betrothal, the marquess affected a sudden health issue. He had to withdraw to Bath to take to the healing waters.

That last effort to stave off the unwanted suitors had

worked, however. No one wanted anything to do with Julie. She spent the rest of the season a friendless wallflower.

Her father was furious, and her chaperone was scandalized. That's how Julie's latest season had concluded.

Julie wasn't looking forward to another season like the last one, but if her father had his way, she would be married before it even started. She feared Lansdowne was now in better health and would resume his suit. Was he the reason for their hasty Hampshire trip?

They arrived an hour before dinner. Julie's stomach was churning in hunger and agitation. She was afraid of what awaited her during the party and resolute not to show her state of rising anxiety. So, she changed and hurried toward the dining room.

"Do not hurry so, young lady. Ladies never hurry." The stern voice of an older woman made Julie pause as she reached the sitting room and was about to open the door.

She turned and saw a thin, white-haired old woman with the ramrod stature only the extremely well-bred possess. She wore a dark blue gown and a sapphire necklace hung on her wrinkled neck.

Julie curtsied. "Apologies, my lady," she murmured to the floor.

"Good, now hold that door open for me, would you?" the old lady commanded in a brisk tone while she shuffled into the room holding a walking cane.

Julie followed, closed the door behind her, and looked about the room to find the same people she'd seen hundreds of times during social events but not a friendly face among them.

Julie ambled toward her chaperone. Mrs. Darling was scanning the room for potential suitors like she always did.

"Look, there's Lord Ashton." Mrs. Darling tilted her fan toward a gentleman standing by the hearth in a group of men. "Isn't he nice?" She smiled artificially.

"He told me that women who read should be muzzled," Julie intoned evenly, although an unpleasant shiver ran down her spine.

Lord Ashton was another one of her suitors. The one she'd driven away with her sharp tongue.

"I don't know about all the women who read, but he wasn't wrong about you," the woman said in disgust.

Julie swallowed a retort and continued her search about the room for an escape.

And that's when she saw him. The most beautiful, impeccably mannered, incredibly charming man in all of London. All of England, perhaps. Her salvation. Viscount St. Clare.

He was also a known rake and libertine. He seduced everything female that moved, and bedded every lord's wife, sister, and daughter. Not only had he shamelessly ruined the reputations of dozens of women, but he also emphatically refused to marry them. He refused to duel over them either.

He was her ideal solution. The perfect escape. He would ruin her and refuse to marry her, as he had done so many times before. She would be free to live her life and wait for John. With those thoughts churning in her head, a calculating smirk tugged at her lips.

She was studying the beautiful face of her future savior when she caught the gaze of another man, standing to St. Clare's left. He was about a half-inch shorter than the viscount, with dark, almost black hair and opaque eyes. Julie couldn't make out his eye color from here, but she knew they were light, though not the viscount's light blue. He was tall and broad-shouldered, with stern features. Ladies probably swooned over his masculine appeal, but something about his cold, opaque eyes, and the way he was looking at her, made Julie shiver uncomfortably. He seemed too harsh, too forbidding, uncaring, just like her father. Julie hastily turned away.

It was uncommon, to say the least, to meet a man for the first time after three years in the social whirl. It wasn't as if men traveled extensively to the Continent with the war raging. Unless he was a soldier. Like John.

She turned to take a peek at him again, but he was gone. Giving one last look about the room, she concentrated her thoughts on St. Clare instead. How was she to seduce him? Should she ambush him or just come out and ask him directly to ruin her? An experienced rake, such as himself, got propositioned by ladies all the time, she was sure. The difference was that she didn't know what to propose. A liaison? A tryst? She had heard the words a few times, but she didn't know what they entailed.

Her thoughts were interrupted when the guests were invited into the dining room. A moment later, a low masculine voice rumbled beside her, addressing Mrs. Darling, and she gave a delighted chuckle in return.

Julie turned and froze in surprise. There, standing by Mrs. Darling, and looking intently at Julie, was the same stranger whose opaque eyes she'd been staring at but a moment ago. She blinked several times while her chaperone performed the introductions. The sitting room was filled with a loud buzz, and Julie was so busy gaping that she didn't hear the stranger's name clearly.

Had Mrs. Darling said *Clydesdale?* The name sounded

familiar. Julie curtsied, then extended her hand when he offered to escort her into the dining room. It would figure that the only person Julie wasn't acquainted with would be the one to accompany her to dinner. He wasn't aware of the rumors.

Julie was seated to the right of the stranger at the table. She sat only one spot away from their host, the Duke of Rutland, which was incredibly odd.

Julie looked at the other side of the table and saw the old lady who'd chastised her for walking too quickly just a few minutes ago. She must be the infamous Dowager Rutland then, the duke's mother. And to Julie's left, her stranger must be none other than the duke's only son.

Julie peeked at him beneath her lashes. He was as forbidding as the first time her eyes met his, but he was looking straight ahead now. Clydesdale. Yes, now she remembered; he was the Earl of Clydesdale and the future Duke of Rutland. Julie's heart started beating uncontrollably fast.

A duke's heir.

He was eligible by her chaperone's standards, and from what she'd heard of him, he regularly avoided events within the *ton*. Until now.

Julie's mouth went dry. Their travel to Hampshire wasn't a coincidence; she was certain of it. Something was very wrong.

The first course started with servings of mackerel with fennel and mint, and everyone ventured into eating and conversation. At the same time, Julie just stared fixedly at her plate.

"You don't like the food?" Clydesdale asked, his voice a deep rumble.

"Oh, no." She frowned. "It's wonderful."

The earl regarded her curiously. "You haven't tried it."

It was bad manners for him to indicate that, especially when she was trying hard to be polite. On the other hand, why should she bother? If her guess was correct, seating her next to him during dinner was a clear indication of his suit. She needn't be polite to him. She should dissuade him.

She shrugged and looked straight into his opaque gray eyes. "I detest mackerel," she said, although it was not the truth.

"You should have said so right away." He gestured for the footman to replace her plate with another dish. She breathed in deeply and delicately put a small piece of the new dish into her mouth. The earl studied her carefully while she chewed. Julie's mouth went dry under his intense perusal, and her throat closed, making it hard to swallow.

"Too dry," she said, as she finally managed to get the food past her throat and took a large sip of her wine.

"Would you like anything else?" Clydesdale asked, his tone all politeness.

"No," she choked out past her still dry throat. "I'll have more wine, though." She raised her glass, and it was immediately refilled.

"I am glad you find the wine to your liking." The earl relaxed in his chair, still watching her.

"I don't," Julie said, irritated. Would the man just leave her alone? "I've had much better." She noticed that a few people beside her were paying attention to their conversation.

Clydesdale regarded her quizzically. His intense gaze was still unsettling. "Have you?" he asked, idly toying with his fork, rolling it between his long, masculine fingers, as if contemplating stabbing her with it.

Julie lowered her gaze to the gesture before meeting his

gaze again.

He smiled coldly as if he'd read her thoughts. "This is port from Douro Valley; the best money can buy. As for the food, Chef Badeaux is the best chef on this side of the English Channel. We brought him from France ourselves and paid him a great deal. So, I know it is not his talent that is causing you trouble." He narrowed his eyes on her mouth. "Maybe the problem is in your tongue—"

Julie's eyes widened exponentially at that statement. It was improper to refer to ladies' body parts directly, but so far, the earl hadn't acted properly at any point.

"Too bitter." With these words, he turned away, leaving her gaping at him.

Julie quickly schooled her features and gulped the *best wine money could buy*, drowning the dry tickle in her throat. Her hunger evaporated like a puddle on a hot, sunny day. She felt decidedly uneasy. The surrounding voices blurred until she heard a single, distinct voice ring out over the din.

"… the Americans are asking for it!"

Julie turned to Lord Bingham, who sat to her right. His face was red, presumably from too much wine, his eyes glinting with excitement.

"They did this on purpose, I tell you. That captain of theirs just shot at our sloop, which was small and defenseless. We—the lords—should not let it stand and press our government to do something about it."

"They think that just because we are at war with Bonaparte, we are too busy to avenge the *Little Belt*," another lord chimed in. He was young and eager to put his tuppence worth into the heated conversation. "But we can do both, kick Boney out of the Continent and show the Americans who they are

31

dealing with."

What were they talking about? Julie frowned in thought. *Little Belt Affair?* Julie read the papers almost reverently, trying to glimpse the battlefield John was on. Hoping to read that the war had ceased, and the soldiers were on the way back home. During one of those times, she'd read about the *Little Belt*, the sloop that attacked off the coast of the United States, which led to several deaths. The affair was under furious debate in Parliament, or so she'd read, blaming the Americans for firing upon a ship on purpose.

Lord Bingham seemed quite pleased with the young buck's agreement. "Absolutely," he said, looking smug. "We should show them who they are dealing with."

More vigorous assertions ensued, hot-headed arguments mixed in with false patriotism by men who would never go to war themselves. Julie felt sick to her stomach.

"Don't you think one war is enough?" The words left Julie's mouth before she could consciously restrain herself. She could never make herself listen to people talking about the war in such a cavalier fashion. Especially young fops who slept soundly at home, while her John had been on the front lines for years. "Considering none of you"—she waved her hand about the table—"are actually going to fight."

Clydesdale cleared his throat next to her. Did he mean to silence her thus? She pretended not to notice.

"Now, see here, young lady," Lord Bingham said in a patronizing tone. "It's not a woman's place to talk about war and politics. This is gentlemen's business."

"No, of course not, I shouldn't let my delicate sensibilities impede a nice supper conversation about murder, now should I?"

Bingham fumed, going red in the face.

"That's enough, Julie." Julie intercepted her father's furious gaze. He looked as if he was ready to murder her himself. "It's not your place to talk to the lords like that! You will apologize."

"Fine." Julie breathed in slowly. Clydesdale was staring at her intently. What she said next would probably seal her fate. A memory of John overwhelmed her clouded mind. "I apologize," she said, feigning meekness. "My countrymen being killed in endless, useless wars should not be my concern."

She knew her tirade wouldn't bode well for her later. Her father looked like he was about to explode. Everyone at the table grew quiet, and women started fanning themselves vigorously. The men were probably disgusted by her behavior, or at least she hoped that was the case.

"My lady—" Bingham began, looking strained.

"It is a complicated matter," Clydesdale interjected smoothly. He looked at her with an inexplicable twinkle in his eyes. "But perhaps you are right, my lady. The supper table is not the best place to discuss issues unfit for mixed company. We should switch the subject to more appropriate topics."

Julie regarded him quizzically for a moment. He didn't seem put out by her behavior, but then again, she couldn't quite guess his thoughts. She chewed worriedly on the inside of her lower lip and turned away. Had she driven him away or not? No matter. She still had another plan.

Julie craned her neck just a little to the place occupied by the scandalous viscount.

St. Clare was sipping on his wine and flirting with the women sitting on either side of him. Justine Thornton—Lady

33

Supe—was whispering something in his ear, pressing her body scandalously close to his arm. No matter that her elderly husband sat several places down from them at the table.

St. Clare was amicable toward both ladies by his side, even making time to wink or smile at those across from him. How was she supposed to spark his interest when every lady at the party seemed to vie for his attention?

Soon, the meal was over. Ladies proceeded to the drawing room, while the gentlemen remained in their seats to have cigars and port and resume their discussions of war and how they should have more of it. Julie turned to see the dowager duchess watching her closely. What could the older woman be thinking of her? Did she approve of her grandson's courtship or not?

Chapter 3

"Your bride is an abomination," the dowager duchess said with a grim expression the minute Robert entered the room.

Robert had to swallow a bark of laughter. "Why do you say that?"

"Hmm, let's see." The duchess pulled a thoughtful face before tapping her fan on her opposite palm along with each item she recited. "She interrupted the gentlemen during supper to offer her unsolicited opinion on a controversial subject that is highly improper for ladies to discuss. She told the ladies in the drawing room that she thinks women are intellectual equals to men. She has an unpleasant disposition, and there's a rumor going about that they have madness running in their family. Must I go on, or have I expressed myself clearly enough?" She looked disgusted to even speak on the subject. "And don't think I haven't noticed the way she talked down to you during dinner."

"You think women are as intelligent as men, too." Robert

raised his brow in a parody of his grandmother, deciding to shift the topic from his unfortunate bride. Since when did his grandmother put any stock in rumors, anyway?

"No, my dear. I think women are *more* intelligent. But we should be wise enough not to show it and definitely not voice it. At least until after marriage."

Robert gave her a sardonic look.

"Honestly, Robert, what was your father thinking? An arranged marriage." The dowager duchess scoffed and turned away. She rarely called him by his given name, even in his childhood. It clearly showed her heightened level of distress.

"Both you and Father were married out of convenience. Both your marriages were arranged by your parents," he intoned, his voice carrying an edge of stone.

"Well, your father wouldn't have chosen wisely without my interference. You know how he is." She waved her hand in the duke's direction. "And he clearly hasn't chosen wisely for you either. He should've asked me."

"I agree. However, what's done is done. The papers are signed. We are betrothed," Robert stated with an air of finality. "Besides, whatever her shortcomings, I am certain she is no match for you." Robert grinned down at his grandmother. "You can make anyone into a proper duchess." He bowed and left her side.

Of course, his father hadn't chosen wisely. He had probably never even met the lady, and he didn't even like Norfolk. He'd done what he always did—struck a handsome bargain. Well, whatever his reasons, Robert was glad for the outcome.

True, Lady Julie was not the wide-eyed young debutante he'd expected her to be. She had this look about her as if she'd seen much of life already and was not impressed. She wasn't afraid to speak her mind, which he admired about her. Most importantly, his father hadn't lied—she was indeed beautiful. He'd realized it the moment his eyes met hers in the parlor. She'd looked directly into his eyes, the way many of his peers avoided doing, and she'd done the same thing at the table. Her directness was as arousing as the rest of her. Her deep blue eyes, plump pink lips, and curvy, feminine figure were the dream of every man. No, bedding her wouldn't be a hardship at all.

Living with her wouldn't be boring either, he supposed. If she continued confronting him, speaking her mind, and not keeping to the corners, their life could be interesting. For a moment, he remembered his maudlin dream of a happy family, a loving wife.

Robert's gaze found his betrothed. She was standing close to St. Clare and leaned in even closer, rising on tiptoe to whisper something into the devil's ear. Much too close for Robert's liking.

St. Clare laughed, and she batted her eyelashes at him seductively. With that one look, Robert took his not yet fully re-awakened dream of a loving wife and shoved it back to the deepest corner of his soul. That life would never be for him.

However, even if he came to terms with the reality that his would be a loveless marriage, he wouldn't tolerate being made a cuckold. Not again.

He made a step toward his intended and the viscount, when Norfolk appeared at his daughter's elbow, grabbed her none too gently by the arm, and dragged her out of the room. Robert stared for a moment before following the couple out.

As Robert walked farther down the corridor, he heard voices from his father's library.

"...incredibly stupid to act like a complete wanton." Norfolk's voice was loud, almost shouting. "In front of your fiancé!"

"My... what?" Lady Julie's voice was small and sounded as if she were terrified. Hadn't the bastard even told his daughter she was betrothed yet? And this was how he broke the news.

Robert had assumed her quiet hostility toward him earlier was due to their arranged marriage. Now he didn't know what to think. He came closer to the library doors, which stood half-open. He could see Norfolk towering over his daughter. She stood there, her arms wrapped around her body, looking small and scared, like a child.

"Didn't he tell you?" Norfolk laughed unpleasantly. "Well, let me be the first to congratulate you, my dear. You are officially betrothed. You"—he paused for dramatic effect—"are the future Countess of Clydesdale."

"What do you mean, officially betrothed?" Lady Julie sounded as if she was choking on the words.

"I mean, we signed the contracts this afternoon, right before supper," Norfolk answered smugly. "We are going to announce your betrothal in front of everyone during the Christmas ball. And you'll be married come January."

The gasp of horror Robert heard from his intended's mouth wasn't exactly what one dreamed of when one imagined telling the lady they were to be married.

Granted, the circumstances were not altogether ideal, but it wasn't like he was a monster. He was an earl, a duke's heir.

Robert took a step back. It wouldn't do to be caught listening in to their private—if loud—conversation. He'd come here thinking the marquess wanted to harm his daughter. Which, given his stance, he still could do, but Robert didn't want to intrude on their tête-à-tête. Not when she would regard him as an enemy as well.

He turned to walk away just when he heard her defiant voice. "I'm not marrying him."

"Yes, you are."

"I'm not!" Her voice shook with rage.

Robert balled his fists. He wasn't exactly expecting her to be enthusiastic about the arrangement, but this, however, was ridiculous.

"What do you think you are doing, you stupid cow!" The marquess's bellow was followed by the sound of furniture falling and a muffled thud.

Robert was inside the room before he could register his legs moving. "That's enough, Norfolk!" Robert stood between the marquess and his daughter.

She was lying on the floor next to an overturned chair in a heap of skirts.

Robert was breathing heavily, from anger, disappointment, and the unfairness of it all. He felt heat creep up his neck to his face. "I think I can take it from here," he said harshly.

Lady Julie was acting like a wanton. She'd openly disobeyed her father just a moment ago, but nothing merited such treatment from her father.

"My lord—" the marquess began, suddenly looking uncomfortable.

"I want a minute to talk to my betrothed if you don't mind." Robert's tone brooked no arguments, so Norfolk murmured his apologies and shuffled away.

Robert turned to his betrothed and regarded her quizzically. Lady Julie scrambled from the floor and stood next to the toppled-over chair. Her chin high, her stance defiant, she stared right into his eyes. She looked like she was ready to do battle. With him. No doubt to avoid marrying him.

Robert raked his hand through his hair.

"When were you going to tell me we were betrothed?" she demanded, breaking the tense silence.

"Honestly? Never." Robert shrugged. "I assumed you already knew. That your father told you."

"Well, he didn't. And I am here to break the engagement."

Robert grimaced at her matter-of-fact tone of voice. "Sweetheart, do you really think there's a better option for you?" he asked, bitterness seeping through his tone. "Your father is determined to give you to the highest bidder. And by the highest bidder, I do mean the highest rank."

"I am not your sweetheart. And I know there is a better option." Her breath came in harsh pants as though she'd been running.

"Truly? And what is it? Lord Lansdowne?" he asked in disgust. "Because I know for a fact that he's your father's second candidate. You are welcome to choose him if you please."

At his words, his intended blanched. She reached her hand behind her and grabbed the back of a chair as if to steady herself. She started to shake.

"I shall not marry him either," she said hastily.

"Are you certain? Because even if I drop you like a hot potato, no scandal is going to matter to him." Robert observed her as she stood silent, not quite knowing what to say. "I don't know what your issues are with me, but I know your father. If you don't believe me, feel free to have a talk with him and find out what is going to happen if I don't take you as my wife."

Lady Julie swallowed audibly, her throat working at the nervous gesture. "Why do you care?"

Robert shrugged. "I don't. Not for you anyhow. But I am in need of a bride. And for many reasons which are my own, I don't want to go through the trouble of courting during the season. You're"—he paused, searching for the right word—"convenient."

A nervous bubble of laughter escaped her.

"That is why I am willing to make you a deal." He stepped closer to her. That was it. If they were indeed to have a marriage of convenience, it was better to get things out in the open. She could decide for herself if she wanted this deal or not. Either way, everyone would leave with their hearts intact. "I'll give you twenty-four hours to think about your situation. Go, talk to your father, to your chaperone, do whatever you need to do to decide whether you prefer me to old Lansdowne. If you decide against me, I'll let you go. No questions asked."

Lady Julie sucked in her breath.

"However, if you decide you'd rather have me, I'll have some conditions."

"What conditions?" Her voice was hoarse. She licked her lips, and Robert was involuntarily drawn to the movement. He cursed himself for his wayward eyes.

"I don't expect affection from you," he drawled, looking into her eyes again. "But I expect loyalty. And what I mean by that is that I shan't be made a cuckold." He stepped closer to her, crowding her. "Second, I expect you to be an exceptional hostess." Another step. "Nothing like your behavior I've observed thus far. If you need polishing, my grandmother will help you, but I'd expect you to try very hard."

By this time, he stood almost toe-to-toe with her. Lady

Julie held her ground; her neck craned back so she could look into his eyes. However, she looked as terrified as a cornered hare.

"And third," he said, dropping his tone a half octave lower and staring directly into her eyes. "I expect you to give me heirs."

Lady Julie, who was staring back at him dazedly, blanched at that statement. Her eyes widened, and she caught her breath. Clydesdale sneered down at her. Would she blanch if it were St. Clare proposing to beget her heirs? She seemed quite taken with the handsome viscount, as half the ladies in London appeared to be.

"That is unless you prefer to be bedded by Lansdowne." He dropped his gaze suggestively to her bosom before looking away and taking a step back.

"And what if I don't comply with your conditions after we're married?" she asked him when she found her voice.

Robert waved his hand in dismissal. "I have plenty of property. One in Scotland, actually. I could just send you there. I'd still need heirs though. That's the sole reason for this whole charade, so maybe I'd throw you into an asylum and petition the court for a divorce on the grounds of insanity," he threatened with a dismissive voice.

He flinched inwardly at his own statement. He'd never talked to a woman in such a cruel manner under normal circumstances. Well, he had once, but she'd deserved it. Lady Julie, on the other hand, didn't.

His threat, however, had the opposite effect on his betrothed. She stood tall and looked him straight in the eyes with a glint of challenge.

"Oh, don't you know?" she sneered back at him. "You just

might have to do that after all." She laughed loudly, without humor, disgust shining in her eyes. "In fact, my sister is currently residing in the York Asylum."

Robert stiffened as he remembered the duchess's words. *Insanity runs in her family*. He hadn't meant to offend Lady Julie thus. He simply wasn't thinking.

"Oh, yes, beware of a lunatic wife. Do you know it might be hereditary? You'll have to lock up your children too, just like my father did." She spat the last words at him.

Robert felt as if she'd hit him. Lock up his own child? Was that the rumor going around the *ton* about Lady Julie? That her father had locked up his own child in an asylum? "My apologies," he said stiffly. "I did not know."

Lady Julie sniffed. "And if you had? Would this all have been necessary then?" she asked triumphantly. "I didn't think an earl would sign a betrothal contract without a proper background check."

"You misunderstood me," Robert answered hoarsely before clearing his throat. "I apologize for the insanity remark; I did not know your sister was held in an asylum. I just wanted to be harsh." He drew out a long breath and raked his hand through his hair.

Lady Julie stared at him in astonishment.

Robert tugged on his cravat; he was extremely uncomfortable. He knew there were rumors about the peculiar Duke of Rutland, his father who preferred numbers to humans, and who was exacting to the point of ridiculousness. Nobody dared so much as a whisper in his presence, but Robert still knew they existed. For a powerful man, such rumors didn't matter at all. For a young lady, however—

"You succeeded," Lady Julie whispered.

Robert took a deep breath. This hadn't gone at all as he planned. This whole marriage arrangement seemed to be doomed from the start. His grandmother was right. She should have been the one to select a bride for him. But it was too late now. The paperwork had been signed, and no matter how much he wanted to dislike his fiancée, he wanted her. He wanted her body in his bed and her defiant spirit in his estates.

"You have till midnight tomorrow to decide," he said after a brief pause. "I need to find a wife soon. I don't want to go through courting in front of the *ton* again. So, I'd appreciate your level-headedness in understanding the situation for what it is. One way or the other, I shall announce a betrothal during this house party. One way or the other, your father is going to marry you off as well. Whether we marry each other is up to you. If you don't tell me otherwise, I'll assume our betrothal is off at the stroke of midnight tomorrow." With these words, Robert turned on his heel and walked away.

* * *

Julie stood in the dark, cold room, hugging herself. The entire situation seemed like a horrible dream.

She was betrothed.

Without her consent, without her knowledge. The earl hadn't even bothered to see her before signing the contract. Julie swallowed audibly. She needed to recharge.

She stepped out of the library and silently padded toward her own room.

All the guests were stationed in the west wing of the house, but for now, they were all entertained in the drawing room, so the hallway was empty. She looked at the doors lining the hall thoughtfully. Was there any way to tell which room belonged to whom? She looked around to make certain nobody was nearby before turning the handle of the door closest to her and peeking inside.

The moonlight from the window lit the room, so she could clearly see the objects inside. She saw ladies' slippers carefully laid on the floor and what seemed to be a chemise on the bed. A lady's apartments, obviously. Julie closed the door and moved on. She wanted to see if she could find St. Clare's room and end this charade once and for all.

Perhaps Lansdowne wouldn't care if she were compromised, but it was possible he would. If he thought she was with child, he might decide not to marry her or wait until he was certain. That would buy her some time.

Clydesdale was right, of course. Her father was desperate to marry her off. But if she just held on a little more, waited a little longer, perhaps John would be back.

What about Mary? The distant thought echoed in her mind, but she squashed it instantaneously.

She had to be realistic. Not one of those lords would do anything to help her. Her only hope was to wait for John to come back. Unless—

Julie stopped in her tracks, contemplating the idea. Unless she made a deal with the earl. He hadn't seemed appalled to find out about Mary. Perhaps he could help her.

Julie shook her head. These thoughts were fanciful. No aristocrat she knew of would willingly associate himself with an idiot. Unfortunately, the seed had planted itself in her mind and refused to let go.

What if the earl agreed to get Mary out? Was she throwing

away the chance to get her sister back by refusing to marry? If she did, what of her promise to John? What of her love for him and his for her?

Your love is the only thing keeping me alive, he'd written to her. What if he didn't have that anymore? What if she belonged to another? Julie shook her head and continued on her way down the corridor.

She searched the next room and another but couldn't find anything distinguishing in any of them. What had she expected? That he'd have *rake* written all over the walls? She opened one more room and finally found the evidence of a male dwelling. It was a neat, dark room, indistinguishable from the others but for the male cape and wig on a chair by the hearth. She opened the door wider to step inside.

"What are you looking for?" Mrs. Darling asked behind her.

Julie jumped and turned around, eyes wide.

"I… er… I was," she stammered, trying to come up with an excuse. "I am looking for my chamber," she finally lied, trying to look confused.

"This isn't it." Mrs. Darling walked a couple of doors farther and opened Julie's room door.

"Thank you." Julie adopted a careless swagger and walked toward her room.

"You were trying to steal, weren't you?" Mrs. Darling asked when Julie entered. "I should tell your father about this. He will be furious," she sneered. "You are a disappointment to him."

Julie swallowed a scathing reply. "Why would I steal?"

"I don't know, maybe you want to be thrown out of here. To be honest, I have no idea why. Being betrothed to a rich and handsome earl is a dream for many." She shrugged.

"Well, I am not one of those many. And I'd rather not marry a man I don't love."

Mrs. Darling laughed condescendingly. "There is no place for love in society marriages, darling. And there won't be in yours." She closed Julie's door, locking it from the outside.

"You are wrong about that," Julie vowed to herself.

She pulled out her diary and leafed through it, turning to the page where she'd described the day John had first kissed her. Goosebumps stole up her arms from the memory, and she shivered in the warm room.

"I love you," he'd whispered after giving her the softest, gentlest kiss. "As soon as I finish school, we'll get married. I promise."

Julie had blushed then. She had been fifteen years old. Although she'd felt much older by that point. She'd been hardened by her experiences earlier in the year. Her mother's death, Mary's disappearance.

Then, in the arms of a boy she'd loved most of her life, she'd felt safe. Now, to keep the dream of marrying that boy and living with him forever, she had to do the unthinkable. Seduce the rake.

She clutched the diary close to her chest and huddled under the blankets with it. "Please, please, please, please, please," she repeatedly begged until she fell asleep.

Chapter 4

R obert was sitting at his desk, drinking whisky and
going over his ledgers later that night, when the
door to his study opened without a knock. Only one
person had the gall to enter his work domain this way, and it
wasn't one of his family members. He didn't look up when
sure footsteps approached him. He continued working when
a moment later he heard a heavy plop in the chair opposite
his.

"Do you ever not work?" Gabriel St. Clare asked from
across his desk.

"You know damn well the answer to that." Robert leveled
his friend with a frank gaze. "Would you like some whisky?"

"I can get it myself. No need to strain yourself." Gabriel
stood and shuffled toward the side cabinet. "How is your
bride-to-be?" He picked up a bottle and studied it. He opened
the decanter, sniffed the contents, and put it back down with
a grimace.

"I guess you should know the answer to that question as

well as anybody. She spent half the night flirting with you." Robert sounded irritated even to his own ears.

Gabriel just laughed. "They all flirt with me, you know that."

"Annie didn't." Robert grimaced even as he said that.

"No, she didn't, did she?" Gabriel paused, bringing another bottle closer to his nose, and looked at Robert over his shoulder. "She did flirt with your cousin, though."

"She did more than flirt if you remember." Robert leaned back in his chair with a sigh. "I think you were right the night of my bachelor party."

"Did I say something clever?" Gabriel picked up his drink, poured a glass, and walked over to the table. "You know I was very much in my cups that night," he said, sitting down.

"You said that there is no such thing as an innocent woman." Robert closed his eyes, the memories of his bachelor party playing out in his mind.

He, blissfully happy, on the verge of the most important day of his life. Gabriel, skeptical, throwing the bawdiest bachelor party of his life. And later Annie—his Annie—on her knees, servicing another man. Not just any man either, but one of his closest cousins. Robert grimaced at the painful memories.

"I'm sure there are one or two," Gabriel intoned dismissively. "I noticed nothing special about your betrothed," he said after a moment of silence. "She is beautiful, her figure is feminine, and she is quite alluring—just like every other lady currently residing under your roof."

"I suppose." Robert stared down at his own glass of whisky.

What Gabriel said was true; she was no more beautiful than most ladies at the party, not too different from any of them. She shouldn't be more alluring, either. And yet she was, at least for him. He couldn't understand why she had this strange pull over him. He didn't want to identify his longing for her. That way lay trouble.

"But the contract is signed, and I don't feel like looking elsewhere. I'd rather not waste my time seeking a bride. She'll do."

"She'll do?" Gabriel chuckled. "I remember you saying that you'd only marry for love, that *ton* marriages are soulless and boring." He waved his hand in dismissal.

Robert looked up at his friend and regarded him ironically. "And do you also remember what happened next?" He raised his eyebrow. "It is better to know firsthand what you are getting into. At least this way, there is no room for disappointment."

Gabriel took a long sip of his whisky. "And does she feel the same way?"

Robert grimaced at the memory of the overheard conversation between his betrothed and her father. He drew a deep, tortured breath. "I don't know. I suppose I'll find out soon enough." He stretched in his seat, joined his hands behind his head, and crossed his feet at the ankles. "Norfolk apparently neglected to mention the fact that we were betrothed before this evening. She was surprised, unpleasantly so, I might add, when she was informed."

"Oh?" Gabriel raised his brow.

"I gave her until tomorrow evening to decide if she wants to marry me. If she agrees, however, I made her some conditions."

"And you think she'll abide by them?" Gabriel sniffed skeptically.

"I don't know." Robert leaned his arms back on the table

and regarded his friend with a level gaze. "Why do I always get the women least interested in me? Just once, I'd like to have a fiancée who's not eager to get into another man's bed."

"Don't be dramatic, Robert. I'd hardly call two a rule. Besides, you know that she won't be found in *my* bed. And if your lady is, in fact, a promiscuous one, she will at least know how to satisfy you in bed." He shrugged comically. "Most proper ladies have no idea how to do that."

Robert laughed dryly. A consolation prize indeed.

"What if she doesn't agree to marry you?" his friend asked.

Robert sighed. "As you said, I have a houseful of proper young ladies to choose from. Perhaps I'll be lucky enough to charm one into marrying me before this dreadful party ends." He looked ahead thoughtfully.

"Why even give her the option? You have a wider choice, don't you? Why not let her go and pick some other lady from the guests?"

"To be honest, I'd rather have her open disgust than the pretense of admiration and affection." Robert shrugged. "I tried that once before. At least, I can expect her to be honest about something." He took another sip from his glass. "I can't believe I was ever naïve enough to believe in marital bliss." Robert put his glass down with a decisive clink.

"Some people have it." Gabriel shrugged. "I suppose we don't fall into that small portion of lucky people." He smirked. "Which, of course, means that we can continue spending our time pleasuring as many women as we want." He raised a glass in salute. "To our luck!"

* * *

Julie was seated next to Clydesdale again the following evening. That preferential treatment didn't go unnoticed by many. Everyone was staring at them with either interest or envy.

Clydesdale was clearly marking her as his, although other than supper seating, he associated with her as rarely as possible.

Julie wondered if this was how he saw their marriage. Spending all their days separately, reconvening during supper, and only for appearances' sake.

No. This would not be her marriage. Not that she planned to marry him, in any case. She glanced down the table where St. Clare was chatting lazily with the ladies beside him. Lady Supe was not seated next to him this time, and Julie could see her glaring at him and his companions from her seat.

This morning Julie had overheard her talking to some of her friends, bragging that she'd spent the night in the viscount's rooms. She'd said that he was staying in the family wing and even described the approximate location. That brief discussion had gotten Julie thinking.

She needed to get caught in the viscount's rooms. Lady Supe obviously desired to repeat her tryst with the notorious rake. All she needed to do was have her and Lady Supe appear at his rooms simultaneously. That way, she'd be caught in his rooms but spend little enough time there for anything to happen.

Julie had written two notes while she was getting ready for supper. One to St. Clare, to come to his apartments after supper, and one to Lady Supe, to meet the viscount fifteen minutes later so they'd be caught. Now, it was only a matter of delivering said notes and waiting for St. Clare in his rooms.

As the supper drew to a close, Julie's knees trembled so hard they barely held her upright. Still, she raised her head high and exited the room. As soon as the ladies settled in the drawing room, she discreetly slipped the note into one of the footmen's hands and asked him to deliver it to Lady Supe. Julie excused herself and walked toward the dining room to repeat the same trick and deliver the note to St. Clare when the door burst open. She ended up face to face with the viscount himself.

"Well, well," he drawled and looked her up and down with narrowed eyes. "Eavesdropping, are we?"

Julie froze for one long moment, her mind going blank. She clutched at the note in her hand. The note she'd written in Lady Supe's name. Which is why she couldn't exactly hand it to him. But she didn't want to stand there and risk running into Clydesdale either. Making up her mind, she took a deep breath and addressed the infamous rake as flirtatiously as she could.

"No, my lord." She smiled. "I was actually waiting for you." She swallowed nervously, hoping he hadn't perceived her to be lying already.

"Were you?" He crossed his arms over his chest and cocked a brow in question.

"It's nothing to be discussing in the open." She looked around theatrically. "Meet me in your rooms in ten minutes." Julie put her hand lightly on his forearm and blinked up at him through her lashes.

The viscount smiled his slow and devastating smile that sent many young ladies' hearts racing. Well, Julie's heart was racing too, although for an entirely different reason. She was frightened out of her wits.

He nodded, then lowered his head so that his lips almost touched her ear and whispered, "See you in ten minutes, sweet." With that, he pushed past her and disappeared down the hall.

Julie couldn't draw a proper breath. She stood, frozen, in front of the dining room until the noise inside finally shook her from her stupor. Gentlemen were walking toward the dining room doors, and it wouldn't do to be discovered snooping. She turned and rushed down the corridor and into the ladies' room. She stood there staring at her reflection and praying, convincing herself that she was doing the right thing. After about ten minutes, she finally emerged and went in search of St. Clare's bedroom.

She didn't want to appear in his room too early. God only knew what would happen if Lady Supe didn't come on time.

What if she never came at all?

Panic gripped Julie in a painful vise. Surely, he wouldn't force her to do anything she didn't want to. He thought she wanted to talk to him, didn't he? Julie took a deep breath to calm her nerves.

She turned the corner to a long hall and wiped her sweaty palms on the skirts of her gown. This wing seemed to have even more rooms than the one she was residing in. "Closest to the far end, next to a huge potted plant and a painting of a ship during a storm," she whispered to herself, reciting the explicit directions she'd overheard earlier that morning.

Julie passed several rooms she deemed to be too far from the far end of the hall. Almost all the rooms had some kind of potted plant next to them.

"Blast!" she muttered to herself. "It's like a dratted hot house in here."

She tiptoed around and looked carefully at the paintings, wary of running into any of the occupants. There was one with peaceful-looking waves during sunrise and another with a ship being built. She scanned the paintings and cursed again—no ship caught in a storm.

Maybe the lady was mistaken, and he was actually in the west wing? No, she wouldn't mistake that. All the guests were in the west wing. That wasn't logical. Julie drew in a deep breath and tried the room next to the painting with peaceful-looking waves. It was the closest to the description she'd overheard, ship or no ship.

She turned the handle, and the door opened. Julie looked around quickly before entering. These were definitely masculine chambers. The walls were dark royal blue, and the bed was covered with blue and silver. The dark mahogany furniture complemented the interior.

So at least she wasn't in the dowager duchess's room. Julie smiled to herself, imagining the duchess's wrath if she caught her there. But her smile evaporated the next moment when she heard movement from the adjoining room. She slowly backed away from the noise, turned at the door, and placed her hand on the doorknob.

Before she could turn it and flee, she was stopped by a deep masculine voice.

"You are in the wrong room." Julie swallowed audibly but didn't turn around. "When you're organizing a tryst, at least try to get into the right chamber," her betrothed said in a casual tone.

Julie felt like a cornered hare. She had nowhere to run, no way out of this ridiculous situation. She did the only thing she could do. She turned to him, raised her chin, and looked

55

him defiantly in the eyes.

"You have quite the nerve." He narrowed his eyes on her and slowly walked forward. "Cavorting with my best friend, under my roof." He snorted.

Julie's eyes widened in surprise. What rotten luck indeed. She hadn't even contemplated that St. Clare might tell Clydesdale about her proposition to meet. How was she to know they were 'best friends?'

"What, nothing to say?" Clydesdale raised his eyebrow.

"I didn't ask to marry you." Julie was surprised to hear her calm voice, although her hands were shaking violently. She clasped them in front of her, hoping the earl wouldn't notice. "I also did not consent to marry you."

"No, you did not." He nodded slowly. "Am I to take this little tryst as your refusal of my bargain?"

Julie swallowed, unable to speak. Since it was clear now that St. Clare would not ruin her, there wasn't much choice, was there? It was either Clydesdale or Lansdowne.

She took a deep breath. "Don't I have two more hours to decide?"

"No, sweetheart," he said in a menacing tone. "Your little outing changes things. You have exactly ten seconds to decide, or I am walking out of here, and my deal leaves with me."

Ten seconds.

Thoughts rushed wildly through her head. She would have to marry Lansdowne if she refused. She would lose John if she agreed.

No, she would lose John either way. But she could still save Mary.

She shut her eyes tightly, willing her rioting thoughts to quiet down.

Chapter 4

***

Robert stared at his traitorous wife-to-be. Another woman he was about to marry. Another woman choosing another man to bed. He watched as emotions raced across her expressive face. She shut her eyes tightly, looking as if she were on a torture rack.

"I have a few conditions of my own," she blurted before opening her eyes again. "If we are to be married, I want them to be written into a contract."

She looked confidently into his eyes, although her hands were fisted at her sides, betraying her nervousness. She had quite the nerve indeed.

"Please." Robert indicated a chair across from him, curious as to her conditions.

Lady Julie took a couple of steps and sat gingerly in the offered seat.

"I'm listening," he said, as he settled in his own chair.

"First, I want your help getting my sister out of the asylum," she said evenly.

Robert blinked. This was the last thing he'd imagined her asking. True, when she had talked about her sister last night, he'd registered the hurt in her eyes, but he'd assumed it was more due to the embarrassment of it all. He'd never imagined this spoiled, self-involved creature actually cared for her unfortunate sibling.

"She would live with us," she continued, "and be treated with respect." She blinked several times.

Robert thought he saw her eyes glistened with unshed tears. He frowned at the thought.

"Go on," he said when she obviously expected an answer.

"I—" She swallowed audibly and took a full breath of air, her chest rising and falling with the effort.

Robert cursed his traitorous eyes for following the movement of her breasts.

"I shall give you heirs, however many you want." She cleared her throat before continuing. This concession seemed to cost her a great deal by the way she pushed it past her tight throat. "And then Mary and I get to live in the country. You'll settle an allowance on us, so we are not to want for anything." She closed her eyes briefly. "I understand you want to prepare your heirs to inherit the dukedom. But I'd ask you to leave the children to live with Mary and me until they are old enough." She looked up at him. "Mary's my sister," she clarified. "And she is not insane." She paused. "She's just… different."

"Anything else?" Robert was touched by her defense of her sister and even more by the insistence to keep their children by her side. He'd expected her to birth them and throw them at him, out of her sight. She kept surprising him at every turn. Maybe he was mistaken about her after all.

Lady Julie quietly shook her head.

"And you agree to all of my conditions?" he asked.

She looked up at him then, her eyes full of pain and grief. "I do," she said with all the conviction of a virgin throwing herself on the sacrificial altar.

"No late-night rendezvous with any of the lords?"

She shook her head.

"It's not enough," he said, getting up from his chair. She followed his movement with a terrified gaze before standing herself. Robert took a step and brought them toe-to-toe. "I want you to show me a gesture of good faith."

"H-how?" She craned her neck to look up at him. At

this distance, their considerable height difference was too noticeable.

"A kiss," he said in a deep voice.

He had the satisfaction of seeing her blanch, her eyes widening. He wanted to ruffle her feathers. Somehow her calm and composed demeanor unnerved him. At least that's what he told himself was the reason for his accelerated pulse. He didn't want to look beyond that. She lowered her lashes briefly, her hands playing nervously with the pleats of her skirts.

"Very well," she said finally, tilting her face up to his and closing her eyes.

Robert smiled to himself. "Oh, no," he said disapprovingly. "No, that won't do."

"What—?" She opened her eyes, looking confused.

"I shall not kiss you like a sacrificial offering. I want you to kiss me," he said smugly.

Lady Julie suddenly turned crimson.

"No need to act all innocent now," he said, taking a tiny step closer to her. "It's not the first time you've been in a room alone with a gentleman, and I assume I am not the only man you've been with."

Despite her behavior, the tryst she'd arranged with Gabriel, and his own past, he somehow hoped she would deny it. Not that he particularly praised virginity. She, however, only downcast her eyes again.

"Go on then," he urged her.

Lady Julie took a deep breath, then stood on her tiptoes and placed a warm, chaste peck on his lips. She was about to pull away when he caught her by the waist and dragged her flush against his body.

"Not so fast," he whispered. She looked at him, genuinely perplexed. "That wasn't a proper kiss. I can't take that kiss to seal the bargain."

Lady Julie placed her hands on his chest as if to push him away, but her hands froze against him. She brought her eyes back to his.

"What do you want from me?" she breathed, looking at him, pleading.

"I've already told you. A proper kiss."

She let out another tiny sigh before getting up on tiptoes and placing her mouth over his. This time, she kissed him with her mouth slightly open, her warmth enveloping his lips.

Before she could pull away again, Robert took control of the kiss, slanting his mouth over hers, and kissed her with a greedy passion. Taking advantage of her parted lips, he pushed his tongue inside and licked urgently at the silky corners of her mouth.

God, she felt so warm, so sweet, so... stiff. He felt her freeze in his arms, not responding to his ministrations. Robert felt his skin heat.

Despite her lack of enthusiasm, Robert felt his muscles tightening and his cock responding happily to the nearness of a warm, soft woman. He needed to coax a reaction out of her. He couldn't—no, he *wouldn't*—marry a woman who was so obviously repulsed by him when his response to her was anything but.

He placed a hand at her nape and tilted her head for a better angle before deepening the kiss even more. She tasted sweet and lovely. Entranced and lost in the feel of her, his hands roamed her body, his tongue exploring her mouth. He thought he actually felt her shy response as her body pressed against his, and he heard her slight moan before she pushed at him with a muffled protest.

Robert reluctantly let her go, panting. No, that was not a response. She didn't want his kisses. He looked up at her. Her lush breasts were moving in a frantic rhythm with her breaths, drawing his gaze. His hands clenched at his sides as he tried to subdue his arousal. He forced himself to raise his eyes, and what he saw was enough to cool his ardor.

She was looking at him with a terrified expression on her face as if he'd just killed someone in front of her. Her color heightened past crimson red into the realms of vermilion. She was breathing heavily, too, as if from exertion or anger. Then she did something that lowered his temperature to that of arctic ice. She wiped her swollen, wet lips with the back of her hand in a gesture of disgust.

Robert hardened his eyes and tried to pull his usual in-scrutable mask back into place. "I was right," he said, settling back in his chair, although it was ungentlemanly for him to sit while she was still standing. "Bitter."

Her eyes lit up in outrage for a moment before the anger died out inside her.

"Do we have a deal?" she asked in a low, slightly hoarse voice.

"We do," he said shortly.

Chapter 5

The next day, Robert gathered his family in his father's study to relate the joyous news. The duke clapped him on his shoulder and murmured his congratulations. He was never very articulate with his feelings, though his brief compliments showed his approval quite well. The dowager duchess, however, was less enthusiastic about the union.

"You must be out of your mind!" she said with a sniff. "That girl is an absolute disaster. She will never be a proper hostess. She can't even carry on a simple conversation."

"The deal is done and sealed, Your Grace. She will be my wife, whether or not you approve."

"Well, I disapprove just the same. She doesn't deserve you, and she doesn't deserve this title." She regarded him stone-faced.

"You said that about the last one." Rutland raised a brow at her.

"Well, wasn't I right about her?" She skewered the duke

with a knifelike stare.

Rutland shook his head and walked to the seat behind his desk.

"Nevertheless," Robert stated loudly, "I need both of your help with introducing her into society as my new countess."

He turned to look at his father and noticed that he'd lost him. The duke could only concentrate on a conversation for brief periods. Once they started to bore him, he went back to his margins and numbers. Robert rolled his eyes and looked at the duchess.

"Well, it doesn't look as if I have much choice, do I?" she asked primly, folding her hands on her lap.

"That's not all." Robert took a deep breath, preparing to drop the most important part of his deal.

"Oh?" The duchess regarded him stonily.

"She's asked me to help get her sister out of an asylum."

"Ha!" the duchess exclaimed loudly. "I knew it. That family looked like it ran in their blood."

"Don't be cruel. We don't know the entire story there."

"I don't need to know the full story; I saw the lady." The duchess's nostrils flared, the only indication in her bearing of a feeling more prominent than indifference.

"She also asked that we treat her with respect," Robert continued. "Which we shall do."

"You cannot make promises on my behalf." The duchess sniffed and looked away.

"I can, and I did. So please, be civil to her," Robert insisted.

"You know what that means, don't you? She will foist that child on me. I shall be the one looking after it, taking care of it, and God forbid, introducing it to society one day!"

"No need to exaggerate—"

"Did you see that girl? She doesn't know how to handle a fork, let alone a child. I bet it is her offspring, not a sister!" The duchess's eyes narrowed on him. "She probably birthed it, and her father threw the poor child into an asylum far from the scandal." The dowager duchess's face contorted in disgust. "That man is without principles. I don't know why you deal with him, Rutland."

Robert's father raised his head at the mention of his name. He was clearly out of the loop of the conversation. Noticing that no input from him was necessary, he went back to his ledgers.

Robert heaved a weary sigh. "None of this is under discussion. I am simply letting you know what is going to happen. So, I'd appreciate your cooperation."

The duchess smoothed the wrinkles of her gown. "Funny how you care nothing for my opinions, and it seems to me, I shall be doing all the work."

"You won't be marrying her." Robert looked at her intently.

"No, but I shall be arranging your wedding, the wedding breakfast, helping her pick out the trousseau, teaching her manners, and sponsoring her and her"—she waved her hand in disgust—"offspring into society when the time comes." She paused and looked at Robert down the length of her nose. "Considering I am always right, I wish you'd listen to me at least once and pick another bride."

"I'll make you a deal." Robert walked over and sat next to her. He took her hands in his and looked at her face intently. "How about I'll take your advice next time?" His lips twitched at a barely suppressed smile.

The dowager duchess raised a brow at him. "Don't you think I'll forget about this."

64

* * *

"I cannot believe you are getting married!" a fiery redhead practically yelled from the doorway.

Julie turned and saw her favorite cousin stomp into the room. Her curly hair tumbling out of her braid, the green skirts of her gown flowing in a rush between her feet, she was a picture of an enraged siren.

"Good afternoon to you too." Julie smiled awkwardly and stood to hug her visitor.

"When did this happen? Why? How?" Evie held Julie at arm's length so she could study her face. "No, start with whom. No, better with why. Although..." She bit her lip thoughtfully.

Julie laughed with genuine laughter for the first time in weeks. "How happy I am to see you, Eves." She hugged her cousin once again. "Please, do sit down."

"Don't tell me," Evie pouted. "I don't even get to be the maid of honor." She raised her brow in defiance. "Do I?"

"You would—" Julie began.

"I know, I am not out yet. Couldn't you have waited until after my come-out ball?" Evie walked to a settee by the window and plopped into a seat. "Well? Am I going to hear the story or not?"

Julie drew in a lung full of air. "It's my father." She blew out her breath.

Evie almost sprang to her feet. "You are marrying your father?"

Julie pursed her lips, trying to swallow her laughter. "Of course not, silly."

"Whew." Evie drew features of relief on her face, though her lips twitched at her own folly.

"He is making me marry the earl." Julie shook her head. "I don't really have a choice. If I don't marry Clydesdale, he is going to make me marry someone else. And trust me when I tell you that someone else will not be any better."

"Clydesdale..." Evie frowned in concentration, tapping her finger thoughtfully on her chin.

"Do you know him?" Julie became instantly curious.

"The name sounds familiar." Evie shrugged. "Of course, I don't get to meet any interesting guests in our household. But Grandpa always has gentlemen come and go." Evie shrugged delicately and threw a loose lock of hair over her shoulder. She looked up at the ceiling thoughtfully. "He's not that tall, gorgeous human being who does His Grace Rutmoor or Rutler's business, is he?"

"Rutland." Julie blinked in surprise. "So, you do know him?"

Evie bit her upper lip in a mischievous grimace. "So, he is gorgeous?" She narrowed her eyes at Julie and pursed her lips.

Julie felt her face heat, as it always did when she thought about her husband-to-be. It was that blasted kiss. Before then, she had no trouble thinking about him in terms of a complete stranger. Now, she couldn't think of anything but his hot lips on her, his agile tongue inside her, and his insistent hands roaming all over her body.

Julie sobered, realizing she hadn't answered her cousin's inquiry. She thought about the earl's forbidden features, his steely, cold eyes. Was he gorgeous?

"Not like John," she finally said sadly.

Evie's gaze turned somber. "I am so sorry."

Julie shrugged and huffed a little humorless laugh. "I had no choice," she said finally. "I have to face the reality that John might never—" She broke off and closed her eyes in agony.

Evie was by her side the next moment. She hugged her fiercely from the side, plastering her cheek on Julie's shoulder.

But Julie resigned she couldn't think of John anymore. It was no use. She couldn't wait on John forever, not while Mary was locked in an asylum. She'd lost everyone she loved in the past five years. She would at least get one of them back.

"Did you tell him?" Evie murmured quietly by Julie's ear.

Julie nodded. "I wrote to him a few days ago." She licked her parched lips. "I can't—I can't think about it," she said with a strained smile. "Because if I do, I shan't be able to—" She swallowed and pulled a committed grimace on her face. "And I have to," she said more quietly, "and," she added with strained optimism, "I get Mary back."

Evie's eyes widened like saucers. "You do? How?"

"I told you, I made a deal with the devil. I need to get something out of it, don't I?"

"That's wonderful!" Evie hugged her with all her youthful enthusiasm. "Oh, how I've missed her." Tears started forming at the corners of her eyes.

"Please, don't cry, Eves, or else I am going to cry too, and we'll both turn into watering pots for the rest of the afternoon." Julie nipped on her lower lip.

"I'm sorry." Evie fanned herself with both her hands.

"Don't apologize." Julie smoothed her hair. "Next time you come to visit, after the wedding breakfast, she will probably be here."

"Oh!" Evie's expression brightened instantly. "She is going to need a completely new wardrobe. Oh, I know, I shall send you all my gowns, so she can wear them before we purchase her new ones! There's a new modiste in town—" She paused and looked at Julie from head to toe. "Who's dressing you for your wedding?"

Julie smiled. She'd missed her little cousin. As a child, she'd shown the potential of being beautiful, but she was utterly gorgeous at seventeen. Her emerald-green eyes contrasted with her bright red hair, white skin, and golden freckles. People said that having freckles was unfashionable. Pure white skin was the golden standard, but those people hadn't seen Evie. She was also blessed with a taste in fashion. Even though she was not out in society yet, she loved buying beautiful new gowns that she fashioned herself.

She was also absolutely exuberant, happy, and excited all the time. It seemed like she was never sad, and people around her always smiled. She was a gem, especially to Julie. When everybody turned their backs on her, and John was far away, Evie was her only friend and confidante.

"Clydesdale's grandmother," Julie said, pulling her thoughts back to the conversation at hand.

"Grandmother?" she repeated with such a grimace that Julie couldn't help but laugh. "Come now, we can do better than that, can't we?" She raised her brow.

"I know, Evie dear." Julie smiled and shook her head. "But I don't want to." She shrugged. "In fact, I want the most hideous-looking gown to emphasize my feelings about the wedding."

Evie narrowed her eyes. "We can work with that. Leave it to me." Evie jumped from the settee.

"What do you mean?" Julie frowned in concern.

"I mean, I shall get you the gown." Evie smiled mischievously.

"What about the dowager?"

68

"Leave her to me, too." Evie winked and practically hopped to the door. She turned as she opened it. "You'll have the most memorable gown. Of that, you can be certain." With those ominous if cheerful words, she left.

* * *

Robert came to London a few days before his wedding. He had business in town that he had to attend to before he retired to Clydesdale Hall for their honeymoon, but that wasn't the whole reason he came to town several days early. Truth be told, he wanted to see his bride.

It was unfathomable and incomprehensible, but since the few days they'd spent in Hampshire—albeit not under the best circumstances—he somehow had missed her.

Missed her? He didn't know what to think of that new revelation. Perhaps because she was different. Fresh. Yes, fresh in that she didn't bother to pretend to be in love with him, but rather showed her hostility quite openly.

He couldn't fathom why she was so obviously repulsed by him. Maybe if she knew him better…

No, he had to shake himself. There was no way he would make the same mistake twice and try to make this wedding, this marriage, into something it was not. It was not a love match.

Nevertheless, here he was in London, on the verge of visiting his bride.

The afternoon of his return to London, he went to the house of one of his mentors and long-time allies, the Duke of Somerset. He'd had a few dealings with the duke regarding their bordering lands. They had similar approaches to farming and mitigating the lands in the north of the country. Somerset had several estates neighboring Rutland's, but he spent most of his time either in London or his southern estate.

His favorite was by the sea in Sussex, with a lovely name—Peacehaven. Robert had spent some time there, and he understood the duke's urge to spend most of his time there since it was as beautiful and peaceful as the name implied. It also meant that when Robert was in his northern estates, he dealt mostly with Somerset's managers while on-site, so he wanted to talk to him directly while he had the chance.

He was welcomed immediately and told to wait in the family room. He entered the indicated chambers and looked around. He'd been in this room several times. It was spacious, decorated in pastel colors, and very cozy. Not at all what one would expect from a duke's grand estates.

Robert wanted something similar for his own home. But of course, Somerset's house was decorated by his late wife and then his granddaughter. Robert paused in his thoughts. Would his new bride feel the urge to decorate his dwelling? He almost laughed aloud at his foolish hopes. Of course not. She wanted to run away from him as soon as an heir was born.

At that moment, he noticed a movement at the windowsill. A bright red string or something familiar was peeking out from behind the curtains. Then the curtain moved, and a beautiful green-eyed girl appeared from behind it.

"My apologies, I did not realize anyone was here," he muttered and sketched a bow.

The girl executed a perfect curtsy. Now, she would be an ideal duchess in a few years. He looked at her intently and realized he'd met her before, the duke's beloved granddaughter. Evelyn or Eva—

"Good day, my lord," the young girl said in her soothing, melodic voice.

"Pleasure, my lady." He inclined his head.

She smiled widely at him. "May I offer you congratulations on your betrothal?" she offered with a genuine expression of delight on her face.

"Thank you," he said with a straight face. Every damned person in London knew about his betrothal, even the ones not yet out in society, it appeared.

"You've got yourself a wonderful bride, don't you think?" She looked at him with an inquiring look on her face.

"I suppose," he drawled.

The girl's eyes narrowed on him. "You don't seem very excited about the prospect," she observed. "You don't really want to marry her, do you?" she asked thoughtfully.

"If you are about to offer yourself as an alternative," he said with a sweet smile, "I am flattered, but I am afraid you're entirely too young for me."

The girl laughed sweetly. "Oh, no, sir. I shan't be marrying anyone like you," she said with a laughing conviction. "I shall marry for love."

Clydesdale stiffened instantly. "That's what I thought too when I was younger."

"Let me guess. Something traumatic happened, so now you are punishing Julie for it?" The girl was so close to the truth that it sent an unpleasant pang through his heart.

It distracted him, so he almost missed the familiarity with which this girl referred to his future wife.

"You know Lady Julie." It wasn't a question, but she nodded, nonetheless.

"And I know she had a chance for a love match too. Before

you came along, that is."

"She didn't have to agree," he countered.

"Of course, she did. You free her sister from an asylum, and you get your heirs. A fair deal."

Robert pursed his lips in displeasure. He didn't like that other people knew about the deal. Of course, he'd told his own family and Gabe, but who was this chatty little girl, and why did she know so much?

"And she loses her love in return." The girl shrugged. "A decent gentleman would have helped her out of her predicament and left her free to marry her true love."

This phrase, *true love*, grated on Robert's nerves. And hearing about this true love of his future wife, who was apparently somewhere out there while she was cavorting with one lord and marrying another, was making him sick.

"If you think—" He didn't get to finish his answer as the duke entered the room.

"Aw, flamebird, here you are," the duke said and walked straight to his granddaughter, giving her a kiss on her forehead. "Run ahead to your studies. Your governess has been looking for you."

He gave her a meaningful stare. She clutched her book to her chest and, with a pout on her face, marched in the direction of the door.

"My lord." She curtsied theatrically as she walked past Robert, prompting the duke to apologize on her behalf.

After the business with the duke was concluded, Robert walked back to his carriage. He stared out the window before deciding on his journey. The words of the girl with flaming red hair were stuck in his mind.

She had a chance for a love match too. Before you came along.

Chapter 5

The duke later clarified that Lady Julie was his distant cousin. Which meant that Julie probably told all of those things to the girl herself.

Confided in her, complained to her.

Possibly cried on her shoulder. Robert couldn't believe it. He was a villain in this story. He banged the roof of the carriage, signaling for the driver to move. He was going to Vanessa's house.

* * *

Julie hadn't seen her betrothed since the ball at his Hampshire estate. After that, she was busy with the wedding preparations, having the Dowager Duchess of Rutland teach her the way of the duchesses.

She did not know where Clydesdale was or what he was doing. Whether he was amusing himself in the company of other beautiful women—not that she cared—or whether he had business to attend to before their marriage took place.

She knew he had arrived in London several days ago. His grandmother had mentioned it to her quite a few times. Even Evie had mentioned he'd visited their household. But he didn't deem it necessary to see his fiancée.

As she was standing in front of the looking glass in her wedding gown, she wondered whether she even remembered his face correctly. His features blurred as the days went by, and with each day, he grew shorter, balder, rounder, his eyes less pronounced, his facial features unclear. He'd demonstrated clearly that he cared nothing for her, and her wedding gown would state what she thought of him.

Julie gave a final twirl in front of the looking glass and

smiled at her reflection. How Evie had persuaded the dowager she should be the one to help Julie with her wedding gown, she would never know.

She knew Evie, though. Everyone loved her. And if she wanted people to do something, they did it. Apparently, even the Dowager Duchess of Rutland.

Evie would make a perfect duchess as opposed to Julie herself. Julie heaved a loud sigh. She looked at the bedside table and remembered the letter she'd stored in the top drawer.

She'd received John's letter just two days ago.

He begged her not to do this, not to marry another man. He vowed that he'd be back soon, just a few more months. She froze in the middle of the room; her gaze blank, remembering the contents of the letter:

You are the only reason I am still breathing, Julie. I dream of you every night. You are my guiding light from this terrible darkness. Do not give up on me, my love. I shan't survive it.

Tears streamed down her cheeks. She closed her eyes in anguish. How would she ever be able to live with herself if something happened to him? What if that was the last communication they ever had?

A knock at her door jolted her back to reality.

"We are going to be late. Everyone is waiting." Mrs. Darling entered the room and stopped mid-stride, staring at Julie in horror.

Looking at her chaperone's stricken face, Julie nearly forgot her woes. She was ready to scream with joy at that reaction. If only she had time to compose herself from the reeling emotions of her betrayal of John.

She cleared her throat and wiped away the tears. "I am

ready."

She walked past Mrs. Darling and into the hallway. Mrs. Darling pulled herself together, and a few moments later, she caught up with her.

"What in blazes were you thinking?" she hissed between her clenched teeth. "The duke's family will be enraged. Your father—"

"I don't care," Julie said stonily. "They took most of my freedom, but they didn't take all of it. Besides, there's nothing they can do now." She shrugged and covered her face with a veil.

All the way to the church, her father was chastising her for her gown and her insolence, ungratefulness, and many other things. Julie kept silent. She might be feeling many negative feelings toward this match. Still, she was grateful to be leaving her bully of a father for good. She'd be happy if she never saw him again. He had ruined her life, and now he was giving her an escape.

She gazed out the window during the ride, looking at the crowded London streets, imagining her riding with Mary the next time she'd be here. She had to concentrate on getting Mary back. That was the only thing that kept her sane.

As they neared the church, their carriage slowed its pace considerably. Julie looked ahead and saw an enormous crowd by the church. People were waiting for a joyous wedding celebration of a duke's heir and his bride. Well, weren't they in for a surprise?

The carriage squeezed itself between the traffic, and they were finally at the steps of the church. Julie saw someone run inside, probably informing the groom of the bride's arrival.

Her groom.

That was the most unrealistic part of the day. The groom was waiting for her in the church. And that groom wasn't John.

Her stomach lurched, and she thought she was going to be sick.

The Marquess of Norfolk handed her down from the carriage, gripped her arm painfully, and led her into the church. An audible sigh of disbelief sounded behind them, and loud whispers of, "I can't believe it," and "did you see what she was wearing?" echoed behind them.

Now that it was too late and they were already in the church, Julie second-guessed her decision to wear this gown. Did she really want to make a statement with her attire and anger not only at her father but her future family as well? Her husband, with whom she'd be forced to live, at least until she gave him heirs, the frightening dowager duchess, and the eccentric duke for a father-in-law?

The doors opened at that moment. Julie, holding on to her father's arm, started walking down the aisle.

The orchestra started playing; the light streamed from behind, casting a vast shadow on their path. She heard the ripple of outraged whispers and gasps. She looked up and saw a tall figure at the end of the aisle. Julie blanched and faltered in her step. Norfolk tightened his hold on her and whispered threats through his clenched teeth.

Suddenly she couldn't hear the music anymore, the whispers, or her father's threats. All she could hear was John's voice, loud and clear as if he were right next to her.

"Promise, you'll wait for me. Promise me."

She closed her eyes. "I promise," she had vowed three years ago.

And now, she was going to break that vow and cover it with another—this one more sacred in front of God. To a man she did not love, a man she didn't even know. She lifted her eyes as she felt herself being handed to a set of firm hands.

The pair of gray, laughing eyes met hers. His features at once hardened, and his face hid behind an inscrutable mask. She felt her icy hands suddenly grow warm in the hold of her betrothed. She stared at his severe and stony face, this man she was going to pledge her life to. And she could barely catch her breath at the sight of him. He probably felt her nervousness because his hold on her hands tightened.

"Dearly beloved," started the priest, and the world went blank.

* * *

The bitter taste in his mouth accompanied Robert all morning on his wedding day. He sensed he was making a huge mistake.

What if Lady Julie was truly in love with someone else, and he was ruining her life? Would her father let her marry that other man if he cried off, or was he saving her from a worse fate? The doubt plagued him all the way to the altar.

The feelings intensified as he entered the church, seeing the throng of people who all waited for his wedding. Everyone except for his bride, who was either late or not coming at all. His nerves got the best of him, and he was ready to call off another of his weddings before it could even start. But all his turmoil stilled once he saw his bride coming down the aisle.

She wore a hideous pitch-black gown with a ridiculously long train. Her gloves, her veil, and even her slippers were also black. Think what he must about his bride, but she knew how to make a statement.

With this ridiculous display of a gown, she showed the *ton*, her father, and most of all Robert what she thought about this marriage.

It was not a celebration; it was a mourning of love lost. He should feel bitter toward her or even angry. Somehow, he only felt admiration and something akin to pride. His lips twitched in laughter as she stood in front of him. He couldn't help but admire this young girl who'd made a deal to marry him so she could get her sister—or as his grandmother thought, her daughter—out of the asylum. This girl didn't care for his title and money and showed it to the world with her mockery of a wedding gown.

His expression completely changed as she lifted her veil, and he saw her pale, troubled face. She was not enjoying the joke, the wedding, or anything that was happening. She was repulsed by the mere idea of being married to him. His eyes took on a stony expression as he stared down at her and saw his entire future. The silent dinners, the cold nights together, the accusation in her eyes every time she looked at him. He almost stopped the wedding right at that moment.

What was the alternative? Marrying anybody else would yield the same results. With one difference, they would pretend affection before the wedding and cuckold him to their hearts' content once they married.

Robert took a deep breath. *Please, God, let this all turn out well.* He took her icy hands in his and squeezed them tight. As if assuring himself that she wouldn't run off, as if assuring himself that he wouldn't run either.

"Dearly beloved," the priest began.

Chapter 6

"To the bride and groom!" sounded the toast of a best man. "Now, you may know that I do not advocate marriage myself. In fact, I probably will not be marrying at all. Why tie yourself to one person for life when you can enjoy multiple a day?"

Clydesdale cleared his throat loudly.

"Right. I digress. Some unions, however, are made in good faith. And I believe that this is one of them. I wish them happiness, whatever that happiness might look like."

"To the bride and groom!" echoed the room.

Julie was sitting on one end of an extremely long table in her father's drawing room, the table used only during balls and soirees. She hoped this was the last time she ever dined in this house.

To her left sat her father, looking smug and self-important. Mrs. Darling was seated to her right, proud that her charge had made the match of the year. A couple of seats down from her sat Julie's only ally, her distant cousin Evie, who rolled her eyes at the best man's toast.

Julie wanted to laugh at the expression on the face of the politest lady she knew, a lady who had yet to make an entry to the *ton*. She was sitting between her father, the Marquess of Stratford, and her grandfather, the Duke of Somerset. Her loving mother sat on the opposite side of the marquess.

Julie looked at them with an unconcealed longing. Some people were just born lucky. Evie had a loving family, a doting grandfather, wealth that allowed her to have anything she wanted, and she was a refined beauty to boot. Lord help the poor fops of the *ton* when she made her entry into society.

Somerset stood at that moment to make his toast. "I've known our lovely bride, Lady Julie, since she was a little girl," he said, looking fondly at her. "Her mother was like a daughter to me. Until my son married, I had no daughters of my own, you see. In a way, that makes Julie my distant granddaughter. And I wish her only the greatest happiness. If I were choosing a husband for Julie myself, I wouldn't have found anyone better than Robert, the Earl of Clydesdale, the future Duke of Rutland. It has nothing to do with his title, although it certainly doesn't hurt."

Laughter broke out around the table.

"Clydesdale is one of the finest men of the *ton*. He is reliable, hardworking, and I know he will treat our Julie right. Now, I know that love matches are not fashionable. I also know that this marriage is one of convenience. But knowing these fine young people who've been joined in holy matrimony, I can see them growing to love each other in the future. And it is my greatest wish for you both. Because love is the most important thing." He raised his glass at that.

"To the bride and groom!" echoed the room once more.

Tears gathered in the corners of Julie's eyes. Somerset had defied society and married a simple Irish girl in his youth. They had one of the most scandalous marriages of his time. They eloped after a brief acquaintance and then spent every minute of their time together. He was devoted to his wife until her last breath and even after. He openly doted on her and never remarried. His son took his cue and also married for love, although into a well-respected family of the *ton*, securing a substantial fortune for his family at the same time. And in a few years, Evie would take up the gauntlet and enter society searching for a love match.

Julie, on the other hand, had lost her love forever. She looked across the table into the forbidden features of her husband's face. She tried to recall what John looked like, but she couldn't remember his face clearly anymore. She tried to imagine him the way he was the last time she saw him outside her balcony doors. But even if she could recall that heartbreaking night three years ago clearly, which she couldn't, he probably looked so different now. Weathered and hardened by the war.

She closed her eyes in misery. That was in the past now. John was now her past. Her future began with this day.

After breakfast was over, Clydesdale came to her side and proffered his arm. They exited, said their goodbyes, and left for his townhouse. Julie had packed all her valises and trunks the night before. She had a completely new trousseau with Madame Deville's help, including sheets, gowns, and underthings. She took all her old gowns with her as well. She did not know what Mary was like now, but she knew she would need new clothes once she was out of the asylum.

The carriage ride was brief but filled with awkward silence.

Since their fateful midnight chat during the Hampshire house party, this was the first time that Julie and her husband had been entirely alone. Julie had so many questions she wanted to ask him, but she did not know where to start or how to approach him. Her mouth was dry, and her thoughts blank.

When they finally arrived at the house, they were greeted by a long row of servants waiting in the hall. They were all liveried in dark royal blue and silver, similar to his bedroom's colors at the Hampshire estate, as she recalled.

Clydesdale escorted her to the first landing on the staircase and turned to his servants.

"I am happy to present you to your mistress, the Countess of Clydesdale." His voice boomed in the hall. Despite his words, his tone implied that he was anything but happy. "Mrs. Post. Please, do the honors."

A middle-aged, plump woman with braided gray hair and a brown gown took a couple of steps forward and curtsied deeply. "Honored to meet you, my lady," she said to the floor. When she looked up, kind, sparkling brown eyes met Julie's. "I am the housekeeper here. Let me introduce the other household staff."

She proceeded to introduce everyone by rank and name. Julie's gaze ran in panic from one person to another. She tried hard to remember everyone's name, but she failed miserably. There were over forty servants, and aside from Mrs. Post herself and the butler Mr. Hudgins, she didn't remember anyone by the time the introductions were over.

"I shall be most happy to give you a tour of the house," the housekeeper concluded.

"That won't be necessary," Clydesdale chimed in.

Julie looked at him questioningly.

"We'll be leaving for Clydesdale Hall on the morrow," he clarified. "I want all of you packed and traveling as early as dawn." He looked at his servants. "And Mrs. Post, please assign a lady's maid to her ladyship."

Julie hadn't taken her lady's maid with her when she left her father's house. She didn't want any memories from the Norfolk house to be carried over to her new life.

"I want everything ready by the time we arrive in Doncaster with her ladyship's... sister. Like we've talked about."

Julie's heart gave a tiny leap at the mention of Mary, and she didn't give notice to the small hesitation Clydesdale made. He intended to go after her right away. Julie couldn't have been more grateful if she tried. She looked up at him with gratitude shining in her eyes.

"Yes, my lord." Mrs. Post lowered her head in obedience.

"Right then." Clydesdale clapped his hands. "I'll show her ladyship to her rooms. Be sure to send the maid as soon as possible." With these words, Clydesdale offered Julie his arm.

"Thank you," Julie whispered as they started up the stairs.

Clydesdale looked at her questioningly, raising one brow.

"For taking me straight to Mary," she clarified.

"That was the deal, wasn't it?" he asked in bored tones. "I always keep my word."

Julie swallowed heavily. She remembered her part of the deal, the part that he probably expected to start on this very night. Her stomach churned as she remembered Mrs. Darling's words the other night as she tried to explain what was going to happen.

"You need to just lie there quietly and let him do whatever he wishes. You shouldn't make any sound or move a muscle. It is going to hurt, but it won't take long. And whatever you do, do not

show your revulsion to him. Act as if nothing is happening. Think of England if it brings you peace."

Julie swallowed again. Mrs. Darling's cryptic words did not comfort her at all. As much as she feared childbirth, thinking about what would happen on this particular night was even more frightening. If what Mrs. Darling said was true, she would have to endure this treatment by her husband every week until she got with child. And then the horrors of the birthing process.

She couldn't think about that, not now. She was getting Mary back. And as soon as the child was born, they would live in the country. All three of them: herself, Mary, and the babe. She let out a deep breath just as they reached the doors to her bedroom. Clydesdale paused, hesitating before opening the door for her.

She entered a spacious and beautiful light blue room with silver trimming. It was exquisitely beautiful, albeit cold and bare as if nobody had lived in it for a long time.

"You can decorate it if you'd like," he said stiffly. "Once we return to London, that is." He hesitated at the door.

"It's lovely," Julie said absently, looking around her room.

"Right." Clydesdale nodded and started out the door before pausing once more. "Ask Mrs. Post if you need anything. Dinner is at seven. Sharp."

"I'll try to remember that," she said, feigning meekness.

He nodded once again and exited the room.

Mrs. Post assigned a young, beautiful girl, named Alice, of about seventeen years old to be Julie's lady's maid. Alice chattered non-stop about how glad she was to move up to this position and how she would be the best lady's maid. She was excited about everything: about Julie's hair, talking about how she'd braid it thousands of different ways, about her wardrobe, and how she looked forward to matching her outfits. Julie just smiled in answer to the girl's enthusiasm.

"There hasn't been a lady in the house for as long as anybody in this household remembers," Alice went on. "We are all so glad to finally have a mistress. Perhaps the master won't be so cold and surly all the time anymore." She went on to chat about every other thing she could think of.

Julie felt stricken that the servants obviously looked to her to liven up the house. With the mood she had been in since the engagement, she doubted she'd be able to brighten up anything. But that would all change once Mary was in the house. That girl could turn the darkest cloud into sunshine; she was that lovely. Julie only hoped that everyone else loved her as much as she did. She prayed that the *ton's* reaction would be less severe this time around. She prayed even more that Clydesdale would keep his word and his family would claim Mary as one of their own.

Julie wore a pale violet gown to supper and asked Alice to make a simple braid of her hair. Alice protested, saying that it was her wedding day, and she should look festive, but Julie resisted. The girl had obviously missed the symbolism of the black wedding gown Julie had worn this morning. This day was not a celebration for her.

Several minutes past seven o'clock, she came down to the sitting room, where her new husband awaited. Unlike her, he wore full evening clothes. He was wearing all black except for a light blue waistcoat, a crisp white cravat, and a white shirt. He was pacing the room, periodically checking his timepiece. He looked up when he saw her and looked her over from head to toe.

"I see you are in half-mourning already. It's a good sign, I hope." He raised a brow, but his demeanor was less than interested, bored even.

"I apologize if that offended you." She smiled tightly.

"It didn't." Clydesdale closed his pocket watch and placed it in his waistcoat before walking up to her and offering his arm. "Shall we?"

Julie took his arm, and together they walked to the dining room. The room was big and spacious, like everything else she had seen in the house. The furniture was humongous and seemed uncomfortable. More to show off the wealth than for people to feel comfortable. Clydesdale seated her on one end of the table and sat across from her, about twelve feet away. She raised her brow at their seating arrangement and looked around at the servants standing along the side of the room. The footmen wore expressionless masks and weren't even looking in her direction.

Julie huffed an impatient breath and stared at the dish in front of her.

"It's not mackerel," her husband said mockingly. "I made certain of it." He bowed to her politely before resuming his meal.

Julie was immediately reminded of the day of their first meeting, and she smiled to herself.

They continued the meal in silence for a while. Julie was waiting for her husband to break the silence. It was the polite thing for a gentleman to do, and when he didn't, she took the conversation into her own hands.

"What time are we leaving on the morrow?" she asked the first thing that came to mind.

"The earlier, the better," Clydesdale replied.

"When would you prefer I be ready?" she tried again.

"The servants will leave by dawn, which means our carriage will be ready at the same time. I shall have someone wake you up so we can leave right after," he said noncommittally.

"I'll be ready by dawn then," she said, staring into her dish.

There was a long silence after that. Julie rummaged through her mind to find any topic of conversation she could discuss with her husband other than the weather but was coming up blank.

"It's a lovely home," she said finally.

"It needs a woman's touch." Clydesdale shrugged and returned to his meal.

Julie raised her head and regarded him curiously. He was treating his meal as if it were the most essential thing in the world, as if it would disappear if he raised his face from it for a moment. His comment, however, made her wonder. Did he want her to be the woman to transform his house into a cozy home? Judging by this conversation and his reactions to her, he wanted her as far away from him as he could throw her, possibly even farther. Julie's head started throbbing, and she continued her meal in silence.

Clydesdale finally spoke only when the torturous meal was over and Julie stood to go back up to her room.

"I'll come by your room in two hours," was all he said.

And Julie wished he hadn't spoken at all.

Chapter 7

R obert knocked on his wife's door at ten o'clock. He had spent most of the evening sitting in his study, staring at the clock. He was supposed to be working, but all he could think of was his wife, waiting for him in her nightgown, in her bed. He couldn't believe how anxious he was about this night. When he'd seen her at supper in that pale violet gown of a modest cut and design, he knew her intention was anything but to seduce him. But he was tempted, nonetheless. One look at those vulnerable blue eyes and all he wanted to do was rip that gown away from her and have her right there on the dining table.

He felt how stiff she held herself during supper, how uncomfortable she seemed. He had never had to deal with this issue. Women always vied for his attention, hung on his arm, and batted their lashes seductively into his face. Now he seemed to have married the only woman in Britain who wanted nothing to do with him.

"Come in," she called from inside the room.

He shook his thoughts from his head. If his guess was correct and she was experienced, then at least he wouldn't have to deal with virginal tears, he thought as he entered the room. Maybe they'd even enjoy the act and each other.

She was standing by the window, looking out into the night. She was dressed in a simple cotton nightgown, buttoned up to her neck with a dressing gown over it. She turned as he entered, her eyes wide, her face pale.

"I understand that this must be—" he paused, searching for the right word, "uncomfortable to do this with someone you, ah, are not attracted to."

She just stared at him, wide-eyed.

"I assume you know what is going to happen?" he asked, unbuttoning his shirt.

She swallowed visibly and nodded.

"Good." Robert started slowly taking off his clothes. "You can get undressed and lie on the bed," he told her as she continued staring at him mutely. "Unless you are enjoying the show." He smiled at her, his smile slow and predatory, and she closed her eyes.

Robert scrubbed his face with one hand. "Julie," he said. "Can I call you Julie? I mean, we are married, and with what is going to happen—"

She nodded frantically, backing away toward the bed.

"No need to act like a frightened hare," he said irritably. "I am not going to hurt you."

"You are not?" she asked as if in a daze.

Robert's head shot up at that. "Why would I do that? I am not an animal," he said harshly. "I don't know what kind of men you've been with." He shrugged.

"I have—"

89

"I don't need the details," he interrupted her quickly. "Just relax."

Julie closed her eyes and started unbuttoning her dressing gown. He stopped his own undressing and stared at her as if transfixed. The gown gaped open, showing none of her skin, just more of the nightgown fabric. But he felt his arousal growing only at the idea of silky white skin beneath all that cloth.

"Wait," he told her as she was about to push her dressing gown to the floor. "Let me."

He came closer to her, already fully naked. She still had her eyes closed. He gently swept her hair back, then pushed her dressing gown to the floor. She stood in front of him in her white flowing nightgown, the material so thin that he could clearly see her nipples beneath it. He cast his gaze downward to the dark triangle between her legs, also peeking through the white cambric. He returned his gaze to her breasts. Her nipples hardened from the cold air, begging for his touch. Robert couldn't help it; he lifted a hand and gently caressed one lovely peak.

Julie recoiled from him instantly. Her eyes flew open, and she looked at him in abject horror.

"Lie back on the bed," he said impatiently.

Her breathing quickened, and she fairly leaped onto the bed and crawled underneath the covers. Robert slowly followed her.

Julie was lying in the center, her knees drawn protectively closer to her chest. She clutched the bedcovers up to her collarbone. Robert scrubbed his face with his hand and threaded it through his hair, not looking forward to bedding a woman so obviously repulsed by him.

He wanted to laugh at his own gullibility. What a fool he'd been to think that open revulsion was better than pretended admiration. He should have picked one of the women who at least pretended to want him. Of course, there was no guarantee they wouldn't act this way on their wedding night as well.

Why was it he couldn't get rid of women willing to crawl into his bed on a daily basis, yet every woman he decided to marry wanted nothing to do with him? They wanted something from him, but whatever that something was, it wasn't him.

With a resigned sigh, Robert crawled under the bedsheets with his wife. She went stiff all over as his limbs touched hers. He tried to coax her to relax, slowly caressing her body. He started off with seductive intent, but sensing her distress, he opted for a soothing caress.

He rubbed her back in circular motions, trying to make her relax to no avail. He kissed her lightly on her neck, her cheek, and saw as she squeezed her eyes shut. Robert moved his mouth over her face, and kissed her tightly closed lids.

"Open your eyes," he whispered against them.

His wife just shook her head.

He couldn't take it anymore. There was no use. He would not force an unwilling woman into an act, deal or no deal. He got up and walked back to his clothes.

Julie sat up and watched him, nervously clutching a bed sheet to her chin.

"No need to fret," he said, putting on his trousers. "I'm not going to touch you." He collected his remaining clothing and moved toward his adjoining room.

"But… what about—" She swallowed, looking distressed.

"Don't worry about that either." With these words, Robert left the room.

He closed the door and stood for several moments, leaning his back against it. He wanted to laugh out loud at his luck. *Open revulsion is better than pretend admiration,* he remembered himself saying.

What an idiot. If he only knew.

Good thing he hadn't broken off his association with Vanessa during his bout of pure stupidity. If he had, he'd have to look for a new mistress on the heels of his marriage. He only wished Vanessa would be with them in Doncaster, not here in London.

He laughed bitterly to himself. It was a good thing all his naïve dreams about a family and a loving wife had already been broken by now. If they weren't, today would have served him a good hard blow.

* * *

Robert tapped his foot impatiently the next morning as he stood next to the loaded carriage, waiting for his wife. She was late, as per usual. The last servants' carriage had rolled away from the house a few minutes ago, and if Julie didn't appear soon, they would have to cut their stops short during the journey, something Robert didn't wish to do. He was about to stalk up the steps and get his wife himself when the front door opened, and Julie stepped onto the porch, a small valise in her hands.

Robert breathed a sigh of relief. "Everything is ready for us to leave," he said and stretched out a hand toward her.

Since the fiasco that was their wedding night, he hadn't

seen her and couldn't quite meet her gaze. Instead of taking his hand, Julie indecisively hovered on the steps.

Robert was forced to raise his eyes to hers.

"Good morning," she mumbled

"Are you ready to get into the carriage?" Robert asked impatiently.

"Yes." She nodded for emphasis and took a tentative step toward him. The footman took her valise from her and loaded it on top of their carriage, while Robert helped her up into it. He was about to close the door when she stopped him, putting a hand on it.

"Careful, you could be left without an arm if I shut the door with your hand on it," he said emotionlessly.

"You are not riding with me?" she asked, her brows drawn together in confusion.

"I'll be out on horseback." He indicated his saddled mare.

"I hoped—" Julie took a long breath. "I hoped we could talk," she finally said.

"It's a long journey, my lady," he said coldly. "We'll have plenty of time to talk."

"We—" She swallowed. It seemed to him that his wife had a great deal of trouble getting out her words. He quirked his brow impatiently. "We are still going to get Mary, yes?"

Robert's brows drew together in a frown before he regarded her trembling lips, her wide eyes.

She was frightened.

She was afraid that he would renege on their deal since she hadn't held up her end of the bargain last night.

"I made a deal, didn't I?" he said coldly. "Never question my integrity again."

He could see she wanted to say something more, but he had

93

no more patience for her. He shut the door and mounted his horse.

The journey to York was going to take about four endless days. He didn't mind long trips, he often traveled from one of his estates to another, and he had a lot to think about on the road ahead.

His miserable wife seemed distressed. She didn't think him a man of his word, on top of not wanting to have anything to do with him. An excellent choice, he scolded himself. Perhaps in time, she'd warm up to him, and they'd be able to at least start working on an heir.

A childless future did not look appealing to Robert. He'd always wanted children, to have someone to love, to teach, to act as his father never did toward him. He understood his own father's emotional limitations. It wasn't his fault. He also knew that Rutland loved him in his own way. But after his mother's death, all the love Rutland was capable of had died with her.

Perhaps, having the loving relationship he dreamed of as a youth was too much to hope for. Could he hope to have a simple *ton* marriage? Without her sleeping around with other men, that was.

She didn't seem eager to hold up one deal she'd made with him. What made him think she'd hold up the other? He looked inside the carriage through the window. Julie was staring blankly at the book she pretended to read. He knew she wasn't really reading because every time he looked at her, she had the same thoughtful expression on her face, and she hadn't turned the page once. Occasionally, she would look out at the scenery and then turn her head back to the book.

They stopped twice to change the horses and have some

refreshments before finally stopping for the night at an inn. Robert booked separate rooms for them and supper in a private dining room.

Julie had mentioned she wanted to speak to him, but they hadn't had an opportunity to do so before now. They had always been in the company of other travelers when they rested during the day.

Their supper was set at nine in the evening when the sun was setting outside the inn walls. Several candles were lit to brighten the room. The table was set for two, and the intimate atmosphere was almost romantic. Julie wore a simple rose-colored dress, buttoned up to her neck, with flaring sleeves. Her wet hair was swept up in a simple bun. She looked lovely, innocent even. Her rosy, lush lips curled in a timid smile as she sat across from him.

They ate in silence for a few minutes, or rather, Robert ate, and Julie just chased the food with her fork about the plate.

"Not hungry?" He raised a brow at her, watching her intently.

A nervous giggle escaped her. "I'm nervous," she said on an exhale. "I've been thinking all day about what I am going to say to Mary once I see her." She shook her head. "I haven't come up with a single thing."

So that's why she'd been quiet and out of sorts all day. Robert nodded mutely.

"I'd also like to talk to you about last night," she blurted.

Robert raised his head and looked at her curiously. "What is there to talk about?" he asked with a frown. His lips pursed disapprovingly.

"I—" She took a deep breath and tried again. "We—"

Robert stared at her, blinking impatiently, wondering if

she'd ever stop mumbling when she talked to him.

"I can't seem to get the words out when I'm talking to you," she laughed self-consciously. "I know we've made a deal. You give me Mary back, and I give you heirs," she stated bluntly.

"There were a few more in between," he reminded her darkly.

Julie licked her lips and nodded. "I remember, and I promise I shall hold up my end of the deal."

Robert leaned back in his chair and studied her dispassionately. "You do know that in order to bear the heirs, you'll have to go to bed with me?" He narrowed his eyes on her and bit the inside of his cheek in thought. "That is if you'll hold up the other part of the bargain about not making a cuckold of me." He raised his brow at this last barb.

"I told you I wouldn't, and I don't break my promises." She grimaced at her own statement, and Robert raised his brows in question.

"Not anymore, anyhow. And I didn't promise you an heir right away," she said defensively. "I just can't—" She swallowed loudly. "It's just... not easy to do that with a complete stranger." She forced out the words.

"As opposed to your long-time pal St. Clare?" He crossed his arms on his chest and regarded her with a sardonic expression. "You didn't seem averse to jumping into bed with him, though you knew him what, a day and a half?"

"Oh." Her face dimmed. "I wouldn't have gone through with it." She placed her fork on her plate and put her hands on her lap. "I just wanted to cause a scandal. One big enough that no one would want to marry me," she whispered.

"And by no one, you mean me." He raised a brow at her.

"By no one," she looked steadily in his eyes, "I mean no one.

That is until…" She trailed off, staring blankly at her hands.

"Until?" He nudged her to continue.

"Until John came back from the war," she said without looking up at him.

John. So, her lover had a name. Robert took a sharp breath in before returning his concentration to their conversation. "War?" he repeated, his brows furrowed. Was he a soldier?

Julie nodded meekly. "It doesn't matter in any case." She looked up at him with a resolute set to her jaw. "I married you, and I am resolved to make the best of this situation."

Robert looked at her, confusion marring his face. It seemed he underestimated his bride. She would not be passive and silent about the issues of their marriage. As things were, she was not even going to avoid his bed forever.

She was determined to make good on their bargain, even though she was so obviously repulsed by the idea. She was resolved not to cuckold him as well, although he'd wait and see until her soldier got back from war to comment on that one. She also seemed determined not to dwell on the past. If that all were true, Robert was ready to retract his opinion of her. Maybe there was more to her than he initially thought after all.

Julie took a deep breath and continued. "I shall not go back on my word—on anything that I've promised you. But as I said, I would like some time to get to know you." She swallowed again. "To get used to the idea of being a wife."

"How much time?" He quirked his brows in question.

"I don't know." She evaded his direct gaze. "A month—or two."

Robert wanted to laugh. "Is a month or two enough to crawl into bed with a man you're repulsed by?" he asked in a sarcastic tone.

"Repulsed?" She shot him a furrowed look. But he brushed it off.

"Very well," he said instead. "Have it your way. You know that the more you put off the inevitable, the longer you'll have to stay with me and not at your own private estate."

"I'm aware." She nodded. "Yet I'd rather wait."

Robert shrugged and resumed his meal.

Chapter 8

For Julie, this was the most nerve-racking conversation of her life.

She still didn't know why Robert had walked out of her bedroom the night before. She couldn't think of a single thing she did wrong. She'd laid there unmoving, her face turned away, careful not to look too distressed by what was happening. She hadn't made a peep. So, she was surprised when he'd scrambled from her bed as if she'd burned him and left her room. Perhaps her facial expressions had shown her turmoil. But was it enough to hurt him so?

Perhaps she should have been more open with him, told him the truth, that she had no idea what was about to transpire. Of course, she knew what she'd been told by her spinster of a chaperone, but that wasn't saying much. She'd said he would lift her skirts and do something to her there that was going to hurt, but she'd said nothing about him fondling her while she lay there half-naked.

She hadn't known he would touch her the way he did. She

hadn't known a strange feeling would shoot through her when he touched her nipple. Julie couldn't help but recoil, but it seemed to infuriate him. What was she supposed to do? She was afraid he would now call off their deal and go straight to his estate without fetching Mary from the asylum. The thought numbed her to the point of paralysis.

When he reassured her fears with that offended look on his face, Julie instantly felt better. He was obviously a gentleman who kept his word, and that knowledge was like a balm to her battered soul. If nothing else, she'd finally get Mary back. And since she'd gotten a reprieve from the marital bed, she would do anything to be a perfect wife for him.

She would look after his estates and stay out of his way. That's what wives were supposed to do, wasn't it? She didn't want him to think she was unreliable. And later, perhaps, if they were better acquainted, maybe the marriage bed wouldn't feel as terrible. If they both felt more comfortable in each other's company, he might tell her what to do.

The thought came, unbidden, of John's tender kisses, his gentle touch. Would she feel that self-conscious half-naked in front of him? If he was the one touching her in bed? She shook those thoughts out of her head. There was no point in dwelling on John. Not anymore.

She was a married woman, and her only hope for John now was that he came home safe and found his happiness with someone else. Her heart was gripped in a cold, harsh vise of envy for the unknown woman who'd eventually become his wife. She swallowed through the lump in her throat. She had no right to him anymore. And he had no right to her.

The rest of the journey was quiet and uneventful. They stopped several times throughout the trip but hadn't dined in private since that first night. She didn't know if private dining rooms weren't available or if her husband had no wish to converse with her privately, and she didn't press the issue. She was a nervous wreck and couldn't hold on to the thread of a conversation anyhow. The closer they got to York, the more jittery she became. Her stomach was tied in knots, and aside from hard bread and some wine, she didn't seem able to digest anything.

On the fourth day of the journey, they finally reached York. When they rode into the city limits, Robert cantered next to the carriage and knocked on the window. She unlatched it and looked at him questioningly.

"Do you wish to have a quick stop at the inn before we go to the asylum? Freshen up a bit?" he asked loudly through the sound of horse hooves and carriage wheels.

"No." Julie shook her head for emphasis. "Mary won't care what I look like. I'd rather get to her as quickly as I can."

Robert gave a jerky nod and rode ahead. With every jolt of the carriage, they were getting closer to Mary. Her heart was ready to sing with joy. At the same time, her head was filled with worry. What did Mary look like now? Would she even remember Julie? What if she was sick?

Julie covered her face with her hands. She couldn't face this turmoil anymore. She needed to see Mary as soon as she could.

They stopped next to a large, old mansion. The gray building seemed dark and forbidding, with the windows all shuttered and draped. Robert opened the door of the carriage for Julie and helped her descend. They walked together to the front doors and waited as their servant knocked.

They waited for a long time before the door finally opened.

A thin, middle-aged, gray-haired woman regarded them curiously from the doorway.

"No visitors are allowed," she said harshly and was about to shut the door in their faces when Robert placed his boot between the door and doorjamb.

"We are not visitors," he said harshly. "We are here to retrieve a patient. Mary Weston. I've communicated through my solicitor about her release."

"Right." The woman grimaced unpleasantly. "You'll have to wait—"

"We'll wait inside." Robert pushed the door open and led Julie in by the arm.

"In that case, follow me."

The woman led them through the dark, damp corridor. There were cracks in the walls, and strange sounds echoed from behind the closed doors along the hall. The floors were dirty, ceilings were leaking, and overall, the place looked hideous. Julie clutched frantically at Robert's arm, and he placed a calming hand over hers. She looked around in horror. She remembered reading an article about the York Asylum earlier that year. It was lauded for its humane practices and excellent keeping. Somehow, looking at the place now, she doubted the article had done the place justice.

The woman led them to a door at the farthest corner of the hall and knocked patiently. "I'll see if the chairman is in," she said as she turned to them. "He is the only one who may discharge the patients," she clarified at their dubious looks.

"Enter," a man called from the other side of the door. The woman went in and quickly closed the door behind her. Robert's nostrils flared in anger in response, and Julie looked at him with undisguised worry.

"Let's go in." Robert nodded at her and opened the door.

The contrast between the room they entered and the hall they'd been in was so drastic that Julie had to look out of the room one more time to make certain they were still in the asylum. The chamber was spacious and richly decorated. At the wall farthest from the door stood an enormous mahogany desk, with a huge, well-fed, middle-aged man behind it. The wall on the left was filled with books with expensive leather bindings, and a plush Turkish carpet decorated the floor. Julie scanned the rest of the room and confirmed there were no cracks in this room's walls or ceilings.

The thin woman turned and looked at them in distaste.

"It's fine, Matilda. Go and get Miss Mary," the man said.

"Lady Mary," Julie corrected him loudly.

"Right, Lady Mary." The man nodded to the woman he called Matilda and turned back to Robert and Julie. "Lord Clydesdale, I presume?" he said with a curt bow.

"Yes. This is my wife, Lady Clydesdale," Robert introduced Julie.

"A pleasure, my lord, my lady. I am the chairman of the York Asylum, Charles Best." He waved his hand toward the seats across from him. "Please, have a seat."

Robert seated Julie before taking his own chair.

"I remember the correspondence from your solicitor, my lord. As far as I understand, you are interested in discharging one Mary Weston." He reached into his desk drawer, looked through some files, then picked one up and placed it on the table before him. "She was admitted here almost five years ago by her father, the Marquess... of Norfolk," he stated, reading something from the file. "You realize that no one but the relatives may discharge lunatic patients?" Mr. Best addressed all his questions to Clydesdale, completely ignoring Julie.

"I am her sister," Julie said, bending a little forward. "I have a certificate to prove the relation—"

"No offense, ma'am, but you cannot be a legal guardian to your sister, only male—"

He was interrupted, in turn, by Robert. "If you'd let her finish, my wife would have told you she can provide you a certificate to prove her relation to Mary, as well as the marriage certificate to me. I am the one petitioning to have Lady Mary discharged and take her under my guardianship."

"I see." Mr. Best took the documents Julie had retrieved from her small valise and set them on the desk.

"We've also petitioned the courts. I have the order signed by the chancellor stating that Lord Norfolk is revoking all association with his daughter, which in turn, makes it possible to petition for guardianship without a court hearing since I am her male relative."

Julie looked at Robert in shock and gratitude. She did not know about the legalities of such a feat; she had no solicitor, and without him, there was no way she would be able to get Mary out. She hadn't known that Robert had already taken care of everything while he was in London. She also realized that his influence in Parliament and being a duke's heir must have helped tremendously, especially on such brief notice.

"Everything seems to be in order." Mr. Best looked through the documents absentmindedly. "We've prepared the discharge documents at the request of your solicitor," he mumbled under his breath and shoved some papers into Robert's face.

"I'll have my solicitor look them over before I sign and hand them back to you," Robert said, collecting the papers.

"You understand I cannot let the patient out of the asylum until you do."

Julie glanced at Robert pleadingly, but he wasn't looking at her. His gaze was concentrated upon the chairman.

"No," he said harshly. "I do not understand. We're here now, and we are taking her home. You know me, and my estate is here in Doncaster. I shall send the documents and a generous sum to repair the old walls and ceilings in your asylum once everything is read and signed. You will not make my wife travel here twice, will you?" he added in a more amiable tone.

The chairman opened his mouth to answer, but at that moment, the air was pierced by an agonized cry. Julie jumped up from her seat, frantically looking around. Robert slowly stood and took her by the arm.

"Don't pay that much attention. The patients here—" the chairman started but was interrupted by another gut-wrenching scream.

Julie ran to the door and yanked it open. What she saw made her blood run cold. Two burly men were dragging a small, young girl by the arms in their direction. The girl was fighting, yelping, and occasionally screaming at the top of her voice, struggling to free herself. When the trio got closer, she saw what she'd refused to initially believe. The girl they were dragging was Mary.

Julie was ready to faint. Her heart throbbed uncontrollably; she started to shake, her lips trembled, but her limbs wouldn't move. Finally, anger overwhelmed every other feeling, and she ran toward her sister.

"Let go of her!" she yelled at the men and made a grab for her sister.

But as soon as the men let go of Mary, she wrenched away

and stared at Julie wide-eyed. Julie couldn't believe her own eyes. Her lovely sunshine of a sister was pale and thin, her hair was a tangled, dirty mess, and her black gown was ripped in places and streaked with dirt. Her face and hands were also smudged.

Tears sprang to Julie's eyes. "Mary," she whispered.

"I don't know you. Go away!" Mary yelled as she looked at her sister, fury burning in her eyes. There was no mistaking the recognition that lit up in her hurt blue eyes.

"Mary," Julie croaked through her dry lips. "Mary, darling, I came to take you home."

"You left me! I hate you. You left me!" Mary cried and tried to run away, but one of the orderlies caught her by the arm and yanked her so hard that she fell to her knees.

"Don't you touch her!" Julie ran to her sister, gently grabbing her by the shoulders and looking tenderly into her eyes. "Mary, darling, I didn't leave you! Father wouldn't let me—"

Mary twisted away and plopped onto the cold, dirty floor.

"You might not take her away today after all," the chairman said drolly from behind her.

Her hands curled into fists. She was prepared to do physical battle with anyone responsible for Mary's current appearance and state of mind. She was obviously neglected, if not abused. If her outward appearance was any indication, these past five years had been horrible for her. An enormous lump kept growing in Julie's throat, tears clogged her eyes, and she was shaking with rage and helplessness.

"You better lock yourself in your room," her husband said furiously behind her. "If this is the state all of your patients are in—"

"Now, listen here! You are not here looking after these lunatics—" There were no more words, but Julie felt the tension crackling in the air, and then the click of the lock on the door behind her.

Julie stretched her arm toward Mary, but the latter flinched away.

"Go away," Mary repeated quietly, looking like a wounded animal.

"Leave." Julie heard her husband's authoritative voice behind her and saw the large orderlies scatter away from him. Next, she watched in astonishment as Clydesdale crouched beside Mary on the dirty floor.

"Mary, my name is Robert." He looked straight into her eyes. Mary regarded him warily. "Has this place been awful for you?" he asked gently.

Mary nodded her answer. A wretched sob escaped Julie; she covered her mouth with her hand.

"I know you don't want to go with your sister, but you don't want to stay here, do you?"

Mary shook her head.

"How about you come with me then?" He carefully reached out a hand to her. "I have an enormous house," he coaxed. "A beautiful garden, and there's a river running close to the house."

Tears streaked Julie's cheeks, unbidden. Mary looked at Clydesdale with almost worshipful eyes. She'd always enjoyed meeting new people. Julie remembered how gleeful she would be to meet someone new; she'd always give them a hug and chatter away about anything. Now, she was regarding him in half fear, half hope. *What have they done to her here?*

"You have horsies?" Mary furrowed her brows.

Robert looked at Julie uncertainly until she gave him a brief nod.

"I do." Robert nodded in affirmation.

"I want to ride," Mary said, still frowning.

"You will ride them, yes," he answered and smiled at her reassuringly. "Will you come with me?" he repeated, his hand still outstretched.

Mary placed both her hands in his huge one, and he tugged her up. Then, to Julie's amazement, he laid a protective hand over her shoulders and squeezed her tighter to him before walking toward the exit of the asylum. He looked at Julie over his shoulder to make sure she followed them out.

Julie's tears dried in astonishment. She strolled behind her husband and her sister, unable to believe the last ten minutes of her life. After five long years, it felt unbelievable to reunite with her sister and discover her in such a pitiful condition. If only she had known the reality of her situation here, she would have married at the first opportunity and tried to get her out. This was a useless train of thought; she shook herself lightly. Besides, no other man who offered her marriage over the past years would have gone as far as Clydesdale had to get Mary.

She knew those men well; even if they got her out, they would have treated her abominably. But Clydesdale—the way he coaxed her into coming with him, the way he hugged the dirty, bedraggled little girl who had been condemned by her own father to the lunatic asylum—told her everything she needed to know about her husband. She was no longer fearful for her future or that of her sister's. He was heaven-sent.

Chapter 9

When Robert first saw Mary, he was speechless. Brainwashed by his grandmother's speculations regarding her origins, he had expected to see an infant, not an adolescent girl. He didn't know her age, but she looked at least twelve or thirteen. This would definitely exclude Julie's parentage unless she'd given birth to her when she was as young as eight years old.

The second reaction was a more substantial, unbridled feeling. It was fury. The girl had obviously been mistreated. The clothes she wore, the way those two men were handling her, her dirty hair, and her thin physical appearance; he wouldn't be surprised if she had been beaten and otherwise abused.

He saw the grief-stricken face of his wife and had an inexplicable urge to hug her and never let her go. The pain marring her features when the girl refused to go home with her, and her tear-stricken look of anguish would probably be etched into his brain forever.

Now, sitting across from him in the carriage, Julie was trying to coax her sister to talk to her to no avail. Mary theatrically looked anywhere but at her sister. Her chubby little hands, so at odds with her overall thin stature, were buried in her dirty gown, her nose in the air. Julie started talking to her in desperation, telling her how they'd traveled from London to get her, about the places they'd stopped, and the people they'd seen. Mary bent her head in curiosity once or twice, but she never once looked at her sister. Julie looked at him pleadingly, but Robert only spread his hands.

"Give her time," he advised the only thing he could.

They traveled in silence the rest of the way to his estate. Mary had spoken only once or twice since leaving the asylum, mostly commenting on something outside the window. Now that she was sitting close to him, Robert took a better look at her.

She had a round face, a small nose, and dry, cracked lips. Her eyes were set close together and had an interesting tilt to them. Overall, looking at her face, one could tell that something about her was different. When the girl spoke, she had a bite to her pronunciations to the point that some words were indecipherable. There was something different about her physical appearance as if her arms were too long for her body but hands too small for her arms. She was not built the way her sister was, with her long-limbed grace and symmetrical features. He understood now what Julie had meant when she had called Mary 'different' in Hampshire. Mary was definitely sound of mind, but she acted like a five-year-old rather than her actual age.

They arrived in Doncaster late that night. Mary was soundly, dozing on his shoulder, snuggled up against his arm.

Chapter 9

Julie was looking out the dark window miserably, though he knew she couldn't see anything. Robert hopped out of the carriage as they reached the Clydesdale estate and took Mary into his arms. She stirred but didn't rouse and snuggled deeper into his chest. He let the groom help Julie out of the carriage, and they entered his country mansion.

He hadn't been home for the entire season, and he'd missed the place immensely. Robert had grown up in Clydesdale Hall, although his father, bound by duty, spent most of his time tending to his dukedom in London. The memories of his lonely childhood overwhelmed him every time he stepped inside the house. He wished to have this place filled up with children and merry laughter, but looking at his wife, he wondered if that was indeed possible or if he'd end up here alone again.

The butler and housekeeper greeted them as they reached the staircase. Robert looked at Mrs. Post and nodded toward the sleeping child in his arms.

"We'd better prepare her a guest bedroom," he said. "The room I asked you to prepare will not do for her."

"Right away, my lord." The woman curtsied and bounded up the stairs.

"What's wrong with the other room?" his wife asked worriedly over his shoulder.

"It's... smaller," he said as he started up the stairs after the housekeeper. "I didn't think to ask the age of the girl; somehow, I assumed she was much younger."

"Why?" she asked in a thoughtful voice.

Robert shrugged noncommittally. "It doesn't matter, does it? Let's just get her to bed."

"I think it'd be wiser if we wash her first," Julie protested lightly.

"You are probably right, but she is so tired, I'd hate to wake her."

They reached the guest room, and Robert put the child on the bed. He turned to walk away, but Julie stood looking at her sister's sleeping frame.

"Shall I show you to your room?" he asked, looking back at her.

"Actually, I'd rather sleep close to her. I don't want her to wake up alone." Julie didn't turn to look at him as she spoke, still staring at her sister.

"I'd say you need to rest as well, and you could also use a bath," he added sardonically.

Julie turned to him at that, her brows raised. She saw his slight smile, and her features cleared.

"I don't want her to wake up in a new place completely alone. But thank you."

Robert nodded and started to walk away, but her next words stopped him in his tracks.

"No, Clydesdale, I mean it."

He turned to her over his shoulder.

"Everything that happened today—" Her voice broke slightly before she continued. "I—thank you."

"You're welcome." He sent her a brief nod and walked away.

* * *

The next day began with a bang, or rather, with a scream. The soul-wrenching cry penetrated the walls of his suite. Robert shot up from the bed, hastily threw on his dressing robe, and ran in the direction of the sound. What he found was as comic as it was tragic.

The door to Mary's room was thrown open; inside stood the bath filled with hot water, but most of it was splashed around the room. Julie stood in the middle of it all, drenched as if she had been doused with a bucket. On the other hand, Mary was actively trying to wrench away from the housekeeper and the young maid who had been assigned to Julie as her lady's maid.

Mary wore a single white chemise, or rather a chemise that used to be white once upon a time and was now ripped in places and incredibly shabby.

"I shan't let you!" Mary yelled at the help. Then she turned and spotted Robert at the door. "Please, don't let them!" she screamed at him. Robert took in the room with an all-encompassing look, then quirked a brow at Julie.

"She doesn't want to bathe," she clarified, something he had already deduced, while shaking some water off her hands.

"I can see that." He stepped closer to her. "But why?"

Julie threw up her hands in frustration. "I don't know."

"You bad!" Mary screamed at her sister. "You hurt me!" Tears sprang to her eyes and streaked down her dirt-smudged face.

"I would never hurt you, darling! I love you," Julie pleaded with her.

"You lie!" Mary looked at her defiantly.

"Nobody will ever hurt you here." Robert moved closer to Mary. "I told you that, remember?" he asked in gentle tones.

Mary nodded slowly, as if unsure.

"Remember, I told you, you'll have your own horse to ride?" he reminded her and saw her face light up. "Right, but you can't ride a horse until you bathe. You need to be clean."

Mary looked at the bath in horror, then at Julie, and back

to Robert and shook her head. Robert had an ugly suspicion settle in his head.

"You don't like the bath, do you?" he asked.

Mary shook her head again.

"Why not?"

"Bad!" Mary practically hurled the word in his face.

"No, it's good, see?" He walked toward the bath and placed his hand inside.

Mary instinctively stepped away.

"Right." Robert turned to the housekeeper. "How about we try a different approach? What if you scrub her with wet towels instead and wash her hair over a basin? I think she'll need some time to get used to the bath."

Mary unconsciously stepped away again. Mrs. Post nodded and hurried to get the towels, wetting them in the bathwater. She took the pitcher and got everything ready next to the washbasin.

"I think we should leave them to it," Robert told his wife, who still regarded the proceedings frozen in the middle of the room. He took her by the arm and started leading her away.

"You stay!" the girl said from behind him. "She go, you stay!"

"I can't stay, love," he said gently. "You need to be washed. These nice women will take care of you. And I shall wait just outside the door."

Mary looked around at the women uncertainly.

"If you are frightened or need anything at all, just call for me," he reassured her. "Do you remember my name?"

Mary shook her head.

"My name is Robert," he said with a gentle smile.

"Rob?" Mary asked quietly.

"Right, you can call me Rob if you like." Robert nodded at her. "So, if you want me to enter, you just say my name."

Mary nodded more confidently this time, and he walked away, drawing his wife with him. When they stopped outside the bedroom doors, she collapsed against the wall.

"She hates me," she said in a quiet whisper. Her eyes glassy, she stared straight ahead, seeing nothing.

"Give her time," he said gently.

A wretched sob escaped, and her shoulders began shaking convulsively.

"She blames me for what happened," she said through her sobs. "And she's right. I didn't fight for her enough, I didn't—" She broke off and covered her face with her hands, unable to stop her sobs.

Robert looked at her mutely. He had never seen a woman cry like that before. A few theatrical tears to manipulate him? He saw that millions of times by several mistresses, especially Annie. His grandmother had never shed a tear in front of him. But this poor, miserable young woman was crying uncontrollably, and he had no idea what to do.

"I wish I could help," he said lamely. He reached an arm toward her, thinking to caress her cheek or pull her hair away from her face but thought better of it and yanked his hand away.

Julie raised her head at that moment and wiped her tears away with the back of her hand. Robert patted himself, looking for a handkerchief, then remembered that he was in a state of half undress and crossed his arms at his chest.

"You helped," she said on a hiccup. "Oh, God, I'm such a mess." She kept wiping away her tears as she talked. "I need to… I'll freshen up and then—" She looked at the door, worry creasing her forehead.

"I think you should stay away for a while," he said gently. "Go to your room, get some sleep, and maybe, later on, you'll be able to get through to her. The Dowager Duchess of Rutland will arrive in a couple of days, perhaps—" He stopped, as she whirled around on him at his words.

"The duchess… is going to come here? Why?"

She looked so stricken with horror and disbelief that he wanted to laugh. His grandmother was a frightening woman for those who didn't know her well, and it was always fun to see what emotion she evoked in other people. But not this time.

"She wants to meet her new granddaughter." Robert shrugged.

"Mary? She is coming here to meet Mary?" Julie's eyes widened even more than he thought possible.

"Yes, well. You don't need to worry; she is a very caring woman—with children," he added at his wife's astonished look.

A nervous chuckle escaped her as she stared at him in disbelief.

"Trust me, she will be good for Mary. Besides, we made a deal. Nobody is going to hurt her under my roof, remember?"

Julie's shoulders relaxed at his last words. Regardless of her feelings toward him, she at least seemed to have come to trust him over the previous five days.

Robert showed her to her room and resumed his place outside of Mary's door. The last thing he'd thought would happen after his marriage was looking after his simple-minded sister-in-law. *How did it come to this?*

Had he imagined a simple life of uninterrupted work, of

116

nights in bed with his wife, and quiet family dinners? He chuckled to himself. Now, who was the idiot in this situation? Nothing ever went as planned. After the incident with Annie, he should have known that having any kind of predictable marriage was not in his cards. Several minutes later, the housekeeper appeared from inside Mary's room.

"Lady Mary is washed. As best as was possible," she added starchily. "Her ladyship left her some of her old clothing, but it doesn't fit right. We fixed what we could for now, but she is going to need new clothing to her size."

"Right." Robert nodded thoughtfully. "I'll let my grand-mother deal with it."

He shrugged and was about to enter the room when Mrs. Post continued, "She has severe bruises all over her body. Some burns, possibly from flogging."

Robert's hand tightened on the doorknob. He'd suspected she'd been abused from the way those two brutes were handling her in the asylum, but hearing the confirmation made his heart clench in fury.

"I just thought you'd like to know," the housekeeper finished lamely.

"Thank you," Robert forced out through the lump constricting his throat.

He entered the room to see Mary sitting on the bed in an old gown that was too long for her and too loose in places. Her lips were pursed in displeasure, and her wet hair was collected in a simple bun. She looked at him miserably. He forced himself to smile, although pity and compassion were fighting inside him.

"Are you ready to see the horses now?" he asked, coming closer to her.

Her face lit up instantly.

"I don't know if you'll be able to ride in this gown, but you can at least pet them and perhaps feed them," he added thoughtfully.

Mary looked at her gown and picked up her skirts. "I want to feed horsy," she said, looking up at him.

"Good." He nodded. "First, you need to eat something yourself. Go to the dining room with—" He looked at the young maid in the room.

"Alice," the young woman clarified quickly.

"Right, Alice. You go with Alice and have breakfast, I shall join you as soon as I change my clothing, and then we can go to the stables."

Mary looked at him, confused.

"Go with Alice," he repeated slowly, pointing to the maid. "Eat."

"Horsy," she said, frowning.

"After you eat." He smiled at her conciliatorily.

Mary stood and slowly walked to Alice, who took her by the hand and led her to the door. Mary paused at the door and looked over her shoulder at Robert but didn't protest. The door closed, and Robert breathed a sigh of relief.

Chapter 10

Over the next couple of days, Julie was busy familiarizing herself with the business of running the house. In her free time, she watched as Mary played with horses, sheep, and other estate animals. In those days, Mary still hadn't taken a proper bath; the maids cleaned her with towels and washed her hair over the washbasin.

Mary hadn't warmed up to Julie either. She spent all her time with Robert, following him around like an enamored puppy, laughing up at him, smiling and showing off her newly mended gowns. She even sat in his study, looking through books by the hearth while he worked. The only times she was separated from Robert was during supper, and only then because it was inappropriate for children to dine with the adults. They didn't want to set a bad example for Mary, especially since the dowager duchess was due to arrive any day.

Julie was glad to see the smiles on her sister's face during the day. She remembered how she'd laughed with her back at the Norfolk estate; they'd played together all day long. Mary loved being outside. They'd spend days climbing trees and collecting flowers. John was often by their side, especially during the summers.

Julie lay awake during the long dark nights at Clydesdale Hall, remembering their happy childhood. But the moment she fell asleep, other, darker memories assailed her dreams. She would wake up in a cold sweat, the memories of her mother and the fateful night of her death lingering in her mind. She knew the dreams were just that, dreams. She knew they were brought on by stress, by finally having Mary back, by being in an unfamiliar environment. Still, she couldn't shake the feeling of ominous foreboding as well.

A part of her also knew that the dreams must have been triggered by the deal she made with Clydesdale. She'd promised to give him heirs, and no matter how terrified she was of the prospect, she'd have to do it sooner or later.

On the morning of the dowager duchess's arrival, Julie met Mary in the hall. Mary had been waiting with a basket of food. Julie was tired from the restless sleep, feeling sluggish and tense. Mary, on the contrary, looked relaxed and content.

"Good morning, Mary." Julie came closer to her sister and smiled, hoping to receive a friendlier reaction than the usual cut direct, but Mary just regarded her mutely. "What are you doing standing out here with a basket?" Julie continued, trying to coax a conversation out of her.

"Pic-nic," Mary said slowly, looking down at her basket.

"Oh, you are going on a picnic?" Julie tried to sound bright. "Alone?"

Mary shook her head. "Rob," she whispered.

Of course, she would go with Robert. She was practically

attached to his hip. Julie was happy about that, surely. She wasn't jealous at all. She was glad that her husband got along with her little sister and was not at all bitter about how much time they were spending together, considering neither he nor Mary spent any time with her. At that moment, the door opened, and she saw the tall frame of her husband entering the doorway.

"Are you ready, Mary?" he asked in a teasing voice.

Mary's features brightened instantly, and she ran to hug her brother-in-law. Robert patted her affectionately on the back. Julie looked at the couple wide-eyed. When had they developed such an affectionate relationship?

"You are having a picnic?" she asked, her voice a little strained as she tried for a smile.

"Yes, you don't mind, do you?" he asked emotionlessly. "Mary asked if we could eat outside yesterday, but we didn't have any food, so I promised her a picnic today while I talk to some farmers."

"Pic-nic," Mary agreed smugly.

"Right." He smiled down at her. "Picnic. Go on, get into the carriage."

Alice trailed behind Mary, out the door, and into the carriage.

"I didn't think you'd mind," Robert said, still holding the door open. "She rarely spends much time outdoors if you are worried about the cold, but surely eating out in the fresh air shouldn't be too bad for her."

"No, I don't mind." Julie shook her head. "I just wish… never mind. It's good that you two are getting along."

"She is a bright child. The tenants love her."

"They do?" Julie's eyes widened in surprise.

Robert just shrugged. "They seem to. Either way, she needs socializing. I think it's good for her," he observed while exiting the door. He paused on the threshold. "I understand you are worried about her, but you don't have to be. I am looking out for her." He tipped his hat in farewell and left the mansion.

Julie was still standing in the doorway, looking at the carriage making its way to the village, when she noticed another carriage coming toward the mansion from the opposite direction. This new carriage was as big as her husband's and had a crest on it. It was led by four magnificent horses and surrounded by outriders on all four sides.

The dowager, Julie thought with a resigned sigh. While Mary was having fun, picnicking with tenants, farmers, and Julie's husband, Julie would have to deal with the cranky old duchess. Only fair, Julie thought again, considering all the years her sister had spent behind closed doors.

While Julie stood there thinking about all the frailties of fate, the carriage stopped right in front of her. The footman put the step down and hurriedly opened the door. Julie watched as the old duchess stepped from the carriage, as regal as a queen. She was dressed in a dark purple gown decorated with gold embroidery, her hair wrapped in a golden turban. Her fingers were covered with rings, with the stones so big that Julie could see them clearly at a distance.

The dowager walked toward the mansion and sailed by Julie as if she didn't exist. Julie tried to curtsy hastily but was distracted by the older woman's brisk pace.

"The hostess always meets her guests inside the house," the dowager duchess intoned severely as she passed her by and walked into the house. Julie took a long breath and closed her eyes. Still better than at home, she tried to convince herself.

At least Mary is here.

* * *

Robert came into the house with a giggling Mary. She'd spent her time breathing fresh air and playing with animals while Robert talked to the tenants and tended to his business. She tired quickly, and thankfully the tenants realized that. After about an hour, she was invited inside to drink tea and partake in some sandwiches and pastries as she waited for Robert to finish his conversations. She looked exhausted and quietly dozed in the carriage, but she perked up as they halted next to the house and even raced him to the front door, giggling. Alice trailed behind Mary, shuffling her feet. She was young and energetic, but it seemed the cheerful young girl had tired her out.

The butler met them in the hall. "Her Grace, the Dowager Duchess of Rutland, has arrived, my lord, my lady." The old man bowed slightly.

"Oh, good." Robert clapped his hands together cheerfully and saw Mary flinch from the violent sound.

"Your grandmother is here," he said gently, trying to offset the reaction he inadvertently caused.

"My grandmother—" Mary said thoughtfully, obviously trying to remember who her grandmother was.

"You haven't met her yet." He smiled at her. "But she is going to love you."

The young maid gave an indelicate snort. Robert turned slowly to her, but she had already adopted a stony face.

"Alice," he said with a tone of authority, "please make sure that Mary wears her best gown for dinner. I shall bring the dowager duchess about to meet her in the nursery."

"Yes, my lord." The girl curtsied and hurried Mary away and up the stairs, while Robert turned and went to his study.

* * *

His secretary was already there as he reached the room, waiting with a heap of correspondence.

"Any news?" Robert asked, settling into the chair.

"Yes, there's an urgent note from your solicitor, my lord," the secretary said with a bow and handed him the missive.

Robert held his breath. He hoped he had finally received the letter he'd been waiting for. He had many things to worry about as it was, but he was waiting on a particular letter about the asylum. Ever since he saw the place's horrendous conditions and witnessed how Mary was treated there, he couldn't get it out of his mind. The moment he'd gotten back to the Clydesdale estate, he'd followed up with his solicitor and asked him to dig up as much information as he could on the place.

So far, he'd come up blank. All the reports regarding the York Asylum praised the institution for its stellar reputation and humane approach. He would have laughed if it hadn't pained him so. The condition Mary was in when they rescued her was by no stretch humane.

Robert opened the missive and read a few lines he found there. His features cleared, and he felt as if he could see the light at the end of a dark tunnel. Apparently, right across the street, almost next door to the York Asylum was another establishment with a similar purpose but with much better execution, the York Retreat. The retreat manager was a highly regarded solicitor and reformist and a whirling storm of a man, Benjamin Tule.

The note indicated that the solicitor had gone to the retreat and saw with his own eyes that the treatment the inmates received there was far different and much better than their next-door neighbors. The retreat servants assured him that Mr. Tule was most interested in reforming all the similar institutions and had even tried to reach out to the York Asylum several times without success.

However, Mr. Tule himself was away on some practice exchange journey. The letter indicated that he'd be back in London by the end of the month and back in York a fortnight or more later.

This wasn't ideal, it was taking too much time for Robert's liking, but at least in about a month and a half, he could meet with the man and perhaps do something about it.

He remembered the well-dressed man in the comfortable, if not luxurious, office of the York Asylum. The contrast between him and bedraggled Mary as she was dragged to them by the orderlies made Robert sizzle with anger again.

"So, you were not even going to come to see me," the stern voice of the dowager duchess sounded from the doorway.

Robert turned his head and saw his grandmother standing just inside the room.

"Apologies. I got distracted, Your Grace." Robert took his eyes off the letter and sauntered to his grandmother. He kissed her hand and helped her settle on the settee by the fireplace.

"I ordered us some tea," she said. "I wanted to discuss a few things with you before supper. I had assumed, as a dutiful grandson, it was your responsibility to seek me out when you returned from wherever you were." The dowager carelessly waved her hand. "Young people and their lack of manners," she muttered under her breath.

The secretary eyed the duchess uncertainly. He'd bowed as she entered and now stood next to Robert's desk, looking uncomfortable.

"As you can see, I am working," Robert addressed the dowager.

"Not anymore." The dowager eyed his secretary stonily until he bowed again and turned to Robert.

"If that will be all, my lord," he said, pushing at his spectacles and settling them higher on the bridge of his nose.

Robert heaved a sigh. "That's fine, we'll continue things on the morrow. My grandmother requires my full attention." He grinned at the dowager, and she just raised a brow.

"Of course, my lord." His secretary bowed, then repeated the action for the dowager's benefit and hurried away from the room.

"Do you have to frighten everyone?" Robert raised one sardonic brow as he settled behind his desk.

"I don't *have* to do anything." The dowager put her hands demurely on her lap and straightened her spine. "However, what I'd like to do now is speak with you about your—" Her lips tightened in distaste at her next words. "About your wife."

"What about my wife?" Robert lounged in his chair in a deceptively relaxed posture.

"How have you been getting along?"

Robert narrowed his eyes. "I don't see how that's any of your business," he said emotionlessly.

"Oh, but it is my business. I need a great-grandson. My son needs an heir."

"Your son has an heir. Me. I, on the other hand, will deal with my heir issues my own way, without your interference."

"My darling boy, this is not your dukedom. I may yet outlive you all. I do not look forward to the process, but with your lifestyles as they are—" She waved her hand dismissively.

"Pardon my dense mind. Are you threatening to murder me if I don't live in a way you approve of?" Robert's lips twitched in a smile as he regarded her.

"Do not be ridiculous." The dowager almost rolled her eyes.

Robert was ready to laugh. It was always refreshing for him when he could crack her stony demeanor. He'd made a game out of it when he was younger, and he enjoyed doing it still.

"What I want to know is if idiocy runs in her family, and if not, why is she not sharing your rooms?" She raised a brow in an intimidating fashion that sent young maidens running in tears.

Robert looked at her with a stony facade. "How I conduct my business in bed is none of your concern. Regarding the idiocy…" Robert shrugged. "I don't think so. Her sister is—"

"Her sister." The dowager looked at him carefully.

"Yes, her sister. You are going to meet her before dinner, and I would advise you to treat her with respect, as part of the family."

"You already told me about the deal." The dowager waved the issue away dismissively.

"It is not just that." Robert cleared his throat. "She has been through enough in her lifetime. She needs kindness in her life."

"In that case, you came to the wrong person." The dowager stiffened even more than Robert thought possible.

"I know you, Grandma," Robert smirked.

"Do not call me that. How many times must I tell you?"

"You raised me, remember? And you were far kinder than either of my parents," Robert said evenly.

"Compared to your father, anyone with a speck of emotion can be considered kinder."

"And that is all I am asking of you." Robert leaned forward, placing his hands on the table.

The dowager tilted her head speculatively. "You care for the girl," she observed rather than asked.

"I do." Robert nodded. "She is… unique. She is not an idiot. She is just—" He shrugged, not quite able to find the right words. "It's difficult to explain. You will see for yourself soon."

"And your wife?"

"Well, my wife needs your support as well." Robert heaved a sigh. "In a different manner. I need her ready to be the ideal hostess in a month's time. You know this season is important to Father. We need to establish an excellent reputation so he can hand over all his business to me without incident."

"It won't be easy with an idiot in the family," the dowager stated dispassionately.

"Right." Robert scratched his chin thoughtfully. "We need to do everything perfectly. And perhaps hold off on people seeing her."

"That would be best," the dowager said and then narrowed her eyes. "I can polish your wife as much as anyone would be able to, but there are some things even I don't have the power to change."

"Such as?" Robert stiffened in his seat.

"Such as… Are you certain she'll hold to her bargain and will not hop around from one gentleman's bed to another?"

Robert held his breath so as not to burst. "I don't know," he said stiffly.

"Well, perhaps if you kept her in your bed, she wouldn't—"

"That's enough, thank you." Robert stood. "Now, if you don't mind, I'll change before supper."

"I don't mind at all." The duchess stood slowly and fluidly.

"I'll escort you to see Mary at a quarter to seven." With a curt nod, Robert exited the room.

* * *

They entered Mary's room just as she settled at her table. Mary shot up from her chair as soon as she spotted them and dashed toward Robert, overturning her chair in the process. She raced into his arms and hugged him tightly. Robert saw the dowager's features strain and finally give up the fight, showing some measure of the shock she must have been feeling.

"Mary, this is the Dowager Duchess of Rutland," Robert announced when the girl lifted her head to look at him. "Your grandmother."

He smiled slyly in the duchess's direction and saw her stiffen like a rod. The dowager did not appreciate the moniker, he knew it. And technically, Mary was not her granddaughter. Curiously, she did not protest this time. Perhaps she was too shocked to say anything at all.

"Grandmother." Mary whispered the word as if testing the taste of it on her tongue. Then she made a hasty step toward her, then another, until she was hugging the dowager's hips. Her Grace's eyes widened, and she turned to Robert as if asking for help. Robert just smiled at his grandmother's obvious discomfort.

"You eat here?" Mary asked as she let go of the dowager's skirts and looked at Robert.

"No," he said shortly, putting his hands in his pockets. "We just came to say hello. You are eating supper here with Alice as always, remember?"

Mary nodded with a pout. Robert noticed the dowager was openly staring at Mary. The girl was obviously not what she'd expected.

"How old are you, child?" she finally asked.

Mary wrinkled her brows and started bending her fingers as if counting. "Eleven," she announced happily after a while. "I think," she amended thoughtfully.

"These clothes are not fit for her station." The dowager turned to Robert.

"I know." Robert nodded. "But since she just arrived, we had nothing suitable for her. Alice and the other maids are sewing what they can, but I expect you to buy her a suitable wardrobe once we move to London."

"London!" Mary's eyes widened dreamily before she frowned. "Father went to London. Never took me," she finished quietly.

"Well, we'll go to London soon," Robert said gently. "Would you like that?"

Mary brightened instantly. Her mood changes were like flashes of lightning, sudden and drastic. Robert was still surprised that she had stayed angry at Julie for so long. The hurt must have been profound for her to keep ignoring her sister like that.

"Now, go on and eat, or your food will get cold." Robert winked at her, turned her by the shoulders, and gave her a nudge toward the dinner table. He turned to see the dowager looking at him curiously.

"You like the girl," she repeated her previous sentiment when they exited the room.

Robert shrugged. "She's my responsibility now; it doesn't hurt to show her a little affection. I expect the same from you."

"We are not an affectionate family, Clydesdale. We are one step from royalty," the dowager answered as she sailed past him and preceded him toward the stairs.

Yes, Robert thought glumly, *I remember.*

* * *

They came down to an empty parlor. Robert consulted his watch to see it was five minutes past supper time. The dowager smirked his way as if she were not surprised at all. A few minutes later, Julie rushed into the room and curtsied hastily.

She wore a violet-blue day gown that accentuated her blue eyes and milky white skin. Her hair was carefully tucked into a simple chignon. The gown had a modest cut, buttoned up to the chin with tiny white pearls.

Ever since they got married, she'd gone out of her way to dress as casually and simply as possible, and somehow Robert still found her enticing. For a moment, he even forgot that she was, yet again, late.

The dowager had no such affliction. "Lesson number one," she said crisply. "The hostess is always the first to attend supper."

"Apologies, there was a mishap in the kitchen—"

"No need to delay us more with boring details." The

dowager sniffed, and Robert saw Julie's eyes widen slightly.

"Shall we?" Robert offered each woman an arm in an effort to dispel the tension, and they all entered the dining room.

"I shall assume the hostess's place tonight," the dowager said as they reached the table. "I have a feeling I'll need to observe Lady Clydesdale's behavior further."

Julie's only reaction was an intake of a deep breath. She didn't protest and sat to Robert's right on the other side of the table from the duchess. Robert swallowed a chuckle.

"How was your day today?" Julie asked as soon as they settled in their seats. She looked up at him innocently, obviously trying to ignore the dowager's disapproving gaze.

"Good." Robert cleared his throat. "Mary quite enjoyed the outing."

The food was brought in at that moment, and he could see the proud look in his wife's eyes. She had ordered the most sought-after foods: roasted duck with vegetables, green peas, and artichoke, tongue, and boiled capers—nothing he particularly cared for, but everything that was considered a delicacy. Robert was more of a traditional meat pies and potatoes kind of gentleman himself. Still, he couldn't fault his wife for wanting to impress the duchess with fashionable meals.

"Why don't you take your wife with you to see the tenants?" the dowager asked.

"It has barely been a sennight. Surely there are a lot of important things for the countess to do," he said and looked up to see Julie studying him intently.

"I rather agree with Her Grace," she said evenly and turned back to her plate. "I think it is time I accompanied you and Mary; it is only right."

She didn't look at him as she spoke this time, just sawed away at her food. Her hair was swept up, baring the side of her neck for his view. Robert couldn't quite avert his gaze from the sight.

"If you wish. I think we can—" he started slowly, and at that moment, Julie brought her fork to her lips and put the piece of food into her mouth.

She licked her lips and closed her eyes briefly in obvious enjoyment, and Robert quite forgot what he was saying.

"We can what?" She turned to him when he said nothing further, and he had to concentrate on collecting his thoughts.

"We can organize a fair or some sort of celebration to welcome you to the estate," he finished lamely.

"It's a marvelous idea," the dowager said. "But it will take quite a bit of preparation. No need to wait for a grand celebration to introduce your countess. We can always celebrate in the spring."

"Quite," his wife agreed. "I can't wait that long to meet the tenants. It's unheard of for the mistress of the estate to not be acquainted with the people for so long."

Robert assumed her eagerness to join them stemmed from her unwillingness to spend all her time with the duchess, and he smirked inwardly.

"Whatever you wish, my lady," he said and resumed his meal.

Next came the dessert. The wine was served, together with fruit and almonds, and some small tart was placed on his plate covered with... cooked fruit? Robert looked in his wife's direction; she was eyeing the piece of dessert with obvious anticipation. Her eyes glowed as she cut the piece and carefully placed it in her mouth. Her tongue peeked out to collect the remainder of the tart off her lips, and Robert groaned inwardly. The suggestive action, the blissful expression on her face, was enough to make his breeches tighten uncomfortably. Would he have to face this torture during every meal?

It didn't matter that he didn't like his vegetables and fruit cooked anymore. From now on, his favorite dessert was watching his wife partake in a fruit tart. For a moment, Robert imagined her putting other, more erotic things in her mouth. His eyes narrowed on the ripple of her throat as she swallowed, then ventured lower to her covered decolletage.

"Did you hear me, Clydesdale?" His grandmother's stern voice brought him back to the table from his thoughts.

Robert started and turned to look at the dowager. "Pardon, I was thinking about something else," he confessed hastily.

"Obviously." The dowager smirked, and Robert felt his neck heat.

Had the dowager witnessed his lustful gazes toward his wife? Had Julie?

"I was saying that despite the additional tutoring that is obviously necessary, your wife is not a lost cause."

Robert shot an amused glance toward his wife and noted her briefly close her eyes as if she were praying for patience.

"I think it is safe to assume she'll be ready for an introduction to London society as your countess in less than a fortnight," the dowager continued.

"Good." Robert nodded. "Rutland probably wants me there earlier. I can go ahead of you and set up the townhouse."

Julie paused with her fork in mid-air. "You want us to travel without you?"

"Yes, I think it best if I go in advance," he answered evenly.

Chapter 10

Julie placed the fork on her plate without eating the rest of her food. Her features darkened. What could possibly distress her about him leaving for London without them?

Chapter 11

The prospect of staying alone with the dowager while Robert went to London didn't sit well with Julie. Nor did his eagerness to leave her.

She knew sophisticated gentlemen often kept their mistresses in London and couldn't help but think that this was the primary reason for Robert's willingness to leave them behind. The thought plagued Julie all evening and well into the next day. The idea of another woman in Robert's arms bothered her more than she was willing to admit to herself.

Julie ordered the servants to fill the carriage with baskets of food, medicine, and other necessary household items in preparation for their outing. Clydesdale was already waiting for them when she reached the hall. He was impeccably dressed in fawn-colored riding breeches, a warm chestnut brown coat and matching leather gloves, riding boots, and a winter hat. He looked as forbidding as he always did.

Julie couldn't help but wonder if she would ever feel comfortable around him. She had never imagined she'd be married to a stranger. She'd always imagined herself with John. The thought of seeing John's face every day was soothing. She knew him so well; she could tell what he was thinking just by looking at him. Julie smiled inwardly in reminiscence. Life with John seemed so easy, while the life she had now with Robert was nothing if not complicated.

Julie was grateful for everything he'd done for her and Mary. She admired him; perhaps she even liked him. She didn't want other women to warm his bed, but would she ever be eager to become that woman herself? Maybe if he wasn't so severe and reserved all the time.

Mary made her way downstairs at that moment, and Robert's demeanor immediately changed. He turned to Mary with unconcealed affection in his eyes, and a smile appeared on his face. It made his eyes light up, and a small dimple appeared at the corner of his mouth, making him look young and carefree. Julie couldn't quite take her eyes off his smile. It made her wish irrationally that he'd smile the same way toward her.

"Shall we?" He interrupted her thoughts as he offered them each his arm, and they set off toward the waiting carriage.

The day was bright, and the sun was at its zenith, bathing the land in a warm, bright light. As soon as the carriage started, Robert began talking about the estate, describing every patch of land they traversed, as if he were showing his lands off to tourists, highlighting all the natural resources, talking about the number of animals in the pastures, relating the numbers of corn and other crop yields for the year.

Julie looked at him in awe. This was the most she had heard him speak ever since they had met. She realized this was what he must have been like with Mary.

At her side, Mary listened to him with her mouth agape. Julie doubted Mary understood half the things he was saying, but her little sister was riveted, nonetheless. Transfixed, even. If Julie didn't know any better, she'd think Mary was in love. Which she probably was in her own girlish way.

Robert, on the other hand, acted like a devoted father. A father neither Mary nor Julie had ever had. Julie couldn't help but feel immensely grateful for that. Mary needed a steady male presence in her life. And oddly, Julie was glad that it was Robert.

They reached the tenants' housing a few minutes later. Robert went on to talk to farmers and workers, while Julie and Mary were left behind to speak to the women, distribute baskets, and inquire about the health of older villagers. To Julie's surprise, Mary protested only a little when Robert left them behind. Then she approached the neighbors unafraid and entered their homes as if they were lifelong friends.

There were no sideways glances pointed her way, and everyone seemed genuinely delighted to see her. This attitude surprised Julie. In Norfolk, people avoided any association with Mary, and in London, Julie was shunned just for the mention of her. Here, people were wary of Julie, though she understood their uneasiness very well. She had been the new mistress of the estate for several days, after all, and she was gracing them with her presence only now.

But what surprised her most was their open affection directed at her sister. Was it a reflection of Clydesdale's demeanor? Perhaps the villagers were looking to him on how to treat Mary, as the people of Norfolk looked to her father. Whatever the case might have been, Julie was glad for the outcome.

While she discussed the tenants' needs and their overall well-being, Mary rested, ate, and drank tea in their houses. Julie watched Mary all the while. She acted differently—relaxed and content. She was not the scared girl who came from the asylum a few days ago; she wasn't the sheltered girl who'd lived on the Norfolk estates either. She was visibly healing and blooming into a confident young lady.

They'd been going around the village for a couple of hours, and Mary was already extremely tired when Robert finally came back to pick them up.

"How was your day?" he asked as they climbed back into the carriage.

"Educational," Julie replied with a tranquil smile.

"And Mary, how was your day?"

Mary placed her head on Robert's shoulder and yawned loudly.

Julie let out a small chuckle. "I am guessing exhausting," she said, still studying her sister's relaxed profile.

Suddenly Mary jerked from Robert's side and plastered her face to the carriage window, shouting something and pointing somewhere outside.

"It's a pond," Robert said in an even tone.

Julie followed the direction of Mary's gaze and saw what had her so interested. The pond was frozen, and there were people, mostly children, skating on it.

"There are people," Mary said with a voice full of wonder.

"Have you never skated before?" Robert asked Mary, and she just shook her head, her gaze glued to the people moving on the pond.

Robert lifted his eyes to Julie's. "Don't tell me you've never skated before either?" He raised a brow to her.

"I did," Julie said tightly, remembering her first attempts at skating as John held her hand, his tender gaze as he did so. She had to clear her throat before she continued. "Our neighbor taught me. But we couldn't quite make Mary cooperate."

"Perhaps she is ready to reconsider." Robert nodded thoughtfully. "I think I have some blades in the attic. We shall go skating tomorrow."

Julie opened her mouth to protest, but Mary fairly jumped in her seat and turned to Robert in her excitement.

"We shall? I want to skate!" She kept jumping excitedly in her seat, and Robert laughed.

Julie was surprised to realize that she'd never heard him laugh before. The deep masculine sound sent pleasurable shivers down her spine. He looked up at her with a questioning gaze, and Julie realized that she'd been staring. She hastily averted her eyes.

"When will we go skate?" Mary kept asking in excitement.

"Tomorrow," Robert repeated and smiled at her. "We'll take our luncheon with us and make a day of it. What do you say?"

"Skate!" Mary turned back to the window where the scenery had changed from the pond to the estate driveway, a smile lingering on her dreamy face.

Julie slid her gaze back to her husband's form. He was also looking out the window, his profile as hard as ever. She almost thought she had imagined the tender exchange between him and her sister just a moment ago and his deep rumbling laugh. There was a lot she didn't know about her husband, she realized. Maybe it was time for her to find out.

Soon after they came home, Robert had left for Doncaster on business and hadn't returned until after dinner. Mary sulked all day long, acting irritable and pouting like a spoiled child. Julie was happy to see her behave that way. Anything was better than the distant gazes and meek behavior she'd witnessed from her when they first brought her home from the asylum.

Julie found herself walking past Mary's nursery for the dozenth time that day. After spending an afternoon with her and the tenants, she hoped they might be on more amicable terms. She couldn't find the courage in herself to test the theory, though, especially without Robert's soothing presence. She decided to wait for him before approaching Mary again but changed her mind abruptly once she heard the dowager's voice coming from the room.

Julie stiffened, afraid that the dowager was chastising Mary in Clydesdale's absence. She stalked closer but couldn't hear the conversation clearly. The door was partly open, and she entered without a knock. What she saw nearly stopped her in her tracks.

Mary was sitting on a windowsill with an embroidery hoop. The dowager was sitting on the same sill across from her, explaining the embroidering method. She looked carefully at Mary's work and was correcting her with unlimited patience. The frown of concentration on Mary's face, and the way her tongue peeked out from her mouth, showed how much she wanted to get it right. Julie's eyes started filling with tears at the sight, but she blinked them back.

"What are you doing, Mary?" she asked gently.

Mary's head shot up as she regarded her thoughtfully, then she turned to the dowager as if asking for help. Julie's heart squeezed in an icy grip.

"Embroidery," the dowager said gently to Mary.

Mary turned to Julie then. "Em-roi-dery," she said slowly.

Julie swallowed her smile. "May I join you?" she asked, coming over to their side.

"Not if you want me to teach you too," the dowager said harshly, not looking her way.

"I'll try my best not to disturb you," Julie said quietly.

She picked up an embroidery hoop from the basket by the dowager's feet, some cloth, and thread, and started working. She sat quietly, working on her patterns and watching Mary work. The dowager was calm and patient with Mary, explaining everything to her in an easy-to-understand manner, repeating herself as often as necessary. She was acting as if she was her real grandmother.

Julie felt the weight of the world lifting from her shoulders. This was an elated feeling. The feeling that she didn't have to do everything alone. That she had allies, people who stood by her and supported her and her little sister. She had a family. After all these years, she finally had an actual family.

By the time supper rolled around, however, the dowager's mood had changed drastically. She became stern and snippy, chastising Julie for every little misstep. It was then that Julie realized Her Grace was not this harsh and cranky with everyone, just with her. She snapped at her for sitting wrong, for eating wrong, for looking in the wrong direction. Although snapped would be too strong a word. She stated her criticism in a cold, emotionless tone, in a way that set Julie's teeth on edge.

By the end of the meal, Julie finally understood why the dowager was irritated with her. At least in part. When the dessert was brought up, she eyed an apple tart with a grimace before looking at Julie with narrowed eyes.

"I tried to be patient with you all this time," she started

slowly, "and Clydesdale asked me to act amicably, so I did."

Julie almost choked on her tart. That was her acting amicably? What was she like when she didn't bother trying?

"But it is clear to me now that you care nothing for my grandson, and I shall not stand for it."

"Surely you know ours was a marriage of convenience," Julie answered diplomatically.

"Well, he could have chosen one of the women who were throwing themselves at him. And trust me, there were quite a few. And instead, he chose you, and I shall never understand why."

"Nevertheless, he did choose me. And with all due respect, whatever relationship we have is none of your business," Julie said more firmly, although her hands shook.

"I know what kind of relationship you two have. No kind," the dowager thundered, which for her was almost like shouting at the top of her lungs. "You don't even know his favorite foods. You've been feeding him tongue and cooked fruit and vegetables—"

"Those are the most sought-after foods," Julie interrupted indignantly.

"Don't you ever interrupt me again," the dowager said as slowly as was possible, emphasizing every word. "I shall not stand for this kind of disrespect in my house."

Julie raised her head at this and regarded the dowager stonily. "But it is not your house, Your Grace," she said calmly, her chest heaving in indignation. She felt her hands grow cold from the iciness of the duchess's gaze. "I do apologize for interrupting," she added hastily after a few moments of silence. Besides, as much as Julie hated to admit it, the dowager was right. Julie had never once tried to figure out anything about her husband. In contrast, he'd tried his best to make certain Mary felt comfortable in his home and that Julie blended in seamlessly as a peer's wife. "All I wanted to say was, he knows what he is doing."

"Of course, he does." The dowager relaxed her stiff stance a little. "His parents weren't the most affectionate lot; his first fiancée was a harlot."

First fiancée? Julie's head shot up in surprise and confusion, and the dowager's face lit up with a satisfied smirk. Julie couldn't identify the feeling that gripped her at the thought of Clydesdale being betrothed to another woman.

"Yes," the dowager continued in an offhand manner. "Since he loved her, it was a hard blow when the wedding was canceled. Not that I was surprised, but nobody ever listens to what I have to say."

Julie doubted that, but her mind was stubbornly stuck on the dowager's previous words. *He loved her.* Julie felt sick to her stomach.

"I suppose he never recovered from that. So, he picked the only woman he could find who wouldn't give him the illusion of love, warmth, and family." The dowager lowered her eyes to her plate. She put a piece of tart in her mouth before chewing slowly as if contemplating the taste. "He detests baked fruit," she said with her usual grimace of distaste thrown toward Julie.

Julie pushed her plate away from her, all the thoughts and unknown feelings simmering inside her. "If you'll excuse me, I am not hungry anymore," she said, getting up from her chair.

"You are excused," came the dowager's stern voice.

Julie hurried away from the room, feeling shame, anger, bitterness, and some other unknown feeling clutching at her heart. She ran into the library and sat by the hearth for hours, staring at the fire and repeatedly thinking of all the things that the dowager duchess had said to her.

She was right. Of course, the old dowager was probably always right, the type of woman who had never made a single mistake in her life. Julie, however, made plenty of mistakes. She'd married the cold and unfeeling earl, or so she thought, and didn't even bother finding out whether there was any depth to him.

She'd been surprised at his affectionate behavior toward her sister and yet she still hadn't made any overtures to get to know him. Even when crafting the menu, she never once thought of what her husband might like to eat; she only thought of what might impress the dowager. Never had she imagined the old dragon would prefer her grandson's favorite foods instead of expensive vegetables and fashionable fruit pies.

Then there was the matter of Clydesdale's first fiancée. *She was a harlot,* the dowager had said when describing her. She understood why Clydesdale never mentioned that to her. Theirs was a marriage of convenience, and he wasn't required to divulge information about his private life to her.

Why then did she have a strange, prickly feeling in her chest at the thought of him loving another woman?

A memory popped into Julie's head. The deal they'd made during the yuletide. The first thing Clydesdale ever asked of her was not to cuckold him. His first bride's betrayal must have cut him deeply. She felt compassion toward him and unexplained anger toward the unknown woman who'd caused him pain.

She might not love him, Julie thought resolutely, but she

could definitely give him the warmth and family that he needed. She would try to become a proper wife to him, whatever that entailed. She tried to divert her thoughts from the inevitable night when she'd be expected to deliver an heir, trying to concentrate on the nights before.

The last time he came to her bed, he thought she detested him, but that wasn't true. Even then, she was simply scared. He evoked strange feelings in her she wasn't sure how to respond to. She thought about his large hands caressing her breasts and shivered. She might not be entirely ready to come to his bed yet, but as she thought about him, his tall frame, his frosty gray eyes, she couldn't help but crave his presence beside her. She might even enjoy his touch. His kiss.

She wasn't certain how to approach him and make herself act differently so he wouldn't leave her bed again without consummating their marriage. If only she were more experienced. If she knew what to do and how to act, perhaps he wouldn't be inclined to leave. It wasn't like she could just ask him, could she?

Julie let out a deep sigh. Maybe she was going about it all wrong. She would never feel comfortable around him if they spent no time together. Yes, she should do what she'd planned from the first and establish a friendlier relationship with her husband. And she knew just where to start.

Chapter 12

The next afternoon, Julie wrapped some meat pies, bread, and wine in a clean cloth and put them in the basket for their outing to the pond. She asked Alice to dress Mary as warmly as possible without bundling her into heavy blankets since she wanted her to have freedom of movement.

Robert met them downstairs with three pairs of skating blades in his hands.

"I hope you wore comfortable boots," he said, looking them over from head to toe.

Mary raised her skirts to her knees, showing off her black leather half-boots.

"Good." Robert chuckled lightly, and Julie was again taken aback by the smooth, silky sound. "Ready?" Robert looked up at her, and Julie smiled in answer.

Once they came to the pond, however, Mary's expression changed. She became guarded, a concentrated frown on her face. She studied the pond and the people around her while

Robert sat her on a log by the pond and tied the blades to her boots. He took her by the hands and tried to help her up. Mary wobbled on her feet, tightly gripping his hands before plopping down theatrically and absolutely refusing to stand on the blades again.

Robert tried to coax her gently to join him on the ice and, after a while, finally gave up and took her blades off. Mary sat on her log and happily observed the proceedings before her.

"I don't know about you," Robert said after a while, "but I came here to skate." He stood up, flashed a smile toward Mary, and walked to the pond.

Julie watched him with a broad smile on her face. He moved assuredly on the ice, gliding, as if he were born there, his form athletic, his muscles moving beneath his clothes, straining against his coat. Julie caught herself imagining his naked thighs as they moved beneath his breeches.

She colored and averted her gaze. She'd only seen him naked once, and it was dark while she was stressed and frightened. She remembered how huge he looked in his naked form, how menacing he seemed to her. She was curious what he'd look like naked in broad daylight. She squeezed her eyes shut, trying to chastise herself for her wanton thoughts. It wasn't as if she'd ever see him naked in the daylight, anyway.

"Are you not going to try?" Robert asked after circling the pond once and stopping in front of them.

Julie smiled at the invitation. He looked so joyful, gliding around children on the ice, almost boyish. Not a trace of the formidable earl was left on his features. She couldn't possibly refuse. She stood and, with a wave to Mary, stepped onto the ice.

148

She hadn't skated in years, and she wasn't that good at it, to begin with. So, by the time she finally made it to the middle of the pond, Clydesdale had already made several laps around it.

"Is that all?" he called mockingly. "Is that as far as you can go?"

That sounded almost like a challenge. Julie dug in her heels and pushed away from the surface, trying to gain momentum as she chased her earl of a husband around the icy pond. Julie laughed, as she couldn't come even close to her husband's speed. She stopped at the side, gripping a nearby tree branch so as not to fall.

She noticed children clearing away, unsure whether they were allowed to share the pond with the master and mistress of the estate. Julie didn't want to make them uncomfortable; it was her duty to make sure everyone felt welcome. But of course, for the children, a couple of aristocrats probably looked threatening.

Julie looked around, thinking of a way to make them seem playful. She saw the snow on the surface of the ice and got a silly idea.

She bit her lip, watching her husband's back as he stood a few paces away from her, shouting something to Mary. She bent down awkwardly, picked up a bit of snow, and rolled it into a ball. Julie glided toward her husband just as he turned to her and threw the snowball right in his face.

Julie gasped and shut her mouth tightly. She covered it with her hands so as not to burst out laughing. Clydesdale sputtered as the snow got into his eyes, nose, and mouth. She was stuck between laughter and embarrassment. She didn't mean to hit him in the face. In fact, she'd hoped he would have time to duck away. She'd just wanted to lighten the atmosphere, and now she worried she'd made it worse. She noticed how the people around her grew suddenly quiet.

Clydesdale raised his hand and slowly, deliberately wiped the snow off his face. "Was that a challenge, wife?" he said, his face stony.

Julie let out a smothered laugh and covered her mouth with her palm tighter.

"Oh, do you think this is funny?" He raised a brow, still looking dark and sinister. Something about the severe features of his wet face brought on giggles in Julie. "If you think," he intoned with his eyes narrowed, "that you will get away with this—"

At that, Clydesdale made a lunge for her, and Julie started with a shriek. The sudden movement made her stumble, but Clydesdale caught her by her waist and drew her to him. Julie was laughing earnestly now, clutched in her husband's protective hold.

The momentum carried them farther. They made a couple of twirls together before Julie tried to disengage herself, resulting in her stumbling again and, this time, falling on the ice.

Julie laughed breathlessly as she tried to sit up, her skirts tangled around her feet. The laughter and slippery ice made her clumsy as she tried to get up to her knees unsuccessfully several times, falling repeatedly. She was about to chastise her husband for not helping her up when she heard an agonized scream from the bank of the pond and saw Clydesdale's face stricken in horror. Before she could turn to see what had happened, he was already halfway to the edge of the pond.

What she saw made her gasp in worry. Mary was running

toward her, stomping heavily on the ice, her hands flailing about her, her eyes filled with tears, screaming for her.

Julie got up and glided toward her hysterical sister when another cry broke out from Mary as she fell to her knees. There was the sound of a crack just before Mary's feet fell beneath the surface of the ice.

Robert reached her at that moment and quickly tugged her out of the icy water before she was even wet to her knees. But Mary was crying inconsolably, screaming, and twisting away from his touch.

"You hurt her!" Mary was screaming against Clydesdale's chest. "You bad!" She was hitting him in his chest and arms and trying to twist away from his hold.

Julie reached their side and extracted Mary from her husband's arms. "Look at me, darling," she coaxed her frightened sister. "Look at me," she repeated more firmly. "He didn't hurt me. I am fine; we were just playing."

Mary wiped her tears with the side of her arm. "Playing?" she said, looking at Julie with sad round eyes.

"Yes, playing. Remember? Like we used to do?" She tried to smile at her sister reassuringly.

"With John?" Mary asked unexpectedly.

Julie was shocked into silence for a few seconds before regaining her composure. She didn't think Mary remembered John. She hadn't mentioned him before. Julie raised her head and saw that her husband had stiffened at Mary's words.

"Yes," Julie said carefully. "With John."

Mary nodded her understanding, wiping her tears away with her shawl, still gasping, trying to calm down. She then came closer to Julie, and for the first time since before she was taken to the asylum, she hugged her.

Julie closed her eyes, lost between agony and bliss, tears streaming down her face. She had dreamed of this moment ever since she'd lost her, and with every passing day, she'd thought she'd never reach it. She hugged her sister closer to her heart, kissing the top of her head, and placing her cheek against her hair. She inhaled her sweet scent. Her little sister was finally in her arms.

"I'll go take off the blades." Robert turned and walked to the bench.

Mary finally twisted out of Julie's arms and regarded her curiously. "Why do you cry?" she asked innocently, looking up at her.

"Because I missed you." Julie kissed Mary's forehead and hugged her close once again, just enjoying her dear sibling's warmth.

After a moment, Julie eased Mary away and looked her over. She seemed unharmed, but her feet and calves were soaking wet. If they stood in the open frigid air longer, they risked freezing her.

"Let's go back to the bank," she said, and at Mary's nod, they shuffled back to the firm, dry land. "And you don't have to worry," Julie added, looking at her husband's form as he took off his blades from his boots. "Robert will never hurt me. He is good."

"I love Rob," Mary said emphatically.

Julie's lips twitched as she tried to stifle her laughter at the quick turn in her sister's mood. "What about me?" she asked playfully.

"I love you," Mary continued seriously. "And Grandmama. And John."

Julie's heart gripped in a painful vise at the mention of her first love. *I love him, too,* she wanted to say but remained silent.

* * *

They reached home quickly, and Robert immediately ordered a hot bath for Mary. He didn't know how Julie would be able to coax Mary into getting into the bath, but he knew it was the quickest way of getting her warmed up.

The maids stripped Mary to her chemise and covered her with blankets while giving her hot tea. Julie hovered about her, fussing and fretting, touching her face, trying to gauge if she was coming down with a fever. Robert stood nearby, watching the proceedings, unable to help.

By the time the bath came in, Mary was sufficiently warmed up so that her teeth weren't chattering anymore, but her limbs were still cold.

"Mary, sweetheart, you need to climb into a hot bath," Julie said, looking at her intently.

"No!" Mary said and shook her head for emphasis.

Julie looked at Robert as if for help, and he stepped closer.

"You are cold. We don't want you to get sick," he said. "You need to get warm and quickly. The only way for you to do that is to get into a warm bath."

Mary gave a decisive shake of her head.

Robert turned back to Julie. She took a deep breath and looked around as if thinking of something. She finally turned and looked at Robert resolutely.

"I have an idea of how to coax her into the bath."

"Very well." Robert frowned but nodded in support. He had no idea what she could possibly come up with.

"I shall need your help," she said quietly.

"Anything," he said without hesitation.

Julie smiled at his answer.

What she did next had him gaping in surprise. She turned her back to him and started slowly undoing her bodice and pushing her skirts out of the way. She backed toward him and asked him to untie her stays. Robert swallowed audibly but complied, slowly undressing Julie in front of her sister. He saw goosebumps cover her skin when his fingers accidentally touched her. His breathing grew frantic, and he felt the heat rise to the surface.

When she had stripped down to her chemise, she came to stand by the bath and stretched her hand toward him. Robert understood immediately. He came closer and took her hand in his.

"Mary," Julie drawled. "Look, I am going to enter the bath, and it is not going to hurt me."

Mary jumped to her feet. "No!" With a yelp, she scrambled to the side of the bath, trying to drag Julie away.

Julie gripped Robert's hand stronger but didn't relent.

"Mary, remember when I told you that Robert would never hurt me?" Mary nodded slowly. "Then he wouldn't help me with getting into a bath if it was bad for me, would he?"

Mary just looked at her wide-eyed. Julie slowly placed one foot, then another, over the bath rim and sat gingerly inside.

"Mmm…" She made a sound of pleasure.

Robert closed his eyes in agony and shifted from one foot to the other. This was torture.

Mary took a tentative step closer to the bath and looked over the rim at her blissful-looking sister. Then, slowly, she stretched her hand toward Robert.

Robert smiled and helped her into the bath. Mary sat

gingerly facing her sister, and Julie grinned, before splashing a few drops into Mary's face. Mary squirmed at first and then giggled happily.

"Now you!" She looked at Robert and made Julie laugh.

"I am afraid the bath is too small," Julie said with a smile and looked up at her husband. God, he loved her smile. When it was genuine, her smile lit up her entire face. He couldn't help but look lower, to her exposed collarbone, her wet chemise billowing in the water, successfully concealing her wet, feminine form. He raised his gaze and saw his wife shyly looking back at him, her face rosy and wet. Robert's breeches tightened uncomfortably.

"I'll ask the maids to get you some towels," Robert said in a hoarse voice before turning away and walking out of the room, the image of his wet wife forever etched on the backs of his eyelids.

* * *

Despite the traumatic experience of watching her little sister fall through the ice, this day had been one of the happiest in Julie's life. After taking the hot bath and scrubbing Mary thoroughly, she braided her hair while exchanging meaningless gossip and chatter. She had dreamed of this ever since the day she woke up to find Mary gone.

She had been fifteen at the time. Her mother's funeral had been the day before, and Julie was in a wretched place. After witnessing the horror of her mother's death, she'd been pale and weak and spent most of her time in her bedroom. She came out of her room only to get Mary, and they would spend the entire day burrowed in bed together, reading and talking.

Mary was Julie's only solace. She would walk Mary back to her bed, return to her empty room and stare into the canopy of her bed until the early lights of the morning, unable to sleep.

The morning after the funeral, as she shuffled into Mary's room, she knew something was different the moment she put her hand on the door handle. She didn't know how she knew. Maybe the smell had been distinct, or the light, perhaps even the air was thinner, signaling the ominous change in the room.

The moment she opened the door, the feeling turned into certainty as she surveyed the empty chamber where her sister used to reside. The coverlet on the bed was different; the curtains were bright orange, not Mary's favorite pink. There were no toys and books by the bedside. Julie stormed into the dressing room, but there was no clothing.

It was empty.

As if somebody had tried to erase Mary's entire essence. As if she had never existed.

Julie raged and screamed and yelled to no avail. Nobody answered her questions and pleas. Her father was nowhere to be found. Her mother was dead, and her sister was gone. She remembered crying herself to sleep every night, praying to be reunited with her little sister, whispering all the things they would do together once she had her back.

Now sitting on the comfortable, warm bed, braiding Mary's hair, she vowed she'd make up for all the lost days, weeks, and years without her sister. She took a deep breath and looked over Mary's careful braid.

"All done." She ran her hand over Mary's head just to feel her warmth beneath her palm. She'd missed touching her sister.

Mary nestled comfortably against her chest. "Will you read to me?" she asked in a sleepy voice.

Julie smiled against the top of her sister's head, remembering all those nights she used to read to her before bed. "Of course. What would you like me to read?"

Mary shrugged, and Julie decided what she would read to her little sister. Her diary. That way, they could both relive their happy days, and perhaps Mary would remember more of the things from her past.

Julie walked over to her room, picked up her diary from her writing table, and brought it with her to Mary's room. She perched on the side of the bed and started reading to Mary from the beginning.

"I always considered my birthday the most important day in my life. My mother would order servants to make my favorite dish, I was allowed to stay up later with my mother as she read to me, to play longer than usual. But that day was relegated to second place the moment my baby sister was born. I saw her wrinkly pink face, her tiny fists, and heard her ugly wail, and I was instantly in love. She was mine."

Julie looked up and saw Mary dozing off, the comforting sound of her sister's voice lulling her to sleep. Julie wondered how Mary slept all those nights in the asylum. She doubted anyone ever read to her there, and her heart clenched at the thought of her in that dirty, drafty place. She was here now. It was all that mattered.

Several minutes later, as Mary slept peacefully on the bed, Julie left her side and walked slowly to her bedroom. She dismissed Alice since she wore nothing more intricate than a nightgown and a robe after the bath. Julie brushed her hair and stared into the looking glass, carefully studying her own features. Her face was pale, framed neatly with her dark curly hair. She closed her eyes and swallowed before collecting her hair in a simple bun.

She was stalling. She'd decided last night that she would finally take steps toward honoring the bargain with her husband. The events of the day had only strengthened her resolve. So, she secured her hair carefully with pins and walked toward the adjoining door to her husband's bedroom. She took a deep breath and knocked lightly. There was no answer. After another shy knock, she entered the dark room. Her husband wasn't there. She let out a breath she didn't know she was holding.

He wasn't there.

A reprieve.

But the thought of waiting another night, of dreading it again, made her palms perspire. No, she'd do it tonight.

* * *

Robert sat at his impressive mahogany desk, twirling a quill in his fingers. He'd been sitting there, pretending to work for several hours now. Ever since he'd left his half-naked, wet wife in the bathtub. His cock twitched just thinking about it.

Robert let out a pained groan. He closed his eyes and saw her happy, glowing smile as she sat in the bath, playfully enticing her sister to join her, completely unaware of the effect she was having on her husband.

It didn't help that he had not had a woman since before his marriage. As the weeks passed, it was more and more difficult for him to keep himself in check. After tonight, he'd be unable to ever close his eyes without seeing her half-naked, drenched body.

His thoughts were interrupted by a knock on the door of his study.

"Yes?" he called without taking his gaze off the quill still clenched between his fingers. He looked up from the thoughts about his wife only to encounter her standing shyly before him.

"I hope I am not interrupting." She smiled apologetically.

Only from the thoughts of you. "No, I was just"—Robert looked around at his forgotten papers on the desk—"finishing up."

Julie made a step farther into the room. She was wearing one of the enormous robes that covered every inch of her, the high neckline of her ruffled nightgown peeking out of it from above. She was wrapped in the billowing cloth, looking like a fluffy cloud. There was nothing seductive about the clothes she wore, but he was seduced, nonetheless.

"Good." She smiled and took another tentative step farther into the room. She looked around as if seeing the room for the first time, and he realized it was, in fact, the first time she had ever come here.

"Is there something that you wanted?" he asked courteously. "Is Mary well? Does she need something?"

"No." She shook her head and smiled lightly. "Mary is quite well. I put her to bed just minutes ago. I don't think the fall through the ice impacted her at all. You were very quick at retrieving her."

Robert nodded silently. *What do you want then?*

"I wanted to thank you—" she started slowly, but Robert interrupted her briskly.

"I thought I told you to cease thanking me."

"—for saving her life," Julie continued as if he hadn't spoken.

"Anyone would do the same," he said with a dismissive wave of his hand.

"Nevertheless." She continued advancing on him, shyly fiddling with her skirts.

"Is that all?" he asked, his voice slightly hoarse. The vision of her in her nightgown did unconscionable things to his imagination. "Is that why you came here?"

"No." She bit her lip before rounding the desk and perching herself on one hip right in front of him. Robert leaned against his seat, creating as much distance as possible between him and his wife. "I thought we could talk," she said, idly fiddling with the papers on his desk and not quite meeting his gaze.

"About?" He narrowed his eyes on her and put his hand on top of hers, staying the motion. She finally lifted her eyes to his.

"About our deal," she whispered.

"What about it?" His blood was rushing through his veins, pounding violently in his head. He was afraid he knew why she'd come.

"I thought it was time we started our marital relations," Julie said, confirming his thoughts.

She'd come to thank him for saving her sister's life, using her body as payment. Somehow the thought made him sick. He wanted her in his bed. Badly. But through the passing weeks, after everything they'd been through, he'd imagined her coming to him willingly. Not because of their deal, and definitely not as a payment for services rendered. It wasn't fair to her, he knew. They had a marriage of convenience, and feelings were never part of the deal.

He felt nauseous for wanting what he couldn't have. Again.

"I thought—" she continued, but he stood abruptly, halting her mid-sentence.

"It's not a good time," he said, walking past her and stopping in front of the fire.

Julie followed in his tracks. "You are probably busy now," she said delicately. "I apologize for interrupting, but maybe you'll come to me after—"

"Why?" He whirled around on her.

"Why?" she repeated, looking perplexed.

"Yes, why tonight?" he asked in a menacing voice that made her step away.

"I told you I needed a few weeks to-to be ready, and now I am."

"Are you?" he asked, advancing on her. "So, you won't recoil from my touch?" He reached out to touch her face, and she instinctively drew away. "That's what I thought," he said darkly, incensed with himself for hoping she wouldn't.

"That's not fair," she said, her eyes glinting in outrage. She took his hand and placed it against her face. "You are frightening me on purpose." She pressed his palm against her cheek, looking him squarely in the eye. "I didn't recoil from your touch," she said defiantly, stepping even closer.

She was a few inches away from him, her chest almost brushing the front of his shirt. Robert's self-control crumbled at that moment, and he drew her sharply against his hard body. She gasped at the sudden motion and put her hands against his chest as if to push him away.

Julie raised her head and looked into his eyes, wide-eyed, as he lowered his head to hers and took her mouth in a scorching kiss. He felt her stiffen in his arms. Her mouth froze under the onslaught of his kisses. He kissed her hungrily, the way he'd wanted to since that first time he'd kissed her in the bedroom of his Hampshire estate, hoping she would gentle in his arms and return his kisses.

Her hands gripped his lapels, and he realized with an ache in his heart that she was holding her breath. He lifted his head and saw that she had her eyes tightly shut. She was disgusted by him, he realized with anguish. While he was tasting her like a ravenous wolf, delighting in the warmth of her body against his, she was enduring his kisses with tightly shut eyes, probably counting the seconds until this was over.

Julie finally opened her eyes and regarded him curiously. She took a deep breath, her lush breasts grazing against his shirt. Robert slackened his hold on her and stepped away.

Julie put the back of her wrist against her mouth, just like she did in Hampshire when she wiped her mouth after the kiss. She didn't move her wrist this time, just held it there for a moment as if he'd bruised her lips.

"Go to your bedroom, Julie," he said, turning away from her and walking back to his desk.

"Will you come to me tonight?" Her voice was unstable. She sounded horrified at the prospect.

"No," he said with bitter resignation. "You are safe from me."

"But I want—"

"Go, Julie!" he said irritably.

He looked at her from beneath his lashes as if looking directly at her would hurt his eyes. She was breathing heavily, her face pale, stricken. After a moment of hesitation, she turned and fled the room. Robert lowered his head to his clenched fists. He really needed to go to London.

Chapter 13

Robert's hot hands were all over her body. He was pressing her close to him while kissing her lips, her neck. His tongue felt like silk on her skin, scorching and soothing her at the same time. Julie felt hot all over. She was clinging to his arms, moaning to get more. More of what, she didn't know; she just never wanted him to stop. His hard body felt so good as she trailed her hands over him. His delicious weight pressed her into the sheets. She raised her head and placed her lips on him, wanting to feel his tongue caressing her lips again.

Julie woke up in her bed, sheets tangled between her legs. Her chemise rode up to her waist, her body hot, her breathing labored. It had been a week since Clydesdale left, and for the seventh night in a row, she'd dreamed of him. That day in the study had turned her whole notion of him on its head entirely.

She had never imagined the cold, dispassionate earl acting that way. Holding her as if nothing in the world mattered, kissing her as if he wanted to devour her. Until he'd dismissed her without so much as a flick of his hand. But ever since, all she could think about was having his hands on her again, having his tongue inside her mouth. She never would have guessed that thought would be so alluring.

He, on the other hand, hadn't seemed to feel any of the feelings Julie had rising to the surface. After he'd dismissed her from his study, he'd gathered his things and left for London the next morning. She couldn't understand how someone could be so passionate and insistent one moment and indifferent the next.

He'd left without even saying goodbye, which was the most frustrating part. Robert had entrusted the dowager with breaking the news to her and Mary. She understood he didn't care enough to say goodbye to her, but he could have at least notified Mary himself. He'd left her a note, but that wasn't much of a consolation to a child who was so wholly attached to him.

He'd said he'd get the townhouse ready for them and that they should follow him in two or three weeks. Perhaps she was reading too much into his behavior. She wished he cared, so she attributed those qualities to him. He'd shown his true feelings by leaving them cold, without a single word. That would teach her to dream of better things.

Julie changed her mind between leaving it alone or confronting him every other hour. She didn't remember the last time she'd gotten so emotional about anybody's actions. It was probably the day her father shipped John off to the army. She thought about the letter she had to send him, notifying him she wouldn't be waiting for him anymore, that she was getting married. She couldn't even fathom the hurt she was inflicting on him with that letter—to be made aware that someone you cared so deeply for was cutting you out of their life.

Julie shook her head. She had no intention of letting Clydesdale do that to her. It wasn't enough that he was her husband; now he occupied every space of her thoughts. She was dazed and confused, and she kept thinking about him at the most inappropriate moments, most notably when the dowager was drilling some rule of conduct into her head. Julie had to do something about that, and fast.

She walked up to the dowager's favorite sitting room and knocked lightly on the door.

"Come in," the dowager said in a harsh voice.

Julie swallowed and opened the door. "Good day, Your Grace." She curtsied and walked farther into the room. The dowager was sitting in a chair by the fire, her legs wrapped in an afghan, her spectacles sitting crookedly on her nose, a book in her lap. She looked as if she had been dozing rather than reading.

"I don't see how this day is any good," the dowager scoffed.

Julie looked out of the window. The icy rain lashed at the windows, the weather gray and gloomy.

Julie took a deep breath and approached the dowager. "I wanted to talk to you about going to London," she said, coming closer and sitting on the settee across from the duchess.

"What about London?"

"Mary keeps asking when we can reunite with Robert," she said evasively. She didn't want the dowager to know how much she wanted the same.

"Mary is a smart child. She knows people with good hearts; she is drawn to them."

Julie swallowed a dig against her since Mary was not as drawn to her, even though she was her sister.

"Yes, well, she misses him, and I think there is no need for us to wait any longer. Traveling with her will take a long time, anyway. Clydesdale will have plenty of time to prepare the townhouse for our arrival."

"Mary can wait. As long as she is occupied here, she won't mind too much for a few days. Why do you want to go to London?" The dowager narrowed her eyes. "Not enough gowns? Or perhaps your soldier is back on leave."

Julie's heart pinched hard at the mention of John. And an unpleasant feeling settled in her midsection at the dowager's tone. She still didn't trust her.

"Have I given you any reason to suspect me of mercenary motives or of infidelity?" Julie blurted out her first thought then bit her lip from saying more.

The dowager regarded her curiously. "No, but there's not much entertainment here in the village. Let's see how you behave among the *ton*." She sat straighter in the chair.

"In order for you to see anything, I actually have to be among the *ton*." Julie stood, done with trying to please the old woman. "I shall order the carriage to be readied by tomorrow if the rain slows. I hope you don't mind." Without so much as a by your leave, Julie strode to the door and exited the room.

She pressed her back against the door and breathed heavily, her heart pumping. She had never acted so disrespectfully to the old duchess, and to tell the truth, she was a bit scared of her. Very well, a lot scared of her.

It didn't matter; tomorrow they would be on their way to London. She could at least mend the relationship with her husband. If they were as amicable with each other as they'd

166

been the past few days before he left for London, living under the same roof as the dowager would be a lot more bearable. Perhaps she could order some new gowns that would entice him enough to finally come to her bed. She imagined his touch on her skin and got hot all over. *I have to stop thinking of him all the time.* She hurried to tell Mary the news of their trip.

* * *

Robert stood on the docks hugging his coat close to his body. It was extremely windy, the rain lashing against his face. He'd been standing like this for what seemed like hours. He'd been in London for several days now, attending Parliament and meeting up with his friends. However, he hadn't done the most important thing he'd set out to do when he made the trip.

Robert had received a note the night before he hastily left for London stating that Mr. Benjamin Tule, the York Retreat manager, who was the only person interested in changing the treatment of people held in asylums, was going to dock there any day. Finding the perfect excuse to escape his wife, Robert had started for London immediately. Only Tule's ship had been delayed due to weather. As a result, Robert had to spend his time in London doing everything else.

Another reason for his London trip was Vanessa. He'd come here with every intention of resuming his relationship with her. To finally feel the comfort of her warm arms and the pleasure of the release he hadn't felt since before his marriage.

Only he didn't do that either. For some reason, he kept stalling and putting off his visit to his mistress. A day turned into a week, so here he was, standing at the marina a sennight later, freezing his bollocks off and thinking that perhaps today wasn't the best day to visit her either.

At that moment, he noticed his solicitor rushing toward him, a thin man in dark clothing walking by his side.

"Finally." Robert let out a deep breath. "I am glad to finally meet you, Mr. Tule." Robert shook the stranger's hand and looked him over.

Mr. Tule wasn't a tall man; he was thin and pale but with strong and confident features.

"A pleasure," Mr. Tule returned. "Apologies for the delay. The weather would not be reasoned with. I've heard that you've asked about me for quite some time."

"Right," Robert agreed. "Perhaps we should adjourn to the carriage and continue our conversation there, lest we freeze to death." His face felt numb from the cold, and his hands were like two blocks of ice. At Mr. Tule's nod, they proceeded into the carriage.

As soon as they settled inside, Robert regarded Mr. Tule intently.

"Tell me, my lord—" Tule started first.

"Clydesdale is fine," Robert interrupted.

"Of course, Clydesdale. You don't mind that we jump straight to business, do you? I am quite tired from the journey." At Robert's brisk nod, the man continued. "Tell me about your interest in the York Asylum?"

Robert rubbed his frozen hands together before answering. "I recently got married—"

"Congratulations, my lord."

"Yes, well, my wife's sister was confined in an asylum for several years until we got her out."

"I am extremely sorry she had to go through that." Mr. Tule seemed genuinely worried.

"While we were in that place, I noticed the poor conditions of the asylum itself, the cracks in the walls, the drafts, the dirt. But that's not the worst part. The way they handled her while bringing her to us—" Robert paused and shook his head at the horrifying memory. "Then, I noticed some bruises, cuts, and burns on her body. From years of abuse, I assume."

Mr. Tule was shaking his head during the recitation.

"I've dug up all the reports, articles, and documentation on the place," Robert continued. "And all of them praise the asylum for being humane, for excellent care, and cleanliness." Robert grimaced in disgust before assuming a severe expression. "All except for one article. From you."

"They are stationed basically next door to us." Tule nodded. "And I have never seen the inmates in their gardens or anywhere for a walk, even one by one. Their doors are always closed; often, we hear screaming. Whatever happens behind those shut doors, many people die every year in that asylum. I don't have evidence to support my claims other than the things I've seen with my own eyes, but that always led to my word against theirs. And lunatics are problematic witnesses, especially if they're dead."

"I am willing to testify against them," Robert said firmly. "I shall take the testimony of our family doctor. He'll do a check-up and confirm my allegations."

"That would be a good start. However, to reform a whole asylum, it needs more than that." Mr. Tule narrowed his eyes on Robert. "How far are you willing to go for this?"

Robert raised his brow. "What do you suggest?"

* * *

Julie was directing the servants to prepare everything for their trip to London when she heard a carriage rounding their driveway. Julie's eyes lit up in excitement, and she ran out the front door.

Was it possible? Was Robert back?

She stopped cold as she saw an unknown carriage stop in front of her. A tall, dark-haired, handsome young man hopped out of the carriage and bowed to her politely.

"Didn't anyone tell you to greet your guests inside the house?" he asked, smiling widely. "Not that I don't enjoy special treatment."

"Oh." Julie woke from her stupor, staring at the stranger's deep brown eyes. "I thought you were Robert." Julie curtsied and looked at him in question.

"Apologies, I must have left my manners back in London. Lord Eric Howard, Robert's cousin."

"Of course." Julie frowned, not remembering Robert mentioning his cousin to her. Then again, he hadn't told her about any of his relatives except for the dowager and the duke. "Please, come in."

They entered the hall together, and Julie saw the dowager's disapproving expression as she stood on top of the stairs.

"You are not welcome here, Eric," she said in her regal voice as she started gliding down the stairs.

Another person who hadn't won favors with the dowager, Julie thought.

"Come now, Aunt. I came to meet Clyde's beautiful bride and to wish them the best since I wasn't invited to the wedding," he said with a charming smile. "With both of us married, don't you think bygones should be bygones?" He raised a brow and smirked.

"I want you out of the house," the dowager thundered, stopping on the final landing.

"Oh, but you are not the mistress of the house, are you, Aunt?" He grinned at her. "Lady Clydesdale here invited me to stay."

The dowager looked at Julie coldly. "Did you now?"

Julie almost flinched under her gaze, but she managed to hold her own. "We can't turn him away this late, can we? Besides, Lord Howard is family," she added with a smile.

Howard smiled back at her, then turned toward the dowager duchess.

"Maybe you should consult with your husband before showing hospitality to his"—the dowager regarded Eric with a disgusted grimace—"family members."

"Well, he is not here, is he?" Julie snapped. "Mrs. Post, please show Lord Howard to his quarters." She turned to Lord Howard apologetically. "We were supposed to go to London on the morrow."

"No apologies necessary. I shan't stay long," he said with a grin.

* * *

Julie spent most of that day in the company of Eric, as he insisted she call him. He was an engaging conversationalist, charming and entertaining. He wasn't judgmental about Mary and was polite and courteous. He told amusing childhood stories of him and Robert. The way he, Robert, and Lord St. Clare participated in mischief in Eton.

"When was the last time you saw him?" Julie asked, curious to know more about her husband. "It's just... it seems like you only knew each other as children," she observed.

"We drew apart after Eton." Eric shrugged. "There was a girl in town. I was in love with her most of my life. Robert knew that." He laughed bitterly. "But he still seduced her and then left her."

Julie furrowed her brows. "That doesn't sound like Robert," she said instantly.

"And you know him so well?" Eric raised a brow. "Forgive me," he continued after a brief silence on Julie's part. "I didn't mean to pry; it just didn't sound as if you two had a love match." He looked at her intently.

"No." Julie shook her head. "Not a love match. But I've gotten to know him well, I think. And he is caring and responsible—"

"Yes, responsible Rob," Eric sneered, a touch of jealousy in his voice. Julie wondered if she'd imagined it.

"Why is the dowager angry with you?"

"Isn't she angry with everyone?" He grinned at Julie charmingly.

"Perhaps you are right." She smiled back at him. "Thank you for telling me all these stories. I enjoy learning more about this family I married into. I know Robert is probably the one who should be telling me all this," she added quietly.

"Anything to help my cousin. I shall be glad to assume any other roles he's neglecting," he said with a lazy smile.

"Look at the time," Julie said, suddenly feeling uncomfortable. "We better get to supper. I wouldn't want to anger the dowager even more."

"No," Eric agreed. "We wouldn't want that."

* * *

Julie walked to the window and looked out at the dark gardens below. She was getting ready for bed and thinking over the events of the day.

The dinner had been awkward. Every time Eric had asked something of Julie, the dowager interrupted him. She threw disapproving glances at him all evening and asked him pointed questions, indulging in monologues preventing him and Julie from conversing.

Eric just brushed it off and winked at Julie, indicating that the dowager's behavior hadn't upset him in the least. All this tension only made Julie more curious about Eric and what past connected him to her family.

She noticed a lone figure standing with a lantern amidst the flowers. She peered into the darkness and thought she recognized Eric's silhouette. She battled for a moment with herself, but curiosity won out. Julie threw on a warm shawl and stalked outside.

The night air was chilly in the garden. She drew her shawl closer and huddled beneath it. Her soft half-boots made a sound on the snow, and Eric turned as Julie moved closer.

"Out for a night walk?" he asked with his usual charming grin.

"You could say that," she said with an answering smile. "And you?"

"Well, I strategically placed myself underneath your window, hoping you'd see me and join me on my walk."

Julie raised a brow at him, puzzled.

"If that hadn't worked, I would have sent you a note," he continued with his lazy smile.

"Why did you want me to join you?"

"Why did you join me?" he countered, and she laughed.

"I wanted to talk to you," she said softly.

"And I was hoping we could skip that part." He took a step closer to her, so they were face to face, only a foot apart.

"Pardon?" Julie had to raise her head to look into his face.

He took her chin between his thumb and forefinger and placed a kiss on her mouth.

Julie drew away, shocked. "What are you doing?"

"Don't act innocent. You've wanted this."

"I most definitely did not want this!" Julie cried, wiping her mouth with her sleeve.

"Oh, please, no need for theatrics. Nobody can see you down here." He moved closer once again.

Julie was frozen in shock and fear, watching him advance on her.

"Those gazes you sent me throughout supper, I know you want me. And I can give it to you too," he said, placing his head so close to hers that their noses were a hair's breadth away. "I can fuck you harder than Robert ever has."

Julie flinched from the vulgarity and was about to draw away again, but Eric grabbed her by the waist and placed a hard kiss on her mouth. He moved one hand to the back of her head so that she couldn't move away. Julie felt his tongue licking at the seam of her lips, and she squirmed in disgust, pushing at his chest.

Eric grabbed her by the hair and kept her face an inch away from his. "Don't struggle," he sneered between his teeth and drew closer again.

"Stop it!" Julie screamed, finally finding her voice. "Stop it! Stop it!" She emphasized each word with a shove of her fists at his chest. Tears of helplessness streamed down her face. Another man was using his physical strength against her, and she couldn't do anything to protect herself.

He placed his mouth on hers once again, and Julie bit him. Hard.

"You bitch." Eric shoved her away and wiped at the blood on his mouth.

Julie stumbled and landed on her bottom in the grass and snow.

"You'll pay for that," he snarled at her, coming closer. "Why do you struggle, anyway? Do you think that your beloved Robert is faithful to you?"

Julie heard a rustle of leaves behind Eric and something that sounded like footsteps. She prayed it wasn't her overactive imagination conjuring up saviors but that one of the servants had come outside and heard the struggle. Eric didn't seem to notice anything, so absorbed he was in his tirade.

"Well, I'll tell you the news, love. Robert has numerous mistresses. Why do you think he went to London? To work? The season has barely started. He doesn't have a thing to do there. He went to indulge in carnal delights you, apparently, cannot provide."

"You are lying!" Julie spat at him, although she wasn't sure of it.

She didn't quite know what he meant by carnal delights, but she'd refused Robert her marriage bed. So what if he went to his mistress?

Eric laughed, a hollow sound, devoid of humor and warmth. "So sure of your dear responsible Robert, are you? Well, let me tell you something. The night I left for Clydesdale Hall, I saw him entering his lover's apartment. The apartment he pays for, by the way."

"I don't believe you." Julie's voice didn't sound as confident anymore.

"Oh, you can ask him. I am sure he will tell you the truth. Ask him who Vanessa is." By this time, Eric stood over her in the shadows. Julie was still sitting in the grass, looking at him wide-eyed. "As for now, I shall show you exactly what he's doing there with her." Eric lowered his hands to her skirts and started lifting them up.

Julie yanked her legs closer to her torso and grabbed his hands to stop his movements. The action upset Eric's balance, and he fell on top of her. Julie shoved at him, but he grabbed her by the hair again.

"You!" They both froze as the dowager's stern voice slashed the air between them. "Get your filthy hands away from my granddaughter," she spat.

Julie was thanking the stars for the timely interruption. She was so relieved that she didn't even notice the way the dowager referred to her.

Eric took his weight on his elbows and regarded the dowager with his steady gaze, still lying on top of Julie.

"You call this whore your granddaughter? Look at her! She was five seconds away from servicing me." He smirked and ran his hand over Julie's breast, making her flinch and dig herself deeper into the cold ground.

A loud crack split the air, and Eric rolled away from Julie, screaming in agony and holding his leg. Julie regarded him in shock, then turned to the dowager to see her holding her walking cane like a weapon.

"Touch her one more time," she said ominously. "And next time, it won't be your leg."

She extended the one side of her walking cane to Julie. Julie grabbed it like a lifeline and was immediately pulled by the dowager to her feet.

Julie started beating at her skirts and straightening them as she got up. Her hands were shaking, her breathing was heavy, and she didn't want the dowager to see her tears and quivering lips. She bit her lower lip hard, but sobs kept escaping her.

"Come, child," the dowager said in the soft tone of voice she only used to address Mary.

She took her by the arm and led her to the back entrance of the house. Julie still shook and sobbed all the way.

"And you," the dowager threw over her shoulder. "I expect you to leave these premises before dawn."

They walked the rest of the way in silence.

The dowager led Julie to her sitting room, sat her in the chair by the fire, and brought her a glass of wine. This was the first time Her Grace, the Dowager Duchess of Rutland, had brought anything to anyone. She didn't even wait on Mary.

"Are you feeling well?" she asked in her usual stern voice.

This harsh voice helped Julie pull herself together. She sipped the wine and nodded.

"I'm sorry I—"

"Disobeyed me, disregarded my advice, invited the snake in against my wishes?" Julie nodded mutely, looking down at her glass. "Well, you've learned your lesson, haven't you?"

Julie placed her wine glass on the floor next to her chair and looked straight into the dowager's eyes.

"You should have told me the truth," she said evenly. "Whatever the truth was. You knew something about Eric. Enough to spy on him, or me. But you still haven't told me a thing."

"What I know wasn't enough to suspect he'd assault you. And it's not for me to tell, Julie. It's for Robert."

"Well, he's not here, is he?" Julie bit her lip and looked away, confident that the dowager had seen the agony and hurt on her face. "He's in London," she said more quietly.

"Don't listen to what Eric said," the dowager said more softly.

"How can I not?" Julie asked, hardly above a whisper.

Not that she blamed him. She raised her eyes to see the dowager regarding her curiously.

"You care for him," she said rather than asked.

Julie stared mutely at the dowager's face.

"Why didn't you say anything to him?"

Julie bit her lip and looked away again. "It's a marriage of convenience. He doesn't owe me anything."

"Nonsense," came the dowager's stern reply. "I happen to know something about marriages of convenience. I've had one myself."

Julie turned back to her and regarded her curiously. "You did?" she asked in a daze, not surprised at the revelation, more astonished that the dowager was willingly sharing information about her past.

"I was in love with another man." The dowager nodded, her gaze concentrated on something behind Julie's back, as if she was looking at her distant past. "Just like you. But unlike you, I had a choice. I could have married the man I loved, but I chose the title over him." She turned her face back to Julie. "I thought that was what you did too. I thought you cared nothing for my grandson, and I resented you for that." She cleared her throat delicately. "And maybe that's exactly how it started for you, but I can see now that you truly care for him… And he cares for you."

Julie lowered her gaze to the hands she clasped in her lap. "I don't think he does," she mumbled. "We—He—He hasn't come to my bed since we got married. I know it's my fault, but… then he left for London after we—" She paused and laughed bitterly. She was about to tell the dowager about the kiss she still dreamed about. The one that drove Robert away from her and into his mistress's arms. Tears scalded the back of her eyes. His betrayal hurt beyond words. She licked her parched lips before speaking again. "I don't believe he cares for me. He left us here, didn't he?"

The dowager stood and patted her on her shoulder. "I know, child. But the worst thing you can do is bury all those feelings inside of you. Don't repeat my mistake. Don't be too prideful to confront him with your feelings."

Julie felt all strength leave her. She needed to pull herself together and take her family to London. She worried she didn't have enough fortitude left for that.

Chapter 14

Robert dropped Mr. Tule off at his house and ambled on to his townhouse. He thought about what Mr. Tule had said to him in the carriage. What he'd suggested would most definitely ruin Clydesdale and especially his wife.

Mr. Tule had said that for the best effect, Robert would need to bring the abuse Mary had suffered in the asylum into the light. And by bringing it into the light, he'd meant to send a letter to the *ton*'s most popular paper. That should gather enough public attention to force the change of governors, allowing Tule to take one of the available seats. In return, that would give him access to monitor the dealings of the asylum more closely and perhaps help find more evidence of mistreatment of the inmates.

Benjamin Tule was a reformist. He was goal-oriented and uncompromising. Robert was sure he'd be good for the asylum. Still, he was also convinced that the details he'd have to recite in the letter would paint Mary in a bad light, leading to a great scandal that would envelop his family and ruin his father's ambitions of having Robert be accepted by his peers.

He'd need to talk to both his wife and father before sending the letter to the papers. As hard as things might be for them, he felt it would be the right thing to do. He hoped his family members would agree with him.

As soon as the carriage drew to a halt, Robert collected the sides of his jacket closer to his body and jumped out of the vehicle. He coughed and hurried up the front steps and entered his townhouse.

He was greeted by his valet, Jensen, at the door. "You have a guest, my lord, in your study." He waved a hand in the study's direction.

Robert moved past him in the indicated direction before asking over his shoulder, "Is there any correspondence for me?"

"On your desk, my lord."

Robert thanked Jensen with a nod and strode into his study.

"Finally, here you are," his friend said in a slurred voice. "Where the devil have you been? I've been waiting for you for hours." Gabriel was sitting behind Robert's desk, drinking his expensive whisky.

"I see." Robert shed his jacket and settled across from Gabriel. "How much of that have you had?" He indicated the bottle by Gabriel's right hand.

Gabriel followed the direction of Robert's gaze. "Not nearly enough." He grabbed another glass from the sidebar and shuffled back to his chair. "Want some?"

"Why not?" Robert leaned back in his chair and scrubbed his face with both hands.

"You look like hell," Gabriel stated, handing him a full glass of whisky.

"Likewise." Robert raised both eyebrows at his friend. "What in the devil has happened to you?" he asked, regarding his friend's disheveled appearance. His hair was mussed, cravat and coat missing, his waistcoat gaped open, and his shirt was misbuttoned. "And what are you doing in my study at this hour?"

"Well," Gabriel said slowly. "First of all, you are supposed to be at home at *this hour*. You are married now, aren't you?"

"So?"

"So? Since I haven't seen you at the clubs, I can only assume you spend all your nights with Vanessa." Gabriel raised his eyebrows. "Didn't you have a holier-than-thou attitude toward marriage vows and fidelity? Smirking at sleeping with married women?"

"I didn't promise her fidelity." Robert shrugged.

"Look, I am not judging." Gabriel put his hands up in mock self-defense. "Who am I to judge anyway, right? Simply curious why you shoved your principles aside. She isn't a picnic in bed, is she? All the proper ones are like that," he continued as Robert kept silent. "Why do you think men keep mistresses after marriage? I've heard horror stories about proper ladies keeping their clothes on in bed, unmoving, not making a sound. It's like lying with a corpse." Gabriel shuddered theatrically, while Robert grimaced. "They say they don't allow their husbands into their beds more than once a week either. Not that you'd want to come more often after that experience." Gabriel laughed with a drunken grimace. "My advice to you, my friend, keep Vanessa. At least she'll keep it interesting for you."

"You are constantly bedding married women. You don't

find them as dull as you describe."

"Well, not the ones who come to me, no. But they are a different breed. Besides, wives are generally not fond of their husbands. They act cold and proper with them and become harlots in my arms." He smiled lazily.

Robert refilled his glass and downed it again. That sounded too close to reality. Julie wanted nothing to do with him. She didn't want his touches or kisses. He remembered the way she'd shrunk away from him the first time in bed. The way she'd reacted to his kiss, her horror-stricken face, the stammering. He was a fool if he'd thought she'd be pliant in his bed. But it was too late. He'd made his bed, and he'd have to lie in it. With his unwilling wife. Forever.

"Why aren't you cavorting with one of those harlots then?" Robert changed the subject from his unhappy marriage. "What are you doing in my house at this hour, Gabe?"

"I *was* with one of the harlots. In fact, I climbed into Ellie Lance's bedroom and was giving her the lick of her life." Gabriel relaxed in his chair. "She was moaning so loudly that even her half-deaf husband heard us. He dashed through the door with a pistol. Thought someone was killing her." He threw back his head and laughed, staring at the ceiling. "Once he saw what was going on, he challenged me to a duel." Gabriel shrugged nonchalantly.

Robert's eyes widened at the matter-of-fact recital of the duel challenge. "You came here to ask me to be your second?" he asked, pouring himself another drink. Robert's voice was getting hoarse, and his throat burned.

"God, no. There is no way in hell I am dueling over the chance to toss her skirts. We didn't even get to the good part."

Robert laughed at his friend's careless attitude. "You are

planning to hide from him," he said rather than asked.

"For just a week or so. He's bound to give up, eventually." Gabriel took a sip of his drink thoughtfully, then chuckled. "Dueling over the honor of a woman who's sucked half of London's cocks. Can you imagine?"

"Maybe you shouldn't have done it under her husband's nose," Robert pointed out.

"I'm five and twenty. I can afford a little adventure."

"You're five and twenty, too young to be shot by a jealous husband."

"That is unfair, isn't it? Why should I pay for her lusty nature? Or his inability to satisfy his wife?" Gabriel shrugged again and downed his drink.

"Indeed." Robert regarded his own drink darkly before tilting it to his mouth and drinking it dry.

* * *

Robert woke up the next morning with a cracking headache. The sun was streaming into his face, hurting his eyes. There was a slight buzzing in his head as he got up and looked around. He'd fallen asleep in his chair, resting his head on his desk. Gabriel was nowhere to be found. *Thank God.*

Robert couldn't deal with his friend's cheerful disposition after the night of drinking. Only two years older, he felt ancient compared to the exuberant, life-loving Gabriel St. Clare, a man without a care in the world.

Robert shuffled off to his room to perform his morning ablutions. The pounding in his head wasn't his only problem. He shivered in what seemed to be a warm room, and his throat felt scratchy. He let his valet dress him and shave him, feeling worse than he had the night before.

After he was presentable enough, he went to his study to encounter his secretary.

"My lord—"

"No time for pleasantries, I'm afraid," Robert said, his voice hoarse. "Pick up a quill. I need you to draft a letter for the papers."

Robert dictated the horrifying details of what he knew about Mary's experiences in the asylum, trying to soften the wording to preserve her dignity as much as he could. Then he folded the letter, put it in his coat pocket, and ordered the carriage ready for his visit to his father.

"A note for you, my lord," the butler said and handed him an envelope. Robert opened the missive and instantly recognized the handwriting.

Come to me at once. The matter is of utmost urgency.

Robert frowned at the note. He walked toward the carriage and turned to the driver. "To Vanessa's townhouse."

* * *

Julie entered the dark and gloomy house. It had taken them eight days to get to London from Doncaster. It hadn't been possible to keep a brisk pace with Mary. She had been sick from all the swaying in the carriage and got tired rather quickly, so they made frequent stops and didn't spend more than six hours on the road a day.

The servants bustled around them, bringing up their luggage, preparing supper, and steaming the water for their baths. The house was thrown into upheaval in a matter of minutes, but by the look of it, everything had been quiet in the townhouse for days. Julie looked around her. She remembered little of the place from the brief visit after the wedding. It seemed... empty.

Mary yawned and swayed lightly into Julie's side.

Julie hugged her closer and looked at the housekeeper. "Mrs. Post, would you mind showing Mary to her rooms?"

"Of course, my lady." The older woman bowed and led Mary away.

"I shall retire as well," the dowager intoned crisply and sauntered toward her rooms, leaning slightly on her cane.

The proud woman rarely leaned on her cane this much, but the eight-day trip had worn everyone out. The dowager had her own lodgings in London, but she'd informed Julie that she'd be staying with them for a while.

Julie didn't protest. The dowager seemed to enjoy Mary's company, and Mary hers. No matter how much the duchess grumbled at Julie and looked at her in distaste, she was family. Much better family, in fact, than Julie's own father. And Julie had started to appreciate her company during the long and challenging trip.

Julie gave the dark hall one more perusal before she turned to the passing butler. "Is his lordship not home?" she asked, although she knew the answer.

"No, my lady," the emotionless butler intoned evenly.

"When did he leave the house?"

"I couldn't say, my lady."

Julie raised her brow in reaction but didn't respond. *He couldn't say.* That could only mean one thing. The butler knew exactly where her husband left and when. He just wasn't inclined to tell her.

They'd spent eight days on the road. Surely, he could spare

a few minutes to greet them, no matter how busy he was. The dowager had sent a letter informing Robert of their arrival before they left for London, so he should have been aware of their trip. Unless, of course, he hadn't been home for days. Julie frowned in thought. With a deep sigh, she ambled up the stairs and into her room. The room she'd spent exactly one night in before, scared and confused.

After a lonely supper and a bath, Julie lay awake in her bed staring at the ceiling. The dowager and Mary had foregone the supper and retired early. Julie, however, couldn't sleep.

The house was quiet. Too quiet.

She'd already gone to check on Mary twice. Something about this empty townhouse triggered the memories of the night Mary had disappeared, of the nights leading up to that. The image of their mother, bloody and in pain, flashed before her eyes. Julie turned and put a pillow over her head.

How different would her life be if she had married John? She wouldn't spend a single night alone and frightened in the darkness, she was sure.

The sound of something snapping or clicking startled Julie, and she sat up in bed.

Was Robert finally home? She stood and tiptoed to the door, leaning her ear against it. Everything was quiet. She sighed and returned to her bed.

Every little sound had her thinking—hoping—that it was Robert coming through the front door. But all her hopes of seeing him had died sometime after her candle burned out. Robert hadn't come home that night.

* * *

The next morning, Julie jumped out of her bed and ran straight into Robert's bedroom. His bed was made up and clearly not slept in. No clothes were on the bed either. He still wasn't back.

She looked out the window. The clouds were gathering over the sky, the weather windy and gray, promising precipitation. She worried her lip, wondering what could have kept him out all night.

Had he spent the night in his clubs? What if he'd spent the time with another woman? What if that's what he'd been doing in London all this time? He had asked her to be true to him, but he'd never made the same promise. Julie's heart clenched at the unpleasant thought.

She slowly went back to her own room, rang the bell for Alice to help her dress, and sat on the edge of the bed. All her strength abandoned her.

Alice walked in, looking bright and happy, a complete opposite of Julie's own sour mood.

"Is his lordship back yet?" Julie's rising hopes were dashed as she regarded her maid's apologetic face.

"No, my lady." Alice curtsied lightly and bustled forward, dressing Julie.

Julie frowned, trying to push unwanted thoughts away. *He is unharmed, and he isn't with another woman.* She repeated it over and over in her mind.

As the morning went by, she wasn't so sure what to think anymore. Her mood darkened even more when Mary seemed to be more withdrawn than usual. She asked about Robert nearly every second, heightening Julie's agitation. Not having answers bothered her more than she was willing to admit.

Her worries and uncertainties showed on her face and

gnawed at her soul if she sat idly by. She knew that. She'd learned that lesson from her unfortunate home. When things were bad, or when she was lonely, scared, and agitated, she worked. So, she got to work putting the townhouse in order.

She ordered the maids to clean up the house, came up with the menus for the upcoming month, ordered some furniture moved around, and made lists of things she needed to buy to make this empty house cozier.

As the afternoon rolled on, winded but surer of herself, Julie went in search of Mary. The fact that Clydesdale couldn't bother to greet them in London didn't mean they couldn't explore the city on their own. They would go shopping, she decided.

She found Mary in her room, sitting on the windowsill, looking out the window into a gloomy garden.

She was hugging her knees, crouched, and swaying slightly as if to calm herself. Since the door was open, Julie didn't bother to knock. She walked into the room and sat beside Mary.

"Good day, gorgeous, want to hear the good news?" she said, gently placing her hand on Mary's back.

Mary turned her head toward her, a grimace of pain marring her features.

"What's wrong?" Julie's eyes widened in horror. "Are you in pain?"

"Yes, pain," Mary repeated, clutching her small fist to her chest.

"Oh, God! Let's go lie down, darling," Julie said and took her gently by her arms. She led Mary carefully to her bed and frantically rang the servants' bell. "Alice, call for a doctor, now!" Julie cried as soon as the girl entered the room.

In several minutes, the house was in an uproar. Maids were running back and forth, bringing clean sheets, boiled water, cloths, and other things that weren't remotely helpful. Several footmen were dispatched to find and bring the doctor.

Mary was perspiring immensely, cold sweat running down her face, as she lay curled up on the bed. Julie didn't let anyone close to her. She was sitting by her side and holding her hand while the dowager assumed her most formidable stance and barked out orders.

"Do not fret, my darling, all will be well," Julie crooned to her sister. "I am right here."

"Rob?" Mary called in an agitated whisper.

Julie bit her lip and tears ran down her face. "He'll be back soon, darling," she whispered and prayed that she wasn't lying.

Mary used to get chest and abdominal pains, but they had never been this severe. Julie was afraid that something was incredibly wrong. What if she did not get better? What if it took too long for a doctor to get here?

Julie had been looking out for Mary ever since her little sister was born. She'd taught her to speak, to read. She was the one who always looked after her when she was sick.

Their mother had been sickly ever since Mary's birth, and all the burdens of motherhood had fallen on Julie's fragile shoulders. Their father had never taken an interest in either daughter.

Julie was supposed to be used to the responsibility of taking care of her little sister. Yet, she was extremely terrified. The only thing she wished, other than for Mary to get better, was for Robert to be by their side. He would know what to do. He would take command of the situation; he would make Julie feel safe.

She closed her eyes and lowered her forehead to Mary's chest, listening to the frantic beating of her heart. "Not now, sweetheart. Not when I just got you back," she whispered.

After about an hour, the doctor finally arrived.

Mary was sleeping by that time, so Julie was reluctant to let him see her, but she didn't want any complications with her condition. She'd had breathing problems since childhood. Her heart would start beating faster, she would have difficulty regulating her breath, and she'd be tired and sleepy. But this time, it was slightly different. Or so Julie thought. She had contributed Mary's melancholy to Robert's absence, but perhaps Mary had not been feeling well for over a day.

What a perfect sister she was, she thought harshly. She should have had her checked by a doctor the moment she got her back from the asylum. But Julie hadn't wanted to scare her. And she hadn't wanted even more doctors to intrude on Mary than they already had.

The dowager entered with the doctor, and they advanced to Mary's side.

"She is sleeping now," Julie started babbling instantly. "Should we wait for her to wake? What do you think is wrong with her? What are you going to do?"

The doctor, a white-haired, kind-looking man, patted Julie on the shoulder. "Relax, child, I'll just need to do a check-up. I might not even wake her."

Julie nodded, appeased, and stepped aside to allow the doctor to pass farther into the room.

"I need you to leave, Julie," the dowager blurted.

"Pardon?" Julie said, staring at the dowager in horror. *Why would she say that?* "I am not leaving her."

"You are too emotional; the doctor needs to do his job."

191

"I am not leaving her," Julie said more firmly, enunciating every word, although she shook inside. She remembered the last time doctors had treated Mary. They did it through bloodletting. The memory of that horrid device, Mary's pale face, and her cries flashed before Julie's eyes, but she refused to let that sway her.

"We are wasting time arguing, Julie. Dr. Grisham is the best in these parts. You have to trust him," the dowager said in final tones.

Julie looked over the woman before her and mirrored her stubborn stance. After their brief tête-à-tête after the incident with Eric, she thought she and the dowager were on good terms. Apparently, she had been wrong. The dowager wanted Julie to learn from her? Well, she'd begin with this. She wouldn't let anyone dictate to her in her own house, much less boot her out of her sister's room when she needed her. She was the mistress of this house, and she'd do whatever she thought right.

"I trust him," Julie said firmly. "But I am not leaving." With these words, she moved past the dowager and closer to Mary's bed.

Julie and Alice had Mary undressed down to her chemise, and the doctor started looking her over. The doctor felt Mary's limbs before he put some metallic objects on her side and midsection. He was about to do the same with her chest when Mary shot up in bed with a startled yelp. A high-pitched scream split the air as she started shoving at the doctor in a panic, eyeing the unfamiliar man by her bedside in horror.

"Mary, dear, all is well," Julie said as she tried unsuccessfully to restrain her. She hugged Mary tight and tried to hold her still, so she wouldn't overexert herself. "Mary, darling, please calm down," she crooned.

"No! No! No! No touch! Bad!" Mary kept shouting through the tears and hiccups.

Julie's own eyes filled with tears before they ran down her cheeks. She had never seen Mary this frightened. This was much worse than her reaction to a bath. What had they done to her in that asylum? Julie's own sobs were as loud as Mary's as she held her in her arms and rocked her on the bed, trying to calm her down.

"Julie," the dowager said sternly. "The doctor needs to continue; you're making things worse."

"I am not leaving her," Julie said as firmly as she could, though her voice was trembling. "I am not leaving you," she repeated into her sister's hair in a broken whisper. "Never again."

They sat like that, hugging each other and crying on the bed for what seemed like forever. Julie heard through her haze a muffled conversation between the doctor and the dowager. She couldn't make out any words, but a few moments later, the door closed, and all was quiet except for the sisters' mingled breathing and occasional hiccups.

"I'm not leaving you," Julie repeated quietly to her dear sister and heard a contented sigh in return.

"Don't give me to the bad doctor," Mary said between hiccups.

"He is not bad. He won't hurt you," Julie whispered against her sister's hair. "I shan't let anybody hurt you."

"I want Rob," Mary suddenly said after a brief pause.

Julie swallowed a lump in her throat. "I know, sweetheart," she whispered back. "Me too."

* * *

Robert stretched and sat up in bed. He reached his hand up to his face and felt a two-day bristle on his chin and cheeks. He looked around the room in confusion. The red wallpaper, the roses at the vanity table, and cherry-red satin sheets covering the bed he was sitting on could indicate only one thing. He was in Vanessa's bed.

By the state of his undress and the fact that he was sitting in her bed, he'd probably spent the night there. The problem was, he couldn't remember anything that had happened the night before.

The last thing he remembered was walking toward her door, knocking—

Then everything was a blur. He thought he remembered entering her home, but that's as far as his memory went.

Now, however, sitting surrounded by her bedsheets, he started remembering the agonizing heat, then the cold shivers and fever-dazed dreams. He dreamed of Julie tending to him. Her cool hands wiping the sweat off his forehead, feeding him soup. He'd even mumbled something to her, something private, something he couldn't remember now. He closed his eyes and let out a pained groan. It was rather apparent to him now that Julie was nowhere near him.

He groaned as he tried to get up. His entire body hurt, and he felt weak and light-headed.

The door opened at that moment, and Vanessa entered the room.

"Oh, you're awake," she said with a lazy smile and trotted seductively to him. She placed a hand on his bristled cheek. "You need a shave," she said with a smile as he pulled away from her. "Do you want me to do it?"

"No, thank you," he said briskly, his voice scratchy. He cleared his throat. "I have a valet for that. Where are my clothes, Vanessa?"

"I asked my maid to have them washed and pressed. They are probably ready for you but—"

"Ask your maid to bring them to me." Robert got up and swayed before catching himself on the bedpost. He looked down and realized that he didn't even have his drawers on. "What happened last night?" He threw Vanessa a narrowed gaze.

"Last night," she said, looking contemplative, "you were quite hot." She smiled as she approached him again and placed her hand on his hard chest. "You should've heard the sounds you made." She dropped her voice to a seductive half-whisper and traced his chest to his abdomen, then ventured lower.

Robert placed a hand on top of hers to halt her descent. "I remember nothing," he said, studying her face.

Vanessa rolled her eyes and stepped away. "Of course, you don't. You came here three days ago and dropped on my doorstep with a high fever." She went to her vanity and studied her reflection while twirling locks of her dark-brown hair.

"Three days?" Robert's voice cracked.

Vanessa looked at him over her shoulder. "You were quite insensible. I had to take care of you, watch over you."

"Thank you," he croaked and closed his eyes. He still felt weak, so he lowered himself to the bed.

"Seems like lately, it's the only way I can lure you to my bed," she said, sounding irritable.

"I am sorry, Vanessa," he intoned. "I appreciate you looking after me, I really do, but… I shall not be coming to you anymore."

"What?" Vanessa turned on him fully, her hands clenched into fists by her sides.

"It's over. That's what I came to tell you."

"That's not what you said in your fever-hazed dreams. You said you needed me. You wanted me." She was seething in anger; it seemed like steam would come out of her ears soon.

"I remember nothing, Vanessa. But I am a married man now. I can't keep coming to your bed."

"That's not what you said last time you were here either. You said nothing would change."

"I was wrong. I'm sorry."

"Don't you dare apologize to me again!" she cried, breathing heavily. "You owe me more than that."

"I know. I brought you a parting gift." He raised his hand to pat his coat pocket, only to remember once again that he was naked. He lowered his hand back to his side. "I'll keep you comfortable for several more months and pay your maid, even though I'm sure you'll find a new protector soon."

"You bastard!" She hurled a small bottle of what looked like perfume at him and missed him by an inch. The bottle crashed against the pillar, spreading the scent of lilac in its wake. Vanessa's breathing slowed down a little, and she walked toward him before kneeling in front of him and placing herself between his legs.

She put her hands on his knees, then moved them higher, caressing his thighs. "You think your pretty little wife is better than me?" She moved closer to him, her breasts chafing against his chest. "I'll show you how good I can be." Her hand reached his cock and squeezed it hard. It twitched and

196

lengthened in reaction.

Robert placed his hands on her shoulders to push her away. "Vanessa…" His voice cracked a little. He couldn't help it; it felt good to have a woman's soft hands on his body.

It had been so long since he'd experienced it. Vanessa lowered her bottom to her heels, settling comfortably before him, and without taking her eyes off him, lowered her mouth to his already erect length. Her mouth was hot and moist, and it felt so good that he didn't want it to stop. Instead, he shot up as if he'd been scalded. Vanessa drew away, looking struck.

"I told you, that's not what I want," Robert said between his teeth. He moved and sat slowly on the other side of the bed, conscious of the fact that he was still not steady on his own two feet.

"Your cock tells a different story," Vanessa said confidently.

"My cock doesn't know better. Please, tell your maid to bring my clothes. I need to leave."

"She'll never be as good as I, you know," Vanessa said, getting up with all the dignity she could muster.

Robert regarded her with a steady gaze. "Perhaps not. But that is none of your business."

Vanessa let out a disgusted breath and left the room. Robert only hoped that it was to bring his clothes. He really didn't feel well enough to traipse around the house fully naked.

Chapter 15

J ulie sat by Mary's bed, looking at her still form, watching her closely, making sure she was breathing evenly. After Mary had calmed down, the doctor went in again to look at her, but Mary refused to cooperate.

She cried for Robert, wept for him to protect her, and Julie's heart seemed to break into tiny little pieces at that moment. As a result, the doctor had promised to visit in the morning in hopes Mary would be in a better frame of mind to receive him.

Julie raised her head at a light knock on the door. A moment later, a vast shadow entered the room. She couldn't see clearly, but she felt rather than saw it was Robert. Julie almost shot up from the chair, millions of thoughts invading her mind all at once. Instead, she stood slowly and regarded her wayward husband stonily.

Robert ran his gaze over her body before fixing his eyes on her face. He looked awful. His beard needed shaving, his clothes were disheveled as if he'd dressed in haste, and his hair was mussed. A strange smell emanated from him. Something sweet, like a perfume. Lilac?

"How is she?" Robert asked in a hoarse whisper, drawing her attention back to him.

Julie swallowed about a dozen scathing remarks. He'd failed to greet them when they arrived in London, had gone missing for days, looked like he'd just come from the den of iniquity where he'd spent the last couple of weeks, and all he said was, *how is she?* No apologies, no *forgive me?*

"Well," was all she said instead.

Robert slowly walked to the bed where Mary still slept soundly and watched her for a few moments in silence. Julie didn't interfere. She just stood across the bed from him, watching the play of emotions on his face: worry, anguish, guilt.

Julie lowered her eyes to her little sister and watched the rise and fall of her chest fixedly.

"I'll go freshen up and come back to sit with her," her husband said in a hushed tone. "You're probably tired and need rest."

Julie just nodded without looking at him. She heard the sounds of receding footsteps and the door being opened.

"Where were you?" Julie said, finally raising her eyes to her husband's retreating back.

Robert turned his head toward her. "It's a long story—" He cleared his throat. "Let's talk about it later." With this, he exited the room and shut the door behind him.

With a loud sigh, Julie settled back into her chair, her limbs heavy, her mind foggy, the stress of the day finally making itself known. She placed her head on her sister's chest, slightly moving with her every breath, and in a few minutes, she was asleep.

* * *

Julie woke up early in the morning because of the sun streaming through the window. She always shut her curtains at night, so she was confused to awaken with them opened.

She sat up and looked around. She was in her room, in her bed, still dressed in her day gown, although her bodice was loosened. She didn't remember coming to her bed last night. In fact, she wasn't planning on leaving Mary when—Robert!

Julie shot from the bed and stalked to her husband's adjoining room. The room was empty and cleaned, as if not slept in. She returned to her quarters and rang for her maid. She needed a fresh start to the day if she wanted to have a confrontation with her husband.

Once she was ready, she walked to Mary's room and heard the voices there. She was about to open the door when it was thrown open. Julie almost collided with Dr. Grisham as he was exiting the room.

"Doctor," Julie exclaimed, startled.

"My lady." Dr. Grisham bowed and walked past her.

Robert was the next to exit the room, his face grim.

"Is anything amiss?" Julie impulsively put her hand on his sleeve.

Robert looked down at her hand before meeting her gaze. "No, all is well. Dr. Grisham has just inspected her. We'll adjourn to my study to discuss this further. I think it's best if you stay with Mary."

"Why?" Julie's eyes widened. "I want to know what is wrong with my sister."

"Perhaps it would be better—" Robert started, but Julie cut him off.

"No, I am tired of all of you treating me like my sister's health is none of my business. It is. It is my only business here."

Robert flinched a little at her words, but he composed himself quickly and nodded. "Do you want to speak to Mary first?"

Julie tried to peer inside the room, chewing on her lip in thought, before looking at the doctor. "I'll speak to her after. I don't want to keep the doctor waiting. Alice can take care of her in the meantime."

"Very well." Robert nodded and gestured for Julie to precede him. They all started down the stairs and into Robert's study.

Julie sat next to Robert on a settee, and the doctor settled on the chair in front of them. They exchanged pleasantries for a few moments before Robert cleared his throat and regarded the doctor with a severe stare. The doctor's gaze seemed to land on Julie as he fidgeted in his seat.

"You can talk freely in front of my wife," Robert said evenly.

"Are you sure? Because I'd be more comfortable—"

Robert glanced at Julie, and she gave him a resolute stare. "Yes, I am sure," he said.

The doctor took a deep breath before speaking again. "I am not here as a harbinger of good news, I'm afraid."

Julie sucked in her breath, and Robert took her hand in his.

"After I left this house yesterday, I did some extensive research and contacted some of my colleagues here in London and sent several letters abroad. Although the letters won't be answered for weeks, I think I have a good idea of what's ailing Lady Mary." He cleared his throat again.

201

Both Julie and Robert regarded him impatiently.

"I'd rather not upset her ladyship," he said, looking pleadingly at Clydesdale.

"Please, go on," Julie said, instinctively squeezing Robert's hand harder.

The doctor grimaced. "What I am about to say is not for a lady's ears," he said carefully.

"Oh, for God's sake." Julie threw up her hands in frustration. "Please, just tell us."

"Very well." The older man cleared his throat and adjusted his spectacles. "It appears to me that Lady Mary was not treated right during her time in the asylum. She has some deep bruising and what looks like burns on some parts of her body and other evidence of abuse."

Julie's mouth fell open, and she felt Robert stiffen by her side. His arm felt like a piece of granite. Of course, she knew or at least suspected that Mary wasn't treated kindly in the York Asylum after the way they'd found her, but *deep bruising* and *burns*? What other abuse was he talking about?

"As I understood from our conversation earlier"—the doctor looked at Julie—"Lady Mary had suffered from maladies of the chest before, but not so severe as last night."

Julie nodded.

"It might be wise to conclude that her condition worsened from the severe neglect and abuse she's suffered as a result of spending years at the asylum."

Julie flinched and stiffened at the words. If only she had found a way to get Mary out sooner. Robert's hand covered hers as if he read her mind and tried to reassure her that there was nothing she could have done. Julie relaxed slightly at the touch.

202

"How can we help her now?" she asked the doctor, her throat dry.

"I am afraid you can't," the doctor stated evenly.

"I beg your pardon?" Robert exclaimed.

"What do you mean?" Julie asked at the same time.

"There's not much known about the maladies of the chest. They usually strike unannounced with very severe consequences for the patient. Lady Mary, on the other hand, has been suffering from it for quite a while. It is known that stress and the overall well-being of a person can worsen the situation, but there are no known cures for it."

"That's impossible. She is too young." Julie heard her husband's voice through the buzzing in her head. His voice sounded far away, although he hadn't moved from the settee they both occupied.

"Yes, well, unfortunately, the disease doesn't differentiate young from old. Besides, Lady Mary also suffers from simple-mindedness." The doctor paused. "Some people in her situation barely live to be sixteen."

Julie felt the blood drain from her face. Her lips felt dry, her tongue swollen. She couldn't say anything if she wanted to. *Sixteen*. Mary would be sixteen in less than a fortnight. Julie felt Robert squeeze her hand, and she was grateful to have him there beside her. She would fall apart if it weren't for him.

"Is there anything we can do?" Robert asked in a hoarse voice.

"Keep her comfortable. Spend time as a family. Make some memories."

Julie felt tears trickling down her face. What the doctor had meant, but omitted to say, was *say goodbye*.

"But she is fine now? She doesn't need bed rest, a special diet, anything?" Robert continued his questioning.

"I am afraid nothing will change her prognosis, for either the better or for the worse." The doctor stood at these words. "I apologize for not being able to do more."

The buzzing in Julie's head grew louder, and the sounds of voices grew distant and blurred as if underwater.

Julie felt Robert's hand slide away from hers, his heat leaving her side as he moved to the door, and she wanted to cry at the loss. But her throat was constricted, and she felt paralyzed. Her world blurred in front of her. The voices sounded far away; the clock ticked loudly in her head.

What seemed like an eternity later, Robert came back to her side. He sat beside her and gently guided her head to his shoulder, encircling her in the heat of his arms. He kissed the top of her head and moved his hands comfortingly up and down her back. Julie heard herself sob, and only then did she realize tears were running down her face. She was sobbing frantically, loudly, gasping for air, clinging to Robert's body.

Mary was dying. She'd waited too long to get her back. And now she was dying. She wanted to go to her. To sit with her and talk until her throat was hoarse. But Mary shouldn't see her looking like a mess. Mary couldn't know. Julie clenched Robert's lapels in her hands as she burrowed farther into his shirt, soaking it with her tears. Robert kept stroking her back in small soothing circles and murmuring nonsense in her ear.

"Shh," he crooned. "It's going to be fine."

But it wasn't. And it wouldn't. Not after Mary was gone.

After a while, Julie finally peeled herself from Robert's side and wiped at her tears.

"I don't believe it's true," she said, her voice gravelly from crying.

"We'll get a second opinion. And third. Or however many we need. Doctors are wrong all the time."

Julie nodded. Now that she was done crying, she could think clearer—the veil of grief lifting from her foggy mind.

Doctors *were* wrong.

In fact, they had predicted that Mary wouldn't live through her first years. When she was slow in walking, they'd predicted she'd spend the rest of her life without being able to walk or talk.

Mary was resilient. She could survive anything.

"We need to—" Julie sniffed and wiped at her wet face.

Robert extended a handkerchief. She blew into it and wiped her face dry.

"We need to tell the dowager what the doctor said. Whether it's true or not, she needs to know the truth… And about the abuse—" Julie stopped as her voice cracked.

"She already knows." Robert grimaced and stood from the settee as if uncomfortable.

"Pardon?" Julie followed her restless husband's form with her gaze.

"She knows. When Mary arrived at the estate…" He took a deep breath. "There were fresh bruises on her. Bruises, rope burns, cuts."

Julie's eyes widened. "Why didn't you tell me?"

"I didn't want to worry you more than you already were. Mary wasn't talking to you; you felt guilty as it was. What would it have changed?"

"I would've—" Julie stumbled for words. "I could've… Maybe I would have insisted on seeing a doctor sooner and—"

"And what? Spent more time crying? I doubt that would

have changed the matter."

Julie swallowed. "Perhaps you're right." She nodded. "No, you are right. It wouldn't have changed things, but she's my sister! I deserve to know everything there is to do with her. I wish you wouldn't make decisions about her without me."

Julie had a bitter taste in her mouth from all the things Robert was keeping from her. She'd lived that life under her father's roof: being ordered around, not being listened to, never being consulted about anything, even her own life. She couldn't do it again.

"And not just about her," she finished her thought out loud.

"I beg your pardon?" Robert threw her a confused look.

Julie shook her head. Right now wasn't the time to get into any of this. Mary needed her.

"We need to go to Mary," she said and resolutely stood from the settee.

Robert nodded and led her out of the room.

* * *

By the time they reached Mary's room, she was sitting up in bed and chatting amicably with her maid. Robert could see relief flood his wife's features at the sight. Mary was better.

He didn't know whether what the doctor said was true, or if his predictions were correct, but he could see clearly that Mary felt better than even this morning.

They'd spent most of the day at home. Mary didn't want to stay abed, and they allowed her to roam about the house a little. The consensus was that she'd just gotten too tired from the trip, but Robert kept it in the back of his head to schedule visits to more doctors throughout the upcoming months.

It was also decided that Mary would take dinners with them from then on. Julie didn't want to spend any time apart from her sister, and to be honest, neither did he nor even the dowager.

Robert was glad for Mary's presence during supper for other reasons too. For instance, he would have felt like sitting on needles. If it weren't for Mary, he couldn't think of how he would dodge the questions regarding where he'd spent the few previous nights. Every time the conversation turned to his activities in London, an awkward silence fell around the table.

Robert didn't want to have to tell them about his illness and how he'd spent three days incapacitated in his mistress's bedroom during the meal.

Of course, a more ridiculous excuse he wouldn't have come up with in his wildest dreams, but that was the truth. Whether his wife believed it was another story entirely. However, there was another reason why he was unwilling to talk about his business in London so far. Because it would involve his dealings and plans with Mr. Tule. And he really wanted to speak to Julie privately first.

"I think it is time we attend a ball with Mary," the dowager said suddenly.

Julie's eyes widened slightly. "I don't imagine we would be well received in any of the ballrooms," she said carefully.

"Isn't she too young?" Robert asked, looking at Julie.

"Is she?" The dowager raised a brow.

"Well, she will be sixteen in less than a fortnight," Julie answered.

"Sixteen?" Robert looked at Mary wide-eyed.

She didn't look a day older than twelve. Robert saw Julie's

lips twitch at the corners at his astonished expression.

"She looks younger, but yes, sixteen," Julie said with a smile.

"Didn't you tell me you were eleven?" Robert raised a brow at Mary in question.

Mary shrugged. "I had eleven birthdays; I didn't have any more."

Julie's face crumpled, and Robert suddenly wished he hadn't asked at all. Of course, she hadn't had birthdays since she was sent to the asylum.

"Sixteen is almost old enough for a come-out," the dowager observed, popping a piece of fruit into her mouth. "Besides, it's not like we are going to wait two years for it," she added quietly.

Julie lowered her gaze to the plate. Robert's heart squeezed in a painful vise. The dowager was right. Mary might not live that long. Robert didn't believe for a second that she would die that young. Still, he would not deprive her of new experiences because of his opinion. What if she didn't live past sixteen? What then?

He saw his wife fight for composure, probably thinking the same thing as he. He reached out, took her hand in his, and gave her a comforting squeeze.

Julie colored slightly at the gesture and hastily turned away.

"Evie is having a coming-out ball soon," she told the dowager. "Hers is probably the only household that will welcome us amicably.

"Evie." The dowager pulled a thoughtful face. "Do you mean Lady Eabha? Somerset's granddaughter?"

"Yes." Julie nodded for emphasis.

The dowager frowned a little before schooling her features. "That sounds reasonable enough. The support from the duke should smooth out our appearance."

"Oh, I am sure of it." Julie visibly brightened. "Evie would love to have Mary at her ball. And she won't let anyone talk badly about her. She loves her almost as much as I."

"It's settled then." The dowager wiped her lips gingerly with a napkin. "We'll need to go to the modiste on the morrow and make sure Mary has the most beautiful of gowns."

"A ball!" Mary said, dreamy-eyed. "Like a princess."

"Yes, a ball." Julie smiled widely.

Mary was first to finish her dinner, as she still wasn't feeling too well, and Alice took her directly to her rooms.

The dowager stood next and regarded Robert down her nose. "I shall retire early tonight. I believe you owe your wife a few explanations." She bowed her head lightly and walked out of the dining room. Robert regarded her defection with raised eyebrows.

He turned to his wife quizzically. Julie just shrugged and stood from the table.

"I am going to my room, as well." She started walking away, but Robert halted her.

"Don't you want explanations?" he asked, raising one brow.

She turned and regarded him coldly. "Do you have any explanations?"

Robert was taken aback by her quiet attack, but he was also surprised and quite pleased that she was expressing her displeasure with him.

"I'll come by your room in an hour, and we'll talk."

Julie nodded and left the room.

Chapter 16

Robert finished his meal shortly after that and went to check on Mary. Mary's disposition brightened immensely once he gave her a bracelet he'd bought her during his first days in London and told her some stories from town.

He promised they'd go to the theater, the gardens, the park, and many other places together as soon as she got better. Mary immediately informed him that she *was* better, making him laugh. He kissed her on the forehead and left her slumbering in peace. With at least one female in his life appeased, he went into his wife's room.

Julie was standing by the window in her dressing gown. She turned as he walked in and regarded him warily.

"I checked on Mary just now," he said, deciding to break the ice. "She seems well."

Julie nodded. "Yes, I read to her after supper, and I think she feels much better than this morning. I hope she gets even better before the ball, although we shan't be able to stay too long. And she'll need new gowns, accessories."

Julie looked up at the ceiling, biting her lip, contemplating the expenses and all the hassle getting ready for a ball would bring.

"I have enough funds. You can buy whatever she needs. And whatever you need."

She shook her head. "My trousseau is still almost untouched."

"I feel you weren't in a celebrating mood when you were ordering your trousseau. Perhaps for Mary's ball, you'll want something different."

Julie let out a strangled chuckle as she met Robert's gaze, her eyes dancing in merriment. Robert smiled, remembering her *mourning* wedding dress.

Julie sobered quickly, though. "I imagine you are not planning on accompanying us to the shops and the modiste." She paused, looking at him intently. "Mary kept asking for you during your absence."

Robert closed his eyes and nodded. "I know. I deeply regret that happened. And I shall. Accompany you, that is."

"Good." Julie turned back to the window.

"Is that all?" Robert frowned at his wife's back.

Julie took a deep breath and clenched her hands into fists by her side.

Robert cleared his throat and moved closer to the window. "I need to tell you something. About what I was doing in London before you arrived."

He needed to tell her about the plans he'd made with Tule. He needed her to understand that if they went through with it, they would be ruined. Not just Mary, but Julie as well. He made a few steps toward his wife.

"Is it about your mistress?" she whispered.

"My miss—What?" Robert halted mid-stride; his head shot up in surprise.

Julie still wouldn't look at him.

"How—What are you talking about?"

"I know you spent all those nights with your mistress," Julie said to the window before she finally turned and regarded him squarely. "I know you went to London to be with her. You came home looking… debauched and smelling of her perfume." Julie's lower lip quivered as if she were holding herself from bursting into tears. "You spent all those nights with her when we needed you here."

"I didn't go to London just to see her—" he started as Julie lowered her lashes and bit her lip, looking like a vulnerable child.

He wanted to gather her up and cuddle her. He wanted to kiss her and soothe all her worries, to tell her he didn't need any mistress, only her. But she didn't want that. She loathed his touch. Only her pride was bruised. At that, he lost his composure.

"Why do you care, anyway?" Robert said, irritated.

"Why do I care?" Julie regarded him with surprise. "You were missing for days! I didn't know whether you were alive or if something had happened to you." Her eyes shone with unshed tears. "Mary was lying in bed, asking for you every blasted day! And when the doctor came—"

She paused, and a sob tore from her body. She covered her mouth with her hand, unable to continue.

Robert closed his eyes in agony. He swallowed against what seemed like a boulder in his throat.

Julie took a deep breath before saying in a more stable voice,

Chapter 16

"We needed you here. *I* needed you. But you..." She trailed away as she shook her head and turned back to the window, a lone tear streaking her face. "The first thing you asked of me in our blasted deal," she continued in a small voice, not looking at him, "was not to cuckold you."

"You never asked the same of me," he said quietly, the excuse sounding hollow to his own ears.

"Well, I am asking you now!" Julie cried as she whirled around on him.

"Fine!" Robert shouted in answer. "Fine, but do you think it is easy for me? Being close to you and..." He paused and closed his eyes. "You can't expect me to wait for you forever."

"I was never asking for forever. Just a few weeks."

"Well, the weeks have passed."

"And I came to you! And you sent me away. Instead of coming to me, you collected your belongings and went to your mistress!" Julie's lip was quivering, her chest heaving. She was clearly holding on to her tears.

"What?" Robert looked at his furious wife's face, realizing that perhaps he had misread her.

Was she jealous of him? Did she want him in her bed? He couldn't understand when that had happened and how he had missed it. He placed a hand under her chin and tilted her face up.

She looked up at him, tears running down her cheeks.

"Don't cry," he whispered. "I haven't been unfaithful to you, I promise. I don't even have a mistress anymore. I ended it with her."

Julie nodded and bit her lip to stop it from quivering. He gave her a soft kiss to stop the trembling.

"I don't know what I should do or how to act," she breathed.

"I thought you would just…" She shrugged lightly.

Robert had no idea what she was trying to say. All he wanted was to soothe her worries and stop her distress. His gaze locked on her lips, then traveled over her feminine form.

His body reacted immediately to the soft mounds of her breasts, to the shape of her curves, even though they were hidden beneath a hideous nightgown. He cuddled her cheek in his hand and gave her another gentle kiss on her lips.

She closed her eyes as if waiting for more. Robert smiled and kissed her again, slower this time.

Julie ran her hands up his chest tentatively at first but became bolder as he kissed her intently, licking at her closed lips, pinching them with his own.

Robert took her hands, resting on his collarbones, and placed them behind his neck, drawing her closer, bringing her body flush with his. His groin hardened even more in reaction to her soft body pressed to his. He parted her lips with his and licked at her slowly, sensually, tasting her. The way he'd wanted to for a long time, ever since they'd struck their bargain.

Julie molded her body to his, clutching at the nape of his neck as if trying to draw him closer. She still didn't answer his kisses but parted her lips to give him better access to her mouth. His body rejoiced at the closeness, at the realization that she didn't freeze or recoil from him.

He ran a soothing hand up and down her spine, still kissing her slowly. One of his hands went to the nape of her neck and tangled in her hair, massaging her scalp. She moaned lightly, and he drew her even closer to him, rubbing her pelvis against his groin, making sure she knew exactly what kind of effect she had on him. She stiffened then but didn't move her body away from his. She didn't take her hands away either.

He drew away slightly and slowly undid the sash on her dressing gown. Then he nudged the gown off her shoulders, and it collected in a heap at her feet.

"Go lie on the bed," he whispered and went to extinguish the lights.

She hastily scrambled to the bed and burrowed under the covers. He undressed quickly and went to lie beside her. The light from the smoldering fire in the hearth was enough to clearly make out her horrified features. She lay still on her back as if afraid to move.

He turned to her and placed his hand on her abdomen, caressing her with his thumb through the covers. She looked up at him, a frightened look in her eyes. But he was determined to not let that stop him this time. She obviously wasn't opposed to having him in her bed, so he'd seduce her, whatever it took.

"You don't have to be afraid of me," he whispered as he tucked a loose tendril of hair away from her face.

He moved half on top of her as she nodded and kissed her soundly on her lips. His hand moved down to her chemise. He bunched it in his hand and drew it up to her waist.

He slowly untied her drawers while still distracting her with his mouth. He broke the kiss, moved the drawers down to her ankles, then took them off and placed them beside the bed. Julie instantly lowered her chemise to cover the patch of hair between her legs.

"You know I'll still need to bare it," he said with a rueful smile.

"I know. Just, not like that. I don't want you looking—and touching—there." Julie was as red as a beetroot.

Robert raised his brows. "Not touching? How do you suppose it will work then?"

"Not… not with your hand…" Julie looked away, mortified. Robert stifled a chuckle.

She seemed nervous and frantic, so he decided not to argue with her. He placed himself on top of her again, positioning his cock between her legs, his head rubbing at her center through her chemise. He heard her suck in her breath, whether in anticipation or in fear, he didn't know and didn't want to guess. He kissed her chin, her neck, and ran his hand soothingly up her sides.

"Relax," he whispered in her ear.

"Can you just… do it?" she asked, biting her lip. "I am too nervous to—" She looked away, embarrassed, the heat creeping up her neck.

He remembered Gabriel's words about proper ladies and their lack of enthusiasm in bed. He sighed and propped himself up on his elbows.

"I can't just do it, Julie. If I don't prepare you, it is going to hurt, and I have no intention of hurting you."

"Won't it hurt, anyway?" she asked worriedly.

Robert raised his brow. "Julie," he said, looking at her quizzically. "You do know what's going to happen, don't you?" he asked, a suspicion smoldering in his mind.

"Of course, I… Yes," Julie answered uncertainly.

"Right." Robert scrubbed his face with his hand. "Have you done it before?"

Julie just blinked up at him.

"You are a virgin," he said with such wonder he believed it translated to his voice.

Julie frowned at him and bit her lower lip. She did that a

lot, he noticed. He leaned over her and freed her lower lip by pulling on it with his own.

He was an idiot. Of course, she was a virgin. He'd let his jealousy and speculation get the better of him before. But that explained everything. Her timidity and unwillingness to go to bed with him, her reactions to his aggressive kisses. At least he hoped that was the reason. He realized that in this case, he'd need more patience to make her feel relaxed.

He had no experience in bedding a virgin, and he'd heard horror stories about the pain and the blood and the women screaming. Robert almost laughed at his thoughts. Surely it wouldn't be that bad. He decided to keep to her wishes as much as he could. The last thing he wanted was to frighten her again.

He kissed her then, slowly, leisurely, until she was moaning into his mouth and clinging to him. Forgetting all about her embarrassment and inhibitions, she moved her tongue inside his mouth and tangled it with his. He groaned in pleasure and drew her tongue fully into his own mouth, sucking on it gently. He slowly raised her chemise up to her waist again and placed himself between her thighs. He rubbed her folds with his hard cock, moving his hips in a suggestive rhythm, rubbing her most sensitive part. Julie swallowed her moan and bit her lip. She closed her eyes and held on to him tightly, looking away.

Robert kissed her exposed ear, then suckled on her earlobe. "No, don't... please," Julie begged as she breathed heavily.

Robert didn't understand why she didn't want him to pleasure her, but he didn't want to argue. Not at this moment.

He returned to kissing her mouth again, her neck, all the while moving against her, bathing his cock in her wetness.

The moment she began to relax, he drew away from her and placed himself at her hot center. He held his cock firmly at her entrance, made a thrust, and… went nowhere. She was too tense, her passage too tight.

"Julie, my sweet," he begged in her ear, "you have to relax."

"I can't." She shut her eyes even tighter.

He turned her to face him and kissed her eyelids.

"Open your eyes, sweet," he whispered against her lips and bit her lower lip. She opened her eyes and regarded him with a frightened gaze. "You were relaxed when I kissed you," he said and kissed her on her lips. He licked at her mouth. "Let me touch you there," he whispered against her mouth. "I promise, you'll like it."

Julie whimpered but seemed to surrender. Robert lowered his hand to her center, marveling at the hot, liquid feeling that greeted his fingers. He teased her there lightly, drawing circles around her most sensitive nub, playing with it. Julie stifled her whimpers and moans, biting on her lip and clamping her lips shut.

"Relax," Robert coaxed, kissing her lips open.

"I can't—"

"You can." Robert placed himself at her entrance again, as he felt her pliant and warm in his arms. He thrust, and a tiny cry escaped Julie as her passage gave way and Robert penetrated her virginal barrier. He thrust again and moved inside her part of the way. She was so tight and hot that he almost lost all reason. He placed his hands beneath her bottom and pushed her hips up to meet his as he gave another thrust. And one more.

Finally, he seated himself fully inside her.

He froze, holding himself up on his elbows, hovering above

her, waiting for tears and recriminations. But she was quiet, holding on to him tightly, a grimace of pain marring her beautiful face.

What a cad he'd been. He had been so eager to get inside her that he hadn't even thought to override her protests of pleasuring her before. He should have made her come before he entered her. He should've prepared her more. But it was too late now.

"Are you hurt?" he asked after a moment.

Julie whimpered in answer.

"I'm sorry," he whispered as he peppered her face with kisses. "I'm sorry. It won't hurt next time. I promise you."

Julie nodded, her eyes closed tight.

Robert moved lightly inside her, carefully observing her features. "Does it hurt?" he whispered close to her ear and berated himself for his stupidity.

Since this was the first time he'd ever bedded a virgin, he didn't know how much it hurt or for how long. Or if he could make her enjoy the act after he'd inflicted this pain on her. He decided to end her misery as soon as he could. He thought the faster he finished the act, the better it'd be for her. He moved inside her as she lay still and unmoving beneath him, with her eyes closed.

Robert shook his head as the words of his friend hovered in his mind. *Quiet and unmoving, like a corpse.* Robert stifled a burst of nervous laughter. This was not how he'd imagined bedding her for the first time, or any time for that matter. Robert thrust three more times and finished inside her. The pleasure of finally having his wife had been diminished only slightly by the hastiness of the act. He withdrew slowly and got up from the bed.

"Where—" Julie sat up in bed, her eyes frantic.

"I'll just be a moment," Robert said and walked into the closet.

He washed his groin from their intimate juices and specks of Julie's blood. He then dipped a clean towel in the washbasin and brought it to his wife.

"Relax," he whispered. "You'll feel better after this."

He slowly wiped her thighs and between her legs as she lay there looking mortified, her body the color of rubies. He kissed her on the lips before moving away and withdrawing the towel. He returned to the bed and lay next to his quivering wife. He hugged her closer to him, running a gentle hand down her sides and back.

"I'm sorry," he whispered again. "I promise it'll be better next time," he said against her shoulder.

Julie nodded and huddled closer to him. He was grateful that she sought comfort in his arms and not away from him. He kissed her hair and held her in his arms tightly until he heard her even breaths.

She was asleep. Good. It meant that he could sleep now too.

Chapter 17

J ulie woke up a little after dawn. She was very warm and comfortable, the back of her head and her back padded by something large and hot. She tried to move and noted the soreness between her legs. The memory of last night came flooding over her. Her skin heated in reaction.

She had been extremely nervous last night. First, she'd been angry and shaking from their confrontation about Robert's mistress. Later, she'd become anxious for an entirely different reason. She was quaking so hard she'd thought she'd swoon. And then he'd kissed her, and all thought evaporated from her dazed mind.

Julie tried to wiggle out from under the covers only to realize that Robert's arm was on her waist, pinning her to the bed and his chest. She should have felt trapped and uncomfortable in his firm hold, but she didn't. She should feel embarrassed with the way she'd let Robert touch her last night, humiliated by the way he'd pushed his way inside her. But regardless of what had happened the night before, she felt safe, protected in the circle of his arms.

Julie relaxed under his weight, leaning against him even more. She marveled at the comforting feel of her husband's body around her. Lying in her husband's embrace, she couldn't quite reconcile what she was feeling. She was really and truly his wife now. A feeling of panic hit her, and she moved to get out from under her husband's limbs once again.

"Mmm—" Robert groaned lightly, and his arm tightened around her.

The backs of her thighs brushed against the front of his, her bottom grazing against his hardening length. Julie's breaths grew frantic, whether from agitation or arousal, she wasn't sure.

He moved his hand to her breast, caressing her taut peak. Julie stifled the urge to moan. It felt surprisingly good. His hands were gentle, and his breath wafted against the nape of her neck. His aroused length hardened even more and moved slowly but rhythmically against the seam of her buttocks. Julie bit down on her lower lip.

Mrs. Darling had told her that husbands didn't like it when their wives moved or made sounds in bed, but it was really difficult with Robert kissing her like he did last night or touching her as he was doing at the moment.

He moved his hand lower, pressing her closer to him, plastering her back even closer to his chest, caressing her body on his way, until he got to her center and cupped her there through the linen of her nightgown. Julie sucked in her breath and almost jumped in reaction.

It felt so good she wanted to press herself firmer into his hand. A wanton thought if she'd ever had one. Her body heated to a fevered pitch. She felt liquid forming between her thighs, right where his hand was cupping her. She felt embarrassed, but it felt too good, lying there in her husband's embrace, trapped between his hard body and his wicked hand.

The door opened at that moment, and a maid entered the room. She made her way to the unlit hearth with sure steps, not looking around. She obviously didn't notice that there were two people in the bed, not just one.

The maid positioned herself in front of the hearth, back turned to the bed. But that was enough for Julie to come to her senses. She struggled her way out of her husband's embrace and crawled out of bed, stumbling in her haste. Robert groaned and turned to his other side without waking up.

The maid turned and made an embarrassed yelp as she finally noticed Robert in her mistress's bed. Julie was throwing on her dressing robe and turned as red as a beetroot, while the maid curtsied and hurried out of the room snickering.

Julie shut her eyes. By mid-morning, every servant in the household would know where Robert had spent the night.

Julie dressed hastily, without help from Alice. She put on her simplest gown, performed her morning ablutions, and went on with her day.

As was her custom, she checked on Mary first.

Her sister was peacefully sleeping, breathing steadily and occasionally murmuring in her sleep. Next, Julie checked on breakfast, conversed with Mrs. Post, made plans for the day's meals, and made a shopping list. Throughout all of that, she couldn't help but think about what had happened last night between her and Robert. The soreness between her legs reminded her of the way their relationship had shifted, not that she needed a reminder.

The more she spent her morning alone, the more panic settled in the pit of her stomach. Regardless of the vows exchanged in the church, this was the moment she truly became Robert's wife. The moment she let go of any hope of ever being with John again.

John. Her thoughts circled back to him rarer and rarer these days. And laying with her husband was the final act of betrayal toward John. She didn't know how she felt about it. Her thoughts were frantic, her feelings a jumbled mess.

She was also nervous to see Robert. She didn't know how he'd react to her. Had she pleased him? Was what she did sufficient for him to never go back to his mistress? That thought nagged in her brain despite her better judgment. What would Robert say to her? She tried to divert her thoughts from the night before, but she couldn't.

All her worries were for naught, however. Besides a greeting and a smile, Robert didn't look in her direction throughout the entire morning meal. He conversed with Mary most of the time, laughing at her displeasure when he talked about how he'd spent his time in London without them.

The dowager interjected a few times with household issues. But she was mostly watching both Julie and Robert closely as if she knew something had gone on between them the night before.

Julie tried very hard to concentrate on her meal and act as if everything were normal, just like Robert did, but she had a feeling that she hadn't succeeded. Every molecule in her body was on a different level of awareness of him. Her left arm felt over-warm just by sitting close to him, and her cheeks were burning whenever he looked at her.

After breakfast, Robert excused himself and left for the

day, leaving both Julie and Mary disappointed by the lack of his company. Whether she liked it or not, her thoughts kept coming back to him. Mary was similarly riveted with Julie's husband, and Julie couldn't be more grateful that she had a strong male influence, at least for a little while in her life.

Julie, however, would not let his strange behavior sour her mood. She spent most of the day with Mary, sitting with her, embroidering with the dowager, reading. She managed some household chores while Mary was resting since she still wasn't back to her full strength, but she mostly wanted to spend time with her little sister. The doctor's horrible words and his ominous prognosis never fully left her mind.

Just before supper, Robert sauntered into the sitting room, where Julie was teaching Mary to play the piano. She'd abandoned the difficult pieces, and they were having fun playing bawdy tavern songs.

Robert came farther into the room and leaned against the side of the piano, his loving gaze on Mary. "I have a surprise for you," he said with a lazy smile. "I just spent the entire day at Tattersalls. And guess what I got?"

"What?" Julie asked, shocked at the sudden announcement, her fingers falling off the piano keys. Tattersalls was a horse auction. There was only one thing Robert could have bought there.

"I bought you a pony, Mary," Robert said with a wide smile. "Happy early birthday!"

Mary leaped up and ran the two steps required to reach her brother-in-law and hugged him fiercely.

"I promised I'd buy you one, didn't I?" Robert said, gently caressing the top of her head.

"Thank you! When can I ride it?" Mary turned her excited

face to Julie.

"It's not here yet, but I couldn't wait to tell you. The pony will arrive in a sennight or so. And it will need to be trained before you can ride it," he said with a smile.

"Ride it?" Julie's eyes widened. Mary was uncoordinated and completely unathletic. She had never been allowed on the horses at the Norfolk estate.

"When?" Mary jumped up and down, holding on to Robert's arms in excitement. "I want to ride! When can I ride?"

Julie's reservations about getting a pony disappeared at that moment. Mary was excited. She was happy. Julie would do anything to keep her little sister happy.

"Well, first, we need to order you a riding habit," Julie said with a smile. "You can't very well ride a horse in your day gown. Let's schedule a couple of appointments at the modiste."

"Riding habit?" Mary frowned, thinking over the unfamiliar words.

"Yes, special clothes that will make it comfortable for you to ride."

"More clothes," Mary said thoughtfully, then looked up at Julie with a wide smile. "You need clothes too."

"I might need some more new gowns, yes." Julie smiled as Mary walked toward her and hugged her side.

"And Rob." Mary looked at him and grinned.

"I think my valet is on top of things regarding my clothing, but thank you for your concern," he said with a chuckle. He placed an arm around Mary and Julie and squeezed them closer to him.

Julie's heart filled with an inexplicable feeling of rightness. That was it. That feeling of safety and happiness. She felt it aching through her heart. The feeling of being surrounded by the most important people in her life.

* * *

Julie finally retired to her room just before midnight. She didn't want to leave Mary, but she was tired, and Julie didn't want to overwhelm her too much. She changed into her nightgown, performed her nightly ablutions, and sat on her bed.

Now that she was alone, she wondered if Robert would come to her. She was strangely looking forward to her marital duties. She knew she shouldn't be. A gentlewoman wouldn't be, especially since it hurt so much, and she was still sore. But she craved the closeness with her husband. She wanted to feel his arms around her again, breathe in his scent, bask in his comforting heat. After a long and tiring day, she'd do anything just to be surrounded by him again.

Just at that moment, she heard a knock on the connecting door.

"Come in," she cried out and sat straight up in bed.

Robert walked in, still dressed in his breeches and his shirtsleeves. He'd shed his coat, waistcoat, and cravat. His collar was gaping open at his throat, showing his bronzed skin. He walked to the window and turned to her, crossing his arms on his wide chest, leaning his left shoulder against the windowsill.

Julie devoured his form with her eyes. How had she never noticed how athletic and strong he was? He was tall and incredibly handsome. And his pale gray eyes were the best feature on his lovely face. They were deep and mysterious.

She could drown in the depth of those eyes. Why had she ever thought him cold and forbidding? How had she missed the spark deep in his eyes?

He studied her in return, and they both stared at each other in silence for a few long moments.

"I hope you are not upset about the sudden gift," he finally said. "I should have talked to you before making an announcement, but I promised Mary to teach her to ride and didn't want to delay it."

Julie shook her head. "No, that was the right decision. I was unsure at first, but seeing the joy on Mary's face made me realize this was the best idea. And she doesn't need to ride a lot immediately, does she?" She paused, studying the coverlet for a moment. "I have to admit, I am looking forward to this new experience with her. I want her to have many more of those." Julie bit her lip and frowned at the thought of Mary passing without experiencing so many things.

Robert was beside her instantly. He sat on the edge of the bed and collected her against his chest. Julie hugged him closer and burrowed into his heat. She felt him rub his chin against the top of her head as she closed her eyes.

This, she thought with a sigh, was exactly what she needed.

"We'll make sure she does," he breathed and placed a chaste kiss on her hair.

Julie sighed, marveling at the feeling of safety and comfort. She could not remember a time she'd felt as at peace as she felt at this moment.

"I also went around making some inquiries." He paused. "About the doctors."

"Oh." Julie looked up at him, still not withdrawing from the circle of his arms.

"My solicitor will find the best ones in England first. And if there is no good prognosis from them, I shall send for someone from the Continent. Don't worry," he said in a softer tone of voice. "We'll make Mary better. I promise."

Julie bit her lip so as not to cry. Robert cupped her cheek and caressed it with his thumb. His gaze traveled from her eyes to her lips and locked on them for a long moment. Julie licked her lips unconsciously and saw his pale eyes darken. He returned his gaze back to hers.

"I need to tell you some things. About the asylum. Are you up to hearing those things?"

When Julie nodded, Robert told her everything he'd done to change things in the asylum. Starting with how he talked to the governors, tracked down reformers, even spoke to other inmates' families while he was in Doncaster, and finishing with his meeting with Tule and his proposal about the letter to the papers. Now, the only thing left was to send the letter that would unleash scandal onto their family and basically make a laughingstock of Mary.

"I was going to talk to you before sending the letter," Robert finished. "But now, I don't think it is a good idea."

Julie nodded mutely. Yes, the best thing for them would be to stay silent and keep Mary protected. To give her the best life possible while they still could. But what about the other inmates? How much longer would they suffer?

"I know what you are thinking, Julie," Robert said, peering into her face. "We shall find another way to help those in the asylum."

Julie smiled weakly. She looked into his dear face and wondered how he could understand her so well. Like nobody else could. She wanted to burrow herself into his comforting heat again. To stay that way forever. Only he took her by the shoulders and slowly eased her away from his body. He stood from the bed then, the loss of his heat like a whiplash. Julie looked at him, puzzled.

"You need to get some rest now," he said, looking down at her.

"You…" She paused and turned a deep red before continuing. "You won't stay here tonight?" she asked shyly.

Robert looked intently into her eyes as if trying to read her mind or peer into her soul. "No, Julie. You need your rest." He cleared his throat and shifted from one foot to another. "Are you sore?" he asked as he lifted his face to hers.

"Oh." Julie bit her lip, embarrassment flooding her cheeks, as she realized what he meant. "Yes, but—"

"I shall not bother you tonight then," he cut her off in as gentle a tone as he could. "You'll need your strength on the morrow. But next time I come to your bed, it will be better." He reached out to tuck a loose lock of her hair behind her ear.

"It wasn't—" Julie shrugged, lowering her gaze. "It wasn't bad," she said, looking down at her fidgeting hands.

Please stay, she wanted to beg. But this intimacy between them was new. She didn't know how he felt about it. Maybe he didn't want to stay with her. So, she didn't ask.

"I'm glad," he said in a tone as if he was stifling a chuckle. "But I hurt you, and you need to recover. You shouldn't be embarrassed to talk to me about it, Julie."

Shouldn't I, though? Even the thought of it made her heart race and her palms perspire.

"It will be much better that way. For both of us." He bent down and pressed a chaste kiss to her cheek. "We'll talk about this later. Now, sleep." With these words, he left the room.

Julie fell back to her pillows with a whimper of disappointment. Yes, she was sore, but even more so, she was tired and heartbroken, and she needed to be comforted.

Robert, on the other hand, probably wanted to be alone. Letting out another sigh, she turned on her side and burrowed even farther into her sheets. It had been a long day.

Chapter 18

J ulie walked along the corridor. It was dark and cold, and she wore nothing except for her old nightgown. She looked down and wondered where she'd even gotten that nightgown from. She stepped farther down the hall, looking around. The house didn't look like their townhouse, but it seemed eerily familiar. The door to her left was cracked open, and light flickered from inside the room as if from lightning.

She walked toward the room slowly, carefully. The moment she entered, she stopped cold. Her mother was on the bed, writhing in agony.

"Mother?" Julie cried as she rushed closer to the bed. She placed her hands on her abdomen, but it was covered with blood. She looked at her hands closer, struck mute with horror. The next moment everything changed. The person on the bed was not her mother anymore, it was her, and the person by the bedside, frantic with worry, was Mary. Julie's eyes widened in horror as she tried to scream.

With a muffled yelp, she sat up in bed. Everything was dark, but she was in the Clydesdale townhouse in London, in her bed. Julie looked around and tried to regulate her breathing. All was well. She was home. Safe.

* * *

The next few days were the happiest of Julie's life. Mary was getting better. She still tired easily, she hadn't had a healthy appetite, but she was not hurting, and her mood was generally positive. Every morning the entire family breakfasted together, then went on to dress shops, museums, or a simple ride in the park. Robert accompanied them everywhere, not that Mary would allow otherwise, and the dowager followed not far behind. They really felt like a family.

After their outings, the women would spend some time quietly either embroidering or gossiping in a sitting room, drinking tea, while Robert worked. After supper, they went to the music room to hear Mary and Julie play or played games in the drawing room. They read together before bedtime, and then Julie adjourned to her room and her husband to his. A simple but happy family life. The one Julie had dreamed about as early as she could remember.

Life seemed perfect. If not for several things.

For one thing, her nightmares were back. She chalked it all up to stress, to the worry that she might be with child, and to the constant dreadful feeling she had that every moment with Mary could be her last. She resolved not to think about it, but she couldn't help herself. She tried to memorize Mary's every smile. Etch into her mind's eye their times together, all her new experiences.

And the second... Well, the second had something to do

with the fact that her husband hadn't come to her bedroom since their first time in London.

Nasty thoughts crept into Julie's mind when she contemplated her husband's absence from her bed. Perhaps he was spending his nights with his mistress. She tried to shove the traitorous thought away.

He'd promised not to, and she should trust him enough to believe his words. He didn't deserve her mistrust. But the only other thought that occurred to her wasn't pleasant either.

He didn't *want* to come to her. He'd suffered through one night with her at her insistence, and now he was avoiding her, not willing to come to her more than he could endure.

She grimaced at the thought. She didn't want to confront him about this again. She knew he would assent to her wishes, spend another night with her, and then what? Would she always come begging for him to bed her? Surely, she had a bit more pride than that.

Besides, he was the one who wanted—nay needed—even demanded heirs. And she wasn't at all looking forward to the birthing process. Bile rose in her throat, and she swallowed against it.

"Look!" Mary cried beside her before she hurled herself at a shop window.

They were walking on Bond Street as was their custom every other afternoon. Julie had started decorating their bare townhouse with new rugs, curtains, and even some furniture. She'd also bought paintings in art galleries and other frivolous things that she knew Robert found quite useless, making their house homier. Mary seemed to enjoy filling their home with anything in her favorite pink and white colors. Robert looked unperturbed, and Julie wanted to have as many reminders of

Mary as possible in her new house.

"Pretty!" Mary intoned dreamily.

Julie, Robert, and the dowager all came closer and looked at what Mary was pointing at. On the windowsill of a small gallery shop, there was a painting of beautiful countryside at sunset, a cliff at the side of the picture, and the sea peeking out at a distance. The painting was bathed in the morning light, making it look almost magical.

"Come, Mary." Julie tugged on her sister's arm. "Let's have a closer look, shall we?"

Mary nodded and bounced on her feet in delight. They entered a tiny but beautiful art shop filled with dreamy paintings, beautiful sunsets, and golden landscapes.

"Good day, my lord, my ladies." The shopkeeper, a plump middle-aged man, came from behind the counter.

Mary walked straight to the painting she adored and pointed to it. "I want this," she said, looking it over.

The shopkeeper chuckled and sauntered closer to Mary. "I am glad you like it. My youngest daughter is the one who painted it."

"Really?" Julie stood beside Mary. "It's beautiful."

"Thank you." The shopkeeper puffed out his chest in pride.

"Do you have more of her work? Can we see it?"

The shopkeeper then made a sweep around the shop, showing all his daughter's works.

They were beautiful. The brushstrokes, the colors, and subjects. Everything was light and dreamy, like in a fairytale. Mary was wooed and wanted to have every painting there was, which was more than a dozen.

As Mary studied the paintings with Robert and the dowager, Julie moved to the little table at the back of the room. There were beautiful antiquities, watches, old lockets, handheld mirrors, and other trinkets. She picked up a beautiful silver pocket watch and opened it. Julie checked the clock on the mantle of the shop and looked back at the watch, frowning. It lagged by about ten minutes. She was about to wind it to the correct time when the shopkeeper appeared by her shoulder.

"It's always lagging, no matter how much you wind it. I really don't know what to do with it," he said with a shrug.

Julie studied the beautiful silver patterns on the cover of the watch, the beautiful mechanism, and smiled.

"I am afraid all of these paintings would not fit into your room," Robert was telling Mary.

"Please, wrap this." Julie handed the watch to the shopkeeper and walked to stand beside her husband. "Perhaps we can hang some at the Clydesdale estate," she said thoughtfully. "And the others. We'll need to decorate those houses too."

Robert looked at her peculiarly before clearing his throat. "Of course. As a matter of fact, we have an estate in Sussex. The view from the balcony is similar to that first painting you picked out, Mary."

"From my balcony?" Mary furrowed her brows.

Robert shrugged. "You can pick any room you like. Several have balconies overlooking the sea."

"The sea," Mary said, her eyes widening in wonder.

"We can go there during the summer, once the season is over, if you wish."

"Hmm. Are all the estates as empty as the London townhouse and Clydesdale Hall? Because if so, we must buy a lot more than a dozen paintings," Julie said with a laugh. She was strangely looking forward to seeing more of their lands and mansions, making them more comfortable and lively.

Her father had four estates, although she mainly grew up at Bedford, his country seat. But none of those places ever felt cozy to her. She didn't feel at home in any of the rooms. Her father didn't allow for any decorations, justifying it with the fact that neither of his daughters would live there long. They were unwanted guests in their own houses.

Now, however, it seemed like she and Mary had finally found a place of their own. Would Robert object to having his own rooms redecorated? She suddenly had an amusing idea.

"I wonder if your daughter would be willing to paint walls rather than on a canvas?" she asked the shopkeeper.

The plump old man perked up at the suggestion. "She would love that. We are actually running out of walls in my house."

"What do you say, Mary? Do you want these landscapes on your walls?"

Mary's eyes lit up in excitement. "Yes! In all of my rooms." She nodded vigorously.

"I would love to have my rooms painted also," Julie said thoughtfully. "The wallpaper seems outdated in both the London townhouse and Clydesdale Hall. I am guessing the countess's chambers are not much different at our other estates either."

"I've never been a countess, and Rutland became a duke when he was two, so you're right," the dowager finally said. She was perusing the paintings while listening to their conversation. "The Clydesdale title didn't have a countess for a long time before you."

Julie bit on the inside of her cheek before turning to Robert. "Would you like your walls painted as well?" At his dubious look, she continued with a smile. "We can ask the girl to paint something more manly than flowers and sunsets. Perhaps a ship or the forest."

"Or horsies!" Mary almost jumped in excitement.

"That's right. We can have horses and hunting dogs painted."

"Dogs!" Mary yelled and started clapping her hands.

Robert smiled at Mary before turning to Julie. "Painting all those rooms in each of my five estates will take a long time. Months." He paused. "Years even."

"Well, we don't have to stay at Clydesdale Hall forever, do we? We can move to a new location after the painter is done with our rooms."

Julie paused as she realized what Robert had been hinting at by stating the timeline.

The deal.

She'd said she'd be moving to her own estate and living separately from him with Mary and the babe the moment after she gave birth. It could be as soon as nine months. She could be with child already and not know it.

Her stomach churned at the idea. But her mind was stuck on the fact that Robert still expected them to move away.

Did she want to move?

She knew Mary would protest greatly, and Julie wasn't sure that's what she wanted anymore either.

"We don't have to decide now," she said and smiled tightly at her husband before turning to the shopkeeper. "We'll just take the paintings for now."

"As you wish, my lady." The shop owner bowed and started collecting the paintings to wrap for them.

* * *

Robert lay on his bed, eyeing the canopy over his head later that night. So far, the stay in London had been going well. He'd done some work on his estates, appeared in Parliament, and escorted his wife, grandmother, and sister-in-law to the theater, shops, and fairs.

Everything was going as well as could be expected. Mary seemed happy; Julie seemed content. Laughter rang inside his house; the meals were filled with female chatter and joyful exclamations. This was what he'd always wanted, wasn't it?

As he tried to analyze his overwrought feelings, he realized it wasn't enough for him anymore. Somewhere along the days and weeks he'd spent with his wife, he'd started craving her affection.

No, he'd started craving her love.

It was a ridiculous thought since he wasn't in love with her. Besides, he'd given up on the foolish notion of love long ago, hadn't he? Those hopes had died with his unfortunate betrothal to Annie.

He'd promised himself he wouldn't indulge in bedding his wife too often. He'd promised himself not to fall under her spell, not to let her be the center of his life. He'd promised himself to maintain distance from her.

She was enticingly beautiful, however. Her laughter was infectious, her smile mesmerizing, and her gaze downright erotic. At dinner, he had to suffer through watching her put all types of food in her mouth, lick her lips, and make satisfying sounds as she tried to entice Mary into eating. Mary didn't care for her sister's theatrics, but Julie enticed an entirely different reaction from Robert.

He imagined her putting her lips around his cock, sucking on it as she made those sounds of pleasure. Licking him up and down his length. He sat across from Julie during meals imagining her taking him in, licking him with her sweet tongue, sucking him in.

His cock was on the ready and on alert with Julie's every sound, move, or gaze. Now that he'd been inside her and knew what she felt like, he couldn't help but fantasize about it. He knew the scent of her orange blossom perfume mixed with the lovely scent of her skin. He could feel the heat of her every time she sat next to him in a carriage.

Lying there, on his bed, he had to revise his feelings. If he didn't crave her affection, then why wasn't he spending his nights with her?

The answer was simple. He didn't want to grow too fond of her.

He liked that she'd started decorating his townhouse as if she planned to stay with him forever, although he knew what their bargain entailed. He adored the smile that lit up her entire face and made her seem hundreds of times more magnificent than she already was. He adored her enthusiasm about their London itinerary, about the plays and other activities. Most of all, he enjoyed their quiet evenings as a family, simply watching her, content and relaxed in their house.

He was already feeling too much for her, and if he started bedding her every night, he knew he would grow obsessed with her; he would crave her more than he already did. Crave her taste, her tiny whimpers. He'd want to make her cry out in pleasure.

Robert felt his cock rise to attention at his thoughts. He reached under the sheets and took himself in hand, imagining it was Julie's touch. He stroked himself lightly, unhurriedly, imagining Julie crouching before him, licking him slowly. He imagined her enveloping him inside her heat, sucking hard—

A strangled moan sounded from the room next to his. Her room. Robert sat up in his bed. Another moan. Or was it a whimper, a cry? His face felt red as another memory flooded him of another time when he came to his woman's room and heard similar sounds. Back then, he'd found Annie crouching on all fours, sucking another man's cock. He shook the thought out of his mind.

Julie wouldn't do that, especially not under his own roof. Something was happening there, so he needed to investigate.

He lunged from the bed and hastily put on his nightshirt. Robert lit his bedside candle and trotted into Julie's bedroom. He knocked gingerly at first, but he entered the room when he didn't receive any answer.

Julie was lying in bed, the sheets tangled between her legs, her hair tossed on the pillow, her nightcap tossed aside. She was writhing as if in pain or in fever, tiny whimpers escaping her slightly open mouth. He moved closer to her bed and noted that her breathing was shallow; she was panting as if after a hard exercise. Her whimpers grew louder suddenly, and then she froze as if about to scream, only the sound didn't emerge, although her body arched slightly off the bed.

Robert put his candle into a candle holder by the bed and placed a hand on her shoulder.

"Julie," he whispered lightly.

Julie started wrenching away as if trying to shake off his hand. Another light scream.

"Julie," he said a little harsher and took her by her upper arms as if about to shake her.

She opened her eyes then and jerked, as if trying to sit up. If

Robert hadn't been holding her, she no doubt would have shot off the bed. She let out a high-pitched scream, her eyes frantic, her breathing shallow. She put her hands on his forearms as if to throw him off her. At the last moment, she seemed to realize where she was and who he was, and she just stared at him, her eyes still wide, her hands still holding his.

"Robert," she said as if she wasn't sure whether this was still a dream.

"Are you well?" he asked, furrowing his brows.

Julie looked around again to make sure that she was indeed in her bedchamber in his house. Then she swallowed and nodded.

"Did you have a nightmare?" he asked gently.

Another nod.

"Do you want to talk about it?"

Julie shook her head, seemingly unable to speak.

Robert looked at her, his brows furrowed, thinking over his further actions. "Are you sure nothing is amiss? Do you need anything, water or…?" He trailed off, hoping she'd finally say something to him.

"Could you… Could you stay here?" she whispered without looking at him.

He nodded, but since she wasn't looking at him, she didn't see it.

"Just to hold me for a bit. If you don't mind," she continued.

Just to hold me. It wasn't exactly a difficult request, but Robert had to swallow hard.

There were other ways he could have comforted her, but if all she needed was the comfort of his arms, he'd give it to her. He'd give her anything.

What had he been thinking about in his bedchamber? He

didn't want to grow fond of her. He almost scoffed aloud. Who was he trying to fool? It was already too late. He'd sell his soul to make her happy, whether she reciprocated or not.

So, he extinguished the light, climbed into the bed, and gathered her against his chest. She placed her head with her tangled mess of hair in the crook of his shoulder and hugged him tightly.

Robert took a deep breath, elated at the feeling of being hugged, being touched by her. Being needed. Wanted. Even if not in an erotic way. Perhaps especially not in an erotic way.

He ran a hand through the silky strands of her hair, smoothing them at her back, gathering them away from her face. Then he kissed her on her hair and squeezed her closer to him.

"Sleep, my sweet," he whispered above her head.

She burrowed even closer into him and stroked his arm, then clutched it tightly before relaxing with a sigh.

Chapter 19

obert came home late the next afternoon.

He was tired from the sleepless night. Julie had spent most of the night tossing and turning, screaming, and struggling in her sleep. Whatever the nightmare she was having, it was scaring the wits out of her, and he had to soothe her for several minutes each time she awoke.

He had some Parliament business with his father in the early morning, and he hadn't seen Julie most of the day. All he'd wanted was to come home, have a hot bath, and snuggle with his wife.

"Mr. Benjamin Tule is waiting for you in the drawing room, my lord." The butler bowed as he took Robert's coat.

Robert froze in the middle of taking off his gloves. "He's here? For how long?"

"Quarter of an hour, my lord. He insisted he'd wait."

Robert finished taking off his gloves and handed them to Hudgins along with his hat and scarf. "Tell him to come to my study. I shall wait for him there," he said, already striding away.

"Robert," his wife called softly.

He raised his head and regarded her standing on the landing, a slight frown marring her face. She descended the stairs, floating slowly along the steps.

He couldn't take his starved eyes off her.

"Is anything amiss?" she asked when she reached him. She raised her hand slightly as if wanting to touch him but checked her movement and returned it to her side. "You seem…" She paused, studying his face. "Worried."

Robert feasted on the sight of her. God, how he'd missed her. All he wanted was to press her into him and kiss her senseless. He tore his gaze from her mouth and looked into her troubled eyes. "I have a visitor. Mr. Tule is waiting in the study."

"Oh," she said, biting on her lower lip. "The reformist? The one who's helping you with the asylum?"

He nodded. "Although who is helping whom is debatable." He smiled slightly before he raised his hand and grazed her cheek gingerly with his knuckles.

She lowered her eyes at the contact before meeting his gaze suddenly. "I'll come with you."

He was about to protest, but she took him by the arm and tugged him toward his study.

"It concerns the both of us," she said resolutely.

Robert didn't want to involve Julie in the asylum's business. He knew it was upsetting for her to deal with. He'd rather solve all the problems and come to her when the issues were dealt with.

Julie, however, looked differently at those same issues. She didn't want to be left out of making decisions; she wanted to be heard, to impact their daily lives. With all her inquiries and her silent support, it was as if she told him: *we are a unit. A husband and a wife.* And Robert couldn't help but bask in the warmth the thought brought him.

Robert settled Julie closer to the hearth and took the chair beside her just as Mr. Tule entered the room. Robert stood and indicated the chair opposite him and Julie.

"Mr. Tule, a pleasant surprise. Please, have a seat."

"I am afraid this isn't a social call," Benjamin Tule said from the doorway and strode inside. "My lady." He bowed over Julie's hand and turned to Robert. "Clydesdale." He bowed shortly and sat on the indicated chair. "I apologize for cutting straight to business, but things with the asylum haven't moved in weeks. You haven't sent the letter to the papers. Are you prepared to make a claim against them?"

Robert shifted uncomfortably in his chair. He hated letting this man down. He was driven and ambitious in the best way possible. He wanted to make life better for the most vulnerable. So did Robert. But he had a more personal matter at stake.

"I am," Robert finally said. "Alas, not at the moment."

"What do you mean *not at the moment*?" Tule shot from his chair.

"Mr. Tule," Julie interrupted mildly, trying to appease his mood, "perhaps you would like some tea, biscuits, or sandwiches?"

"No, thank you," he said absently, returning his gaze to Robert.

Robert took Julie's hand and squeezed it comfortingly. "I have to apologize, Tule. I should have informed you right away, but some things have changed."

Tule raised his brow in irritation.

"My sister-in-law." Robert cleared his throat. "She is ill. The doctor says she might not recover. Although we are not particularly inclined to believe this, we'd rather take all the precautions and not upset her. At least not while we are in London. I don't want her time here to be filled with finger-pointing and scandal."

"I've never heard of you running from scandal before, Clydesdale," Tule observed dryly.

"I never have," Robert said evenly, still holding onto Julie's hand.

She weaved her fingers with his, a tiny gesture of support that gave him the confidence he was doing the right thing.

"And I still wouldn't, had this been solely about me."

Tule looked at Julie then and frowned. "I understand your pain, ma'am. But please understand the pain of those who are still in the asylum. Your sister is out; she's safe now. But the way she suffered…" He shook his head.

Robert felt Julie tense, and he tightened his jaw. Tule was too good at what he did, pressing on others' weaknesses to get what he needed.

"Hundreds are suffering the same way as we speak."

"That's enough, Tule," Robert growled. "Please, don't upset my wife more than she already is."

"What about the people in the asylum? Aren't they upset, hurt?"

"This decision was difficult for us, believe me," Robert tried to appease the reformist. Still, he wanted Tule to know that he was firm in his decision. "Mary is the one who's suffered, and she is the one who will suffer most when the truth comes out. I don't want her to be distressed. I feel for all the people who are suffering there. But who is to say that a few weeks would make a difference?"

Tule stood at that. "I see your mind's made up then?"

"I want to help you. I really do."

"You are the one who sought me out, Clydesdale. You took me off the ship from the Continent, dragged me to your carriage to talk about reforming the asylum—"

"And I still want to do it. You need help from a lord of the realm, and you will get it. But I have a family to think about first and foremost. I'm sure you can understand." Robert stood, indicating the end of the discussion.

Tule bowed shortly and stalked out of the room.

Julie sighed heavily.

Robert looked at her troubled profile. She was biting the inside of her lower lip. She did that every time she was distressed. He walked toward her, crouched in front of her, and looked up into her deep blue eyes.

"I know what you're thinking," he said mildly, as he took her hands in his and caressed them with his thumbs.

"People disapprove of us anyway," she said, shaking her head. "They will never accept Mary. Maybe it wouldn't matter if the article came out." She shrugged and looked away.

"Do you really believe that? You know perhaps more than anyone that society is a wake of vultures. We shan't be able to leave the house with her. They look at us disapprovingly now, but they will spout unpleasantries, not at me…" Robert trailed off.

"At her," she said and closed her eyes.

Robert stood and tugged her to her feet. "Come here," he said as he enfolded her in a hug. "We're doing the right thing for Mary," he whispered as he pressed her cheek against his waistcoat, stroking her hair.

Truthfully, he wasn't so sure they were, in fact, doing the right thing anymore. *Are we being selfish?* Julie snaked her arms around his back and pressed herself closer to him. He kissed the top of her head and nuzzled into her hair.

"How about this?" he asked, his voice muffled against her hair. "We wait until after the ball and send the letter then?"

Julie drew back and looked up at him again. "It's not like we are going to be invited to any other household after that," she said with a light smile on her lips.

"Right. Mary will experience her ball, and we'll spend the rest of the season quietly enclosed in our home."

"And we can send the letter in a little over a sennight."

"Yes." Robert smiled at her gently.

Julie raised her face to his, stood on her tiptoes, and kissed him on the lips. The gesture was so unusual that Robert froze for a moment, not moving, not reacting.

This was the first time she'd willingly kissed him on her own accord. Instead of drawing away when he didn't respond, she ran her hands up his chest, gripping at his shoulder with one hand. With the other, she cupped the side of his face, lowered it closer to hers, and placed an open-mouthed kiss on his lips.

Robert felt her shyly licking at the seam of his lips, and he almost lost all control right then and there.

He grabbed her by her waist and pressed her closer to him, rubbing his rising erection against her belly and lower. He opened his mouth and possessed her in a fierce kiss.

His starved senses immediately reacted to her heat, her scent, her essence. He backed her slowly against his desk while kissing and caressing her. She moaned into his mouth and ran her hands through his hair, making him groan. Robert started raising her skirts up, all the while caressing the insides of her thighs. Julie pressed closer to him, so lost in passion that she didn't protest at his ministrations.

"Here, hold this," Robert said against her mouth and handed her the bunched-up skirts.

She took them and regarded him mutely as he lowered himself to his knees in front of her. He untied her drawers and took them off.

She stood in front of him in her half-naked splendor, her silk stockings tied at her thighs with red ribbons, her skirts at her waist, the lovely patch of dark hair in her most intimate place bared to his gaze. He couldn't believe this was his shy wife, the one who insisted they make love in the dark with her chemise on.

Robert took her by the hips, sat her down on the edge of the table, and spread her knees. He heard her intake of breath, saw the frantic rise and fall of her chest, but she didn't protest. She just watched him with her passion-filled eyes, hazy and unfocused.

He ran his finger along the seam of her intimate lips back and forth, then spread her folds with a circular movement. Julie moaned as she closed her eyes and threw back her head. Robert smiled as he lowered his mouth and placed a wet kiss at her center.

"Robert," Julie gasped breathlessly and jerked in reaction.

Robert placed her knees on his shoulders as he settled more comfortably between her legs. He licked at her folds, listening to her moans, feeling her juices trickling down his chin. He pushed his tongue inside her and was rewarded with a pleasure-filled moan.

Her hands were tangled in his hair, pulling away and pushing him closer all at the same time. He moved his tongue in an erotic rhythm, then trailed it higher to her most sensitive nub. He circled it with his tongue repeatedly until she whimpered and squirmed in his arms. He took her bottom firmly in his hands and pressed her against his face as he sucked on her nub lightly at first, then firmer, making swirling figures with his tongue.

He felt her pulsing from the inside as she tensed in his arms. Julie gave a tiny scream as she came, but he didn't stop, drawing the last pulses of orgasm out of her.

He finally let go of her and got up from his knees as he felt her pliant and warm against him. He wiped her juices off his chin and licked his lips, collecting the last of her taste. She looked at him with hazy, heavy-lidded eyes, breathing heavily, just coming out of her first proper orgasm.

Robert slowly undid the falls of his breeches and let his arousal spring out of its constraints. Julie watched him, not taking her eyes off his straining cock. He moved closer to her, his cock pointing at her stomach, and placed his hands on either side of her on the table.

"Touch it," he said in a hoarse whisper. "Touch me."

Julie took him in hand, slowly at first, gingerly, as if she was afraid to hurt him. Then she moved her hand experimentally up and down his length. Robert sucked in his breath and closed his eyes.

"Harder," he said in a hoarse voice. "Squeeze me harder."

Julie obeyed, and he moaned in delight.

She ran her hand lower and took his sack in one hand while she kept exploring his length with the other.

"God, yes," he moaned as she continued her exploration. "Run your thumb over the head," he instructed in between hisses of breath.

Julie slowly obeyed, spreading a tiny wet spot on top of his cock. What he truly wanted was for her to take him into her mouth. To lick him and suck on him. But he didn't dare ask that of her. Instead, he took her hand in his and guided her the way he liked, squeezing him and running her hand up and down.

"Guide me inside you," he said when he finally couldn't take it anymore. A few more stimulations and he'd undo himself right there in her hand. But he wanted more. He wanted to feel her heat, to feel her from the inside.

Julie did as he asked, placing him at her center, uncertainly. Robert grunted approval and entered her in one hard thrust. Julie gave a soft yelp and grabbed him by the shoulders to keep her balance.

God, it was heaven inside her wet, tight embrace.

"Hold on tight to me," he whispered as he thrust inside her once more. And again.

He kept moving in and out of her again and again with a force he had never used with her. She moaned with his every push, meeting his every thrust with the movement of her hips.

He took her firmly by her buttocks and rammed into her with a ferocity that had her screaming. He heard sounds of flesh meeting flesh as he moved over and over again, but she felt so good he couldn't stop himself.

She was meeting his thrusts enthusiastically, moaning when he pushed into her to the hilt, so he knew he wasn't hurting her. Aside from that, all reasoning left his mind. All he knew was the delight of having his wife roughly on his desk, the

252

way she felt inside, the way she clutched him closer to her, her intimate flesh drawing him further inside. He heard her breathy moans and screams of ecstasy. He felt himself ascending to the next level of consciousness as she pulsed around him, pulling his own orgasm from him.

Robert finally came down to earth and opened his eyes. He was holding his wife by her buttocks, his cock still inside her, his chin on her shoulder. She was likewise holding on to his bare buttocks, her legs around his hips. His breeches must have dropped somewhere in the process of the vigorous lovemaking. They were both breathing heavily, their clothing soaked in sweat and their intimate juices. Julie's hair tumbled entirely out of her coiffure.

Robert slowly raised his hands to her head, moved her hair away from her face, and pushed it behind her back. He then took her face in both his hands and gave a soft, fleeting kiss on her parted lips. Julie closed her eyes as if soaking in his closeness, breathing in his scent.

"God, I've missed you," he said, caressing her cheeks with his thumbs.

Julie smiled, her eyes still closed, then turned her face into his hand and gave him a kiss on the inside of his palm. Robert chuckled lightly at her blissful facial expression and hugged her close once again.

"Come now, we have to change for supper," he said against her hair.

"Mmm…" A breathy moan was her only reply.

Robert chuckled again and gave her one more kiss before disengaging from her and drawing on his breeches.

Chapter 20

J ulie lay in the bath, enjoying the feel of the steamy hot water on her skin. She was pleasantly numb after the vigorous lovemaking in Robert's study.

She'd had no idea that the marriage act could be so delicious. She had no words to describe the feeling. The way he'd stimulated her with his mouth… The thought made her feel a tingle low in her abdomen.

God, she wanted him again. She moaned and moved in the water, trying to shift her thoughts from Robert and his skillful hands, tongue, and other parts. She opened her eyes and shook her head. It didn't help. She giggled like a little girl, splashing the water in the bath.

What he did to her was beyond shameful and in broad daylight to boot! Somehow, she couldn't scrounge up an ounce of shame or embarrassment. She took a sponge, doused it with soap, and scrubbed her skin as painfully as she could to keep her mind from wandering back to Robert and all his delightful parts.

Dinner was a torturous affair. If she'd felt self-conscious after the first time they'd made love, this time she was completely mortified. She'd acted like a helpless wanton, screaming and moaning in delight while clutching his buttocks. What did he think of her now? Julie was sure she spent the entire dinner covered with every shade of red visible to the human eye.

She had paid little attention to the conversation as it flowed around her, only able to notice Robert's glances her way. Wave after wave of heat covered her body every time he did so.

Since Mary got tired easily these days, they spent a short time in the parlor playing cards after supper and retired early. Julie was worried for Mary and didn't want to tire her out. At the same time, she had another, more selfish reason to retire early. She wanted to spend some more time alone with her husband. She wanted to know if he was pleased with her after what happened in his study. Would he be disgusted by her wantonness?

She sat at the vanity table, brushing her hair when Robert came into her room. He walked behind her and placed his hands on her shoulders.

"You are beautiful," he breathed, and Julie colored again.

She cast her eyes down. "I have something for you."

"I am sure you do," Robert said, his gaze oddly intent.

Julie stood and walked to her bedside table. She opened one of the drawers and pulled out the tiny gift she'd gotten him a few days earlier. She'd been waiting for the perfect time to give it to him. She turned toward him, feeling shy. How did one make a gift to one's husband? Was it always this awkward?

She took a step in his direction and extended her hand.

Robert looked at her hand as if it were something alien. His brows were furrowed, his mouth pressed into a thin line.

"A gift?" he asked as if he did not know what that implied. "What for?"

Julie smiled at his odd reaction. "Do I need a reason to give my husband a gift?"

Robert scratched his chin. "I don't know. I've never had a husband."

Julie let out a nervous chuckle. "Take it."

Robert complied and opened the small leather box, staring at the gift for a few seconds. Inside lay the battered and bruised silver watch with beautiful patterns. Julie bit her lip nervously.

"It's a watch," she said finally.

Robert slowly took it out of the box and looked at it carefully.

"The shopkeeper said that this watch has some of the finest craftsmanship," she explained. "But the problem is, it seems to lag several minutes, no matter how many times you wind it. I immediately thought it would be perfect for you. So you don't wait for Mary and me too long."

Robert's lips twitched for a moment before he let go of a bark of laughter. He enfolded her in a swift hug and kissed her on her forehead.

"It's never a labor to wait for you, darling," he breathed.

Julie gazed into his eyes, the rest of the world melting away, leaving just the unfathomable depths of his silver eyes.

He lowered his head slowly, deliberately, until he was a hair's breadth away from her. Julie couldn't wait anymore, so she took the last step and put her lips on his. Robert instantly took over the kiss, licking at her, grazing her lips with his teeth, and Julie couldn't help but imitate him. She shaped her body to his and clung to him tightly, taking more of his taste, his scent into her senses.

The world whirled around her as Robert took her in his arms and laid her on her bed. Julie instantly covered her body with a coverlet, and Robert smirked at the action.

He ripped his shirt off his shoulders and took off his breeches and smalls, walking toward her with dark purpose in his eyes.

"I hope you don't mind doing it with the candlelight burning?" he asked as he climbed onto the bed. He lowered the coverlet from her body, slowly at first, before yanking it off the bed entirely.

Julie gasped a little, watching the intense fire burning in her husband's eyes. He raked her with his gaze, devouring her with his eyes.

"Take off your chemise," he said in a hoarse voice.

Julie's hands trembled when she obeyed. She drew her chemise over her head and laid it on the floor beside the bed.

She was completely naked to his gaze. He was looking at her as if she were a banquet and he was a starved animal. She shivered a little, and at the same time, her body was covered with heat. He crawled on top of her and caged her with his arms and legs. Then he lowered his mouth to hers and took her in a slow and sensual kiss.

Julie couldn't help but moan and arch into him, her breasts chafing against his hard chest. She heard him make an approving sound in the back of his throat, but she couldn't help but feel self-conscious.

It was different somehow, in his study. When they both seemed crazed with passion. Now, lying in her bed, under his soft ministrations, she couldn't help but feel uncertain.

"Robert," she whispered against his lips.

"Mmm," he growled into her mouth and continued his sensual assault.

"Robert, wait," she tried again, and he drew back a little.

"What?" he asked in a whisper, his gaze still locked on her lips.

She placed a hand against his cheek and felt his rough stubble grazing against her palm. He leaned into her touch, and she caressed his stubbly cheek with her thumb, marveling at the sensation.

"Is it acceptable?" she asked shyly.

"What?" he asked, looking confused. He bore his weight on his left arm, and with his right, he trapped her hand between his cheek and palm. He turned his head then and kissed the inside of her palm, then moved lower to her wrist, grazing it slightly with his teeth before soothing it with his tongue.

Julie closed her eyes at the pleasant sensation. "That," she moaned. "The sounds I make. I can't stay silent when you kiss or touch me the way you do."

"Why would I want you to be quiet?" He looked at her in confusion.

"Mrs. Darling said…" She frowned in thought. "She said that I ought to stay quiet and unmoving while a husband… does what he does." She bit her lip as she heard him laugh. Heat crept all over her body.

"Who is this Mrs. Darling, and what makes her an authority on husbands and what goes on in the marriage bed?" he asked teasingly.

"Well, she's not." She hesitated. "She's a chaperone."

"Ahh, so her main job description is to make sure nothing

improper happens between her charge and a gentleman."

Julie nodded, feeling confused.

Robert lowered his head and nipped on her earlobe. "Is she married?" he whispered into her ear, making her shiver.

Julie bit her lip again and shook her head. Robert sucked on her lower lip and licked it slowly.

"Well, what happens between a husband and wife in bed is absolutely improper," he said when he raised his eyes to her.

Robert kissed her mouth again, then drifted to her chin. He suckled on her neck, licking at her tiny pulse. "I love the sounds you make," he whispered against her neck. "I love the way you move against me," he said between peppering tiny kisses all over her neck and face.

"You do?" She couldn't hide the confusion from her tone and felt him smile against her skin.

"My sweet girl," he breathed as he looked up at her. "I want you to enjoy this. I need you to enjoy this. And I want to know when you do."

Julie looked at him unblinking.

"Every time I do something you like, I want you to tell me so."

Julie swallowed nervously.

"Let's try it, shall we?" He grinned at her then, looking absolutely smug. "When I kiss you or touch you the way you like, say *yes*. If I do something you don't like, say *no*."

Julie nodded, and Robert lowered his mouth to hers. He licked at the seam of her lips, and when she opened to him, he swept his tongue inside her mouth with a groan. He licked at her mouth while his hands drifted down her body. The sensation sent shots of pleasure through her. She couldn't help but writhe beneath him.

"Yes?" he asked when he finally raised his head.

"Yes." Her voice was breathless to her own ears.

"Good." He smiled wolfishly and moved down her body, sucking on her neck, nipping on her collarbone.

Every time he raised his eyes to hers, she would answer yes. He lowered his head and took her nipple inside his mouth. She felt a tingle grow through her body, and something hot and liquid gathered between her thighs.

"No!" she cried, clenching her thighs in reaction. Despite the indecencies of this afternoon, she felt shy suddenly.

Robert raised his head and looked at her in confusion. "Are you sure?" He raised his brow.

Julie bit on the inside of her lower lip and shook her head.

"How about I try that again, and you'll see whether or not you like it?" he said with a sly smile. "I promise, you are going to like it." His last words came out as a whisper as he lowered his mouth to her nipple again and sucked it lightly.

She moaned and arched her spine, bringing her breast farther inside his mouth. Robert chuckled and swirled his tongue around her nipple, then sucked on it again, harder this time while his other hand caressed her other breast. She felt him raise his head and look at her face, although her eyes were closed and her head was thrown back.

"Did you like it?" he asked with a self-satisfied smirk in his voice.

"Yes," Julie breathed without looking at him.

"Do you want more?" he asked as he lowered his mouth to her other breast and took her nipple inside.

"Yes, oh, God, yes," she whimpered, not feeling embarrassed at her wanton behavior anymore.

He pleasured her breasts as his hand trailed down to her

center. He played with her there, tickling, circling, flicking her sensitive nub until she couldn't help but moan and arch into his hand. He raised himself over her then and licked her mouth, parting her lips with his tongue, drawing her own tongue. In the next moment, he thrust two fingers inside her core. She arched against him, and a bolt of pleasure shot through her as her nub connected with the heel of his palm.

"Yes, that's right," he whispered against her lips. "Ride my hand. Ride me good and well."

Hearing him saying it made her blush all over, but she couldn't help it. Her hips moved as if on their own accord as she did as he asked, rode his hand, and pleasured herself against him until she couldn't control any part of her body anymore.

A white-hot pleasure shot through her, and she tensed, pulsing all over. He kept moving his hand against her and licking at her parted lips, swallowing her cries inside his mouth until the last of the waves deserted her, and she felt limp and boneless.

He spread her legs wider and settled fully between them. She felt the hot rod of his arousal against her, and in the next moment, he was inside her, thrusting deep and hard.

Being filled by him was like nothing she had ever experienced before. She felt content, complete. He withdrew all too soon before thrusting again, his pelvis meeting hers with a violent smack every time he seated himself inside her to the hilt.

He moved thus for several minutes, breathing hard, sweat trickling down his forehead and across his chest. The bed creaked with his every movement, her hips moving to meet his thrusts.

She clutched at him, her fingers sinking into his skin, her legs wrapped around his hips. She felt as if she'd be lost in the void if she didn't hold on to him like an anchor. His every thrust was met by her loud moans and cries. She didn't care that they could be heard because she couldn't control them anyhow. Another wave of pleasure accosted her, and she lost all sense of time and space and existence.

When she finally opened her eyes, Robert was still on top of her. She could feel his arousal still inside her, softer now. She was pleasantly anchored by his weight, her legs still wrapped around his hips, his face pressed against her cheek.

The position was oddly vulnerable and comforting at the same time. She wanted to stay this way forever. But Robert withdrew and rolled away, leaving her empty and cold.

As he lay on his back beside her, she curled against his side, placing her head on his shoulder to feel his heat again. She was afraid he would pull away again. Instead, Robert kissed the top of her head, and she felt him smile against her as he drew her closer.

* * *

A week later, Julie stood on the pedestal at the modiste in a beautiful deep blue gown that matched her eyes, with a low-cut bodice and bare shoulders. It was the last day of fittings before the Somerset ball. Mary had already tried on her gown and was dozing peacefully on the sofa.

Julie glanced at the looking glass and could barely recognize herself. The bright blue color perfectly suited her; her bodice's low cut clearly emphasized her round breasts. She knew Robert would like it; she'd noticed the way his gaze always fell to her bosom when she wore a gown like that. She also knew it would result in a passionate night of lovemaking. She grew damp between her legs just thinking about it.

The modiste grunted something under her breath and disappeared behind the curtain. No doubt to bring more pins and needles to prick Julie with.

The scent of lilac perfume warned her that someone had come up behind her.

"You look beautiful in that dress." A woman appeared in the periphery of her vision, but Julie didn't turn to look at her. "No wonder Robert chose you as his wife."

Robert.

Julie knew the woman had used her husband's first name on purpose, to emphasize her intimate relationship with him. Julie slowly turned and regarded the woman before her.

She was not tall but extremely curvy. Julie had nice hips and breasts herself, but she had nothing on the woman before her. Her bright red gown emphasized her every curve, and her breasts were in danger of falling out of her low-cut bodice.

"I dare say he did not know about the idiot in your bloodline," she said, flinging one of her dark-brown curls back. "Otherwise, he wouldn't risk his reputation so."

"In that case, I presume you don't know him very well," Julie said calmly, although she was shaking on the inside.

She recognized the perfume, of course. She'd smelled it on her husband the day he returned from his prolonged absence when they arrived in London.

The woman in front of her just laughed musically. "I presume you know who I am?" She regarded Julie with a smirk. "Vanessa Vanderburt, at your service. Or rather, at your husband's service." She smiled lazily. "And I know him a lot better than you think you do. Why would he continue visiting me if I didn't?" she said with a nonchalant shrug.

"He doesn't," Julie answered evenly. She looked beyond the woman's shoulder, wishing the modiste would come back already.

"Oh, but he does. Quite often, I might add. Where do you think he spent the nights of your arrival to London? Where do you think he spends his afternoons?" She touched the curly lock of her hair as if standing still was not an option. "He rarely spends the night, but he is always looking for an excuse to do so."

Julie felt as if she was going to be sick right on the woman in front of her.

"I don't believe you," she said in a hoarse voice. "So you can save your breath." She turned away from her, hoping the woman would take a hint and leave her alone.

"Are you so certain then?" the woman asked, coming to stand at Julie's side. Julie turned and regarded her quietly.

"Are you sure he tells you everything about his desires in bed?" the woman asked. "Because I am sure he does not. Because he knows you will never fulfill them."

"You know nothing about my relationship with my husband."

"Oh, on the contrary." The woman smiled cruelly, her smile not quite reaching her eyes. "He told me you are cold and unfeeling like a fish. He said that you would never be as good as I." She looked Julie up and down. "With your proper attire and behavior, you could never fulfill his desires. Thus, he needs me."

Julie let out a breath and regarded her mutely. The modiste finally appeared from the curtain, blinking twice as she saw

264

Chapter 20

the two women together.

"Ahh, Miss Vanderburt, have you come for a new gown?"

"Certainly." She smiled blandly. "My man loves to spoil me," she said as she looked up at Julie with a challenge in her eyes.

"Give me a minute then, I need to finish with Lady Clydesdale."

The modiste seemed unaware of any undercurrents going on between her two clients. She shuffled past them to her table to grab something, and Vanessa took this moment to lean closer to Julie and slip an envelope into her hand. Then she scoffed at Julie and exited the room.

265

Chapter 21

Robert stalked the hall of his London townhouse like a beast. He hadn't seen his wife since this morning, and he missed her dearly. The urge to see her and hold her in his arms was overwhelming.

Robert had never in his wildest dreams expected that she would become such a passionate and uninhibited lover. That first night when she'd insisted her nightshift be left on her, when she tried not to move and bit her lip to keep from crying out, it seemed like it was a completely different woman. And yet, she was the same. Only now she could playfully bite him on his neck and shoulders, sometimes deep enough to leave marks on him.

He would chuckle to himself, finding another mark she'd left on his body in the looking glass or during his bath. She didn't mind making love in the candlelight anymore. In fact, she unashamedly watched him now, devouring him with her gaze.

She seemed curious to give him pleasure and seemed

earnestly delighted when she found another one of his erogenous zones or when she did something that made him groan. She was playful and giddy in bed. It was never dull to bed her.

Robert knew she was attached to him, she was attracted to him, and she definitely found bedding him pleasurable. Still, he wasn't ready to test the limits of said attraction.

It was one reason he kept their interludes to the bed and otherwise tried to spend as little time as possible in her company. Since their lovemaking had transformed after the incident in his study, he'd stopped sharing his plans with her anymore, discussed nothing concerning estates or anything else, and kept their conversations brief and polite.

He was afraid that she'd tire of him, and more to the point, he was worried that the more she knew him, the more her attraction to him would fade. And he didn't want to be too used to her, too dependent on her when that happened.

Women loved to spend time with him in bed. Other than that, he'd yet to meet a woman who loved his intellect or character. That she hadn't insisted on spending more time with him and seemed quite content with their arrangement was proof enough.

Then there was the issue of her first love. The soldier, John. He tried to push the thought of him away and almost succeeded. But every so often, he would look down at the sleeping form of his wife and wonder if she would still be so content in his arms if John were back?

Some days he would sit in his study, discuss his work with solicitors, sit in Parliament, or drink at his clubs. All he wanted was to go to his wife, no matter where she was or what she was doing. Just to look at her, to speak with her, let the cadence of her voice wash over him. To make love to her on the closest piece of furniture, to brand her with his scent, his body, impress upon himself that she was his and only his. Which, of course, she was; she was his wife. No matter if she loved him or not.

But it did matter. Because as much as he tried to deny it, the truth was simple. He had fallen in love with her.

Idiot.

He heard footsteps on the top landing of the stairs and looked up. His wife stood there, wearing a shimmering blue gown with bared shoulders and a low-cut neckline. Her coiffure was swept up in a crown on her head, with two or three loose tendrils hanging out in strategic places. Julie wore the sapphire jewelry the dowager had given her to wear, a family heirloom that fit her perfectly, long white gloves that complemented white beads in her hair, and a white and blue fan.

She took one step down slowly and looked back. That's when he noticed Mary was right behind her. The girl smiled openly, puffy white skirts clutched in her fists.

She was wearing a white and silver high-waisted gown, white gloves, and a coronet with white roses on her head. She looked absolutely the picture of innocence. She did not know what awaited her in the Somerset ballroom, but she did not care.

This was her debut. She was a flushing and giggling debutante like a regular girl, happy to make her come-out.

Robert cleared his throat. "You look wonderful," he said with a note of wonder in his voice. "Both of you."

"Why, thank you, my lord." His wife looked at him coyly from beneath her lashes. Mary just giggled an answer.

"Shall we?" Robert offered each of them an arm when they made it down the stairs.

"What about the dowager duchess?" Julie asked, looking around the room.

"She went on without us. Rutland sent a carriage after her. She decided it'd be best if she made an early appearance, seeing how we are always late." He looked pointedly at his wife. "Besides, she thinks her early appearance will ease the way for us."

"I agree." Julie smiled before playfully tapping his arm with her fan. "But we are not late. Check your watch." She smiled widely at him.

"I did." Robert returned her smile with his gentle one. "And even by my superior watch, we are still late."

Julie compressed her lips to keep from smiling.

"Are you nervous?" Robert turned to Mary.

She shook her head.

"Excited?" He grinned down at her.

Mary nodded vigorously. "My first ball!" she said, her eyes glinting.

"Indeed." Robert settled them both in a carriage and climbed up behind them.

* * *

Julie wanted desperately for this night to go smoothly for Mary. In the carriage, Mary kept playing with her dance card, flipping it this way and that, explaining to Robert repeatedly that this was where her suitors would write their names to reserve a dance with her.

Julie bit nervously at her lip. She'd explained the importance of said card to Mary earlier this evening when they were getting dressed. Mary had looked so delighted to hear that gentlemen would line up and write their names to save a dance with her. Julie looked at her husband worriedly. She was afraid that Mary's card would remain empty throughout the night.

Her thoughts were interrupted as the carriage drew to a stop, and they alighted in front of the Somerset townhouse.

There was a big crush of people outside, even more so on the inside. The place was filled with white flowers surrounded by branches of greenery. The whole area was covered with white and green hues aside from the yellowish lights of candles.

It was obvious that Evie was the main decorator of the ball. She had impeccable taste, and the house looked as pure as innocence.

Julie did not have time to contemplate the beauty of the house, however. The moment they reached the receiving line, they were whisked away by a footman who had instructions to bring them to the library.

"Finally, you are here!" Evie cried. "I was beginning to worry I was going to have to walk down there by myself."

"What are you talking about?" Julie wrinkled her brow for a moment before taking Evie's hands in both of hers. "Oh, Eves, you look wonderful!"

And she really did.

Her fiery red hair was swept up in an intricate chignon. A few wisps of curly hair hung from her temple and at the nape of her neck. She wore an ice-green chiffon dress with a layered skirt and beaded lace bodice.

For adornment, all she had was a silver chain with a pearl drop, long white gloves with ornaments at the ends, and a matching fan adorned with tiny pearls. She had a white lily in her hair, and her coiffure was kept in place with the pearl pins.

She looked like a young princess of nymphs from a fairytale. Serene and regal, while her glowing green eyes, mischievous smile, and fiery hair gave away her passionate nature.

"Thank you." She curtsied to Julie and Clydesdale and took Mary by the arm. "Mary and I shall make our come-out together," she said triumphantly.

"Evie, you can't!" Julie's eyes widened with shock. "We agreed we shall go in earlier and let the dust settle before you follow."

"Yes, I know. You all worry too much," she said with a nonchalant wave. "But I've discussed it with Grandpapa, and if those people want to be in my graces, they must accept my friends. And if they do not, I don't care to be accepted by them."

"This is very kind of you, Lady Eabha." Robert finally made his presence known. "But you need to marry well, and a tight association with us might hurt your chances."

"I shall marry for love," Evie said, her eyes bright with youthful certainty. "And I shan't fall in love with a person who judges people without getting to know them. Now, please, leave us debutantes alone." She waved her hand slightly in the door's direction. "We need to prepare before our entry. And you need to be there when we make our grand entrance." Evie looked at Mary and winked. Mary giggled back and hugged her tightly.

"Your dress is pretty," Mary whispered, taking a piece of chiffon in her hand and rubbing it lightly between her fingers.

"You have excellent taste, Merr," Evie was saying as Julie

and Robert backed away from the room.

As soon as they were out in the hall, Julie clutched Robert's arm. "Do you think we are doing the right thing by leaving them alone?" she asked worriedly.

Robert placed his hand over Julie's where it rested on his arm and looked down at her. "Lady Eabha definitely has strong Montgomery blood in her veins. I don't think she would take no for an answer. Besides, she might be right. Nobody would dare to cut the Duke of Somerset's granddaughter. So perhaps Mary is in better hands with her than with us."

"Will they dare cut the Duke of Rutland's son?" Julie raised her brow at him.

"It's different." Robert looked ahead as they came to the front of the receiving line. "Mary is now my family. She is not Somerset's. Where I, by bringing my underaged simpleminded sister-in-law to a ball, am committing a faux pas, he, in turn, is graciously showing the *ton* how to react to my ill decision."

Julie mutely nodded as they came closer to the Duke of Somerset and exchanged pleasantries.

Several moments later, Gabriel, Viscount St. Clare, appeared at Robert's elbow.

"Where's our debutante?" he asked after they were done with the greetings and pleasantries.

"They are waiting for an opportune moment to catch everyone off-guard," Robert said quietly.

"They?"

"Yes, Somerset's granddaughter is making her come-out and is dragging Mary with her."

"Is she now?" Gabriel wrinkled a brow. "Daring little

creature. Have I met her before?"

"Oh, you would remember her if you saw her," Julie said with a smile.

Nobody forgot beautiful Evie after a single glance. Julie fanned herself lightly while studying Gabriel as he shrugged, looking nonplussed.

He had gorgeous golden hair, his eyes were icy blue, his features symmetrical and chiseled, as if carved by a sculptor. She shifted her gaze toward her husband's forbidden features.

They were like an angel and a demon, forces of light and darkness. Only for her, the force of darkness held more appeal. She remembered the first time she saw them both and how she'd thought Gabriel superior in his physical appearance, almost overlooking Robert altogether. There was no overlooking him now.

Finally, the music trumpeted, and the butler announced the debutantes. A hush fell over the ballroom, and the roomful of people's gazes was riveted to the top of the stairs.

Two figures slowly made their way down. Evie floated down the stairs, her skirts shifting as if she was not stepping down the stairs but moving on clouds, her back straight, her neck long, her lips smiling. Mary held on to her arm, again, as different from Evie as night from day. She was clumsily making her way, looking down, and holding her skirts in her other hand. Evie smiled at everyone in the room, periodically smiling down at Mary with encouragement.

Julie was looking at the pair so intently that she forgot she was in the middle of the ballroom surrounded by five hundred or so people.

A low whistle brought her back to the ballroom floor.

"That is Somerset's granddaughter?" St. Clare asked in a

low voice. "Exquisite."

Julie looked up at him and blinked.

Gabriel studied Evie with narrowed eyes, his gaze sweeping over her from head to toe, like a hunter studying his prey.

"Careful, St. Clare," Robert said in a menacing voice. "The girl is Julie's cousin. Which means she is under my protection as well as Somerset's."

"Oh, please, Robert." Gabriel gave a charming smile. "As if I need to hear threats from you to know who's off my menu. Besides, innocents are not my forte. Unless they are not as innocent as they seem," he added with a smirk.

Robert threw him a dark stare, but Gabriel just laughed and threw his hands up in mock defense. "Come, now, Robert. You know I would never ruin a girl you care for. Have some faith in me. And she doesn't look like the kind who'd fall for my charms anyhow," he said with a shrug.

"She's not," Julie said with a proud smile. "Robert, let's go greet them; they're almost down." She tugged him toward the foot of the stairs.

Several moments later, the ball started in full force. The musicians struck the dancing tunes, and couples moved on to the dancefloor. Gabriel claimed Mary's first dance while an army of suitors instantly moved over to surround Evie.

Robert was right. Nobody dared cut the granddaughter of a mighty duke. Not even making a come-out with an idiot could mar the night for Evie. She smiled at everyone politely while regarding them from beneath her lashes, fanning herself lightly.

Julie smiled to herself. Evie would be a force to be reckoned with.

As for Mary, after the dance with Gabriel, Robert signed his name on her dance card for the second waltz. Julie suspected he did it on purpose. Just so that her card didn't remain empty. Having performed his duty by his friend for the night, Gabriel moved on to his own more pleasurable pursuits. Whatever they were.

Mary, Robert, Julie, and the dowager duchess stood on the sidelines, a tiny little island everyone took care to avoid. Nobody had given them the cut direct so far; they were cordially avoided instead.

"Clydesdale."

Julie jumped as she heard a familiar male voice. She couldn't quite place it before she turned and regarded the Duke of Rutland.

"Your Grace." Julie sank into a curtsy and pushed Mary's hand down with her so that her sister curtsied too.

"Your Grace," Robert said in a solemn voice. "I don't believe you've met my sister-in-law, Mary."

Mary smiled up at him with her usual smile, and when Robert clarified the duke was his father, she came up to him and gave him a hug. Julie bit her lip at the expression of surprise on the duke's face.

"I didn't expect to see you here," the dowager said in a dry voice. Although Julie fancied she saw a flicker of curiosity on the elderly woman's face.

"Clydesdale came down to me earlier this week. Insisted I attend. Something about lending support for the family." Rutland shrugged and looked ahead as if staring into the void.

"Thank you," Robert said a little hoarsely, and Julie squeezed his arm in a comforting gesture.

"I told you when we met," the duke said matter-of-factly. "If there's anything more important than reputation, it is family."

Julie felt her eyes water. How different he was from her own father. She'd always heard that Rutland was peculiar but also cold and uncaring. She thought him so too when she met him at the fateful Christmas house party. Especially after she'd heard that he and her father had negotiated their children's betrothal. Now, however, she'd have to revise her view of him.

He cared about Robert. It was obvious. And by extension, he now cared about Julie and Mary.

After a short, polite talk, Rutland accompanied Mary around the ballroom, just to make sure that everyone saw his approval of his son's actions and of his daughter-in-law and her sister. Robert explained Rutland disliked crowds and that coming here tonight was a great show of support on his part. Julie felt so warm inside she was about to burst with joy. Was this how it felt to have an actual family?

The first bars of a waltz interrupted her reverie. Mary was intercepted by the Duke of Somerset for the dance, and Robert slowly turned to Julie at that moment and asked her to dance.

"It's not fashionable to dance with one's own wife," she whispered lightly, fanning herself vigorously, for she suddenly felt hot.

Robert grinned at that. "And we are such a fashionable family, are we?"

Family. The word stole her breath. Paired with the way he looked at her with humor and gentleness shining in his eyes, she could not refuse him even if he'd asked her to jump off a bridge into a freezing lake.

Besides, he was right. Chances were, they would never be invited to another ball again after tonight's escapades. She placed her hand on his arm, and they moved onto the dance floor.

They were drawing gazes from the crowd, Julie noted. People started whispering behind their fans the moment they passed them by. Julie held up her head and pretended not to notice.

As they stepped into the dance, Julie was taken into the world of a fairytale. She had her prince, clasping her in his arms, twirling her around a beautiful ballroom, looking at her as if they were the only people in the world.

He was an elegant and sure dancer. Julie didn't have to think about steps or following the music. She magically followed his lead as if she were born in his arms. They danced in silence, occasionally smiling at each other and just enjoying the closeness.

Now that they were alone, however, Julie remembered her earlier confrontation with Robert's former mistress. At least she hoped Vanessa was his *former* mistress. She hadn't had the time to study the envelope that Vanessa had slipped into her hand. Julie had been busy with Mary all day, and later it had just slipped her mind. Now, however, all kinds of thoughts were whirling inside her mind.

She didn't believe Vanessa's words for a moment. Of course, she didn't. Why the nagging headache in her skull then? Julie started feeling flustered and hot.

"Is anything amiss?" Robert looked at her, his gaze troubled now.

She shook her head and smiled slightly. "I think I was too nervous for Mary's sake. And now all the twirling and the smell of flowers are making my head spin a little."

Julie didn't lie. The scent did make her nauseous. Anything else they would have to discuss later, at home. The waltz was coming to an end, and Julie was grateful for that.

"Do you want me to escort you outside?" Robert asked, still frowning down at her.

"Don't you have the next dance with Mary?"

He nodded sharply at that, and she smiled.

"I'll cool down in the corridor a little, but I shall meet you after the dance?"

Another nod from her worried husband. At that moment, the music ceased, and Robert took her by the arm and silently led her away from the dance floor.

Julie left the ballroom as soon as Robert took Mary for the next dance. She felt hot and a little nauseous. The hotness was definitely the result of a packed ballroom and dancing in her husband's powerful arms. But the aromatic smell of flowers and people's perfume was adding to the sensation, making her ill. She stood with her back to the corridor wall and fanned herself.

She heard the music and knew that Mary's waltz with Robert was underway. She smiled to herself, thinking of her tall and muscular husband dancing with her tiny sister, and she wished she could see them dance. She took a couple of deep breaths, getting ready to re-enter the ballroom and witness Mary's dance with her favorite man when she heard steps coming down from the side of the ballroom. The steps reached her, and she was seized violently by the arm.

"You little bitch, how dare you," the familiar voice sneered in her ear, and the next thing she knew, she was being dragged away down the corridor, then thrust into an empty room.

Chapter 22

"How dare you humiliate me in front of the *ton*?" Julie's father spat in her face, his spittle flying toward her; she flinched instinctively. "You took that idiot from the asylum and thought what? That you would be lauded for that? And now you bring her to a ball and flaunt her in front of everybody? I'd have killed her if I knew you were stupid enough to do it!"

"I, humiliate you?" Julie found her voice at the threat to Mary's life. "You humiliated yourself when you sent Mary away." She tried to steady her voice, but she couldn't hold the emotion from it. Tears burned the backs of her eyes. "She is your daughter!"

"I don't know that!" he screamed. "She is probably a bastard. My children would never be born idiots."

"The only idiot in our family is you!" she hissed between her teeth.

Norfolk made a grab for her, but she danced away just in time.

"Don't you touch me," she said emphatically. "I am not your property anymore, and neither is Mary. We are out, and we are happy, and if you come near either of us one more time, I shall shoot you with my husband's pistol!"

Julie walked past the astonished marquess triumphantly, although her hands were shaking.

Norfolk was so surprised by her behavior that he didn't even say a word to her.

Julie entered the ballroom, an enormous smile on her face. It didn't matter that people avoided them anymore; it didn't matter that they'd been gossiped about. The confrontation with her father somehow made her feel free and powerful. She had always been under his shadow. Her mother's death, Mary's disappearance, John's exile to the Continent—everything bad that ever happened in her life was because of him.

Now she was free.

She sought her husband with her eyes and met his worried gaze. She smiled widely at him before the silhouette of a large man blocked her view. She raised her eyes and saw Eric, Robert's cousin, sneering down at her. Julie expelled a deep breath. Would this night ever end?

* * *

After the dance with Mary, Robert looked about the room, searching for his wife. If she were truly well, she would be back by now, wouldn't she? He wanted to sweep Mary and the dowager into the carriage, find Julie and take them home. This ball was dreary enough. And Mary had gotten enough excitement to last her a year.

At that moment, his gaze found Julie, and he relaxed

instantly. His relief turned to dread and then rage as he saw who she was talking with. *Eric.*

The bastard dared to talk to his wife. Robert turned hot with rage. His hands shook from the desire to either throttle the bastard or shake the stuffing out of him. However, he couldn't leave his place because Mary was hanging on his arm, obviously tired, and the dowager was somewhere across the ballroom chatting to an old friend.

Julie seemed to be speaking amicably to his hated enemy, completely unaware that her husband was shooting daggers with his gaze toward her companion.

Eric placed a hand on her shoulder, gently, as if on his lover, and Robert took an unconscious step forward. Julie thankfully shook off his hand, gingerly too, and his eyes narrowed at the action. She wasn't shaking him off in disgust; it was as if she was trying to be circumspect. His suspicion turned to certainty when she looked around in agitation, then met his gaze, threw a few words to Eric over her shoulder, and walked toward him.

By the time they arrived home, Julie was her old self, smiling and chatty. Once they tucked Mary in, Robert went to his room, undressed, and listened to the sounds in his wife's room. She was freshening up, and her maid was helping her get ready for bed.

As soon as the door closed behind Alice, Robert opened the connecting door of their bedchambers and walked into Julie's room. She was still sitting at the vanity, combing her hair. She raised her head as he walked in and regarded him with a slight smile.

Robert walked slowly behind her and placed his hands on her shoulders.

"Is something wrong?" he whispered, staring at her troubled reflection.

Julie didn't raise her eyes. She placed her comb on the table, stood from her chair, and turned to him.

"No, all is well," she said as if she doubted her own words. She looked up to him then, and he saw a tiny frown marring her features. "It's just been an eventful day."

"I know." Robert furrowed his brows. "I saw you talking to someone before we left…" He trailed off, waiting for her to pick up the thread, and she did.

"Oh, you mean Eric?" She grimaced a little.

"Eric?" Robert repeated, his tone dry.

"I need to tell you something." Julie turned away and walked slowly to her bed. She sat on the edge, her hands folded on her lap, her gaze fixed on the floor.

"Yes?" Robert followed his wife with his gaze.

"He came to the Clydesdale estate while you were in London," Julie answered evenly.

"What?" Robert stepped forward, his hands clenched into fists by his side. Eric had been at his estate, with his wife, while he was away? And nobody told him? "Why didn't I know about this?" he asked hoarsely. It seemed like his worst nightmare was repeating itself.

Julie cleared her throat. "I was going to, but then Mary got sick, and later, when we talked, we…" She colored a little. "Well, you know. And it just slipped my mind."

Robert gave a disbelieving huff. "Slipped your mind?" He raised his brows in irritation. "How come *Eric* slipped your mind while you remembered to question me about Vanessa?" Robert's eyes widened as the realization dawned on him. "He was the one who told you about her, wasn't he?"

Julie didn't move and didn't indicate she'd heard him, not even with her breath.

"What else did the bastard say?" Robert's gaze was fixed on his wife's unmoving profile. He shook his head as if to rid himself of the unpleasant revelation.

Julie finally raised her head and regarded him solemnly. "He said that you seduced the girl he loved," she said with a frown between her brows. "That you ruined her and left her."

"And you believed him?" Robert growled the question.

"Of course not!" Julie cried in irritation as she shot off the bed. "I would have confronted you sooner about it if I did."

"What did he do?"

"What?"

"What the devil did he do while he was on my estate?"

Julie cleared her throat lightly. "Nothing happened. The dowager came in just in time."

"Just in time to what?"

"He... uh, he—" She raised her eyes timidly to his. "He tried to seduce me," she finished lamely.

"Did he succeed?"

Julie's head shot up at that. She stared at him, her mouth agape. "Are you seriously asking me that?"

"Well, you seemed pleasant enough when you talked to him today. You are calling him *Eric*—"

"How dare you?" his wife interrupted him with a quiet growl. "How dare you accuse me of that when you were the one in London visiting your mistress!"

"My former mistress, and I think we covered that already."

"Yes, and I believe you!" Julie cried in irritation as she shot off the bed. "And yet you seem to think that I would be seduced by your cousin. Under your own roof, with Mary

283

and the dowager sleeping in the next room. Is that really what you think of me?"

Robert just looked at her in silence.

Julie sniffed lightly. "It is what you think of me." She shook her head and closed her eyes. "I was trying not to create even more scandal than we already were by fighting with him at the ball. I didn't want to ruin Mary's night, but you know what?" She opened her eyes and looked at him with pure anger in her eyes, and something else, something akin to hurt. "I'll tell you exactly what your cousin did." She made a step toward him, "He kissed me." Step. "Forcibly." Another step.

Robert flinched and stepped back.

"And he wanted more." She stopped almost toe-to-toe with him. "He pushed me down and raised my skirts—" Her voice was breaking, and her eyes glinted with tears.

"Julie." Robert's voice was hoarse. He didn't know where he found the strength to even speak. His insides were quivering with rage, self-hatred, and pain. He reached for her, but she twisted away from his touch.

"No," she said, tears now running down her cheek. "No, if it wasn't for the dowager, I wouldn't have been able to stop him." She was wiping her tears away from her face. "And all the while you were in London, doing God knows what—"

Robert couldn't take it anymore; he reached her in one long stride, grabbed her by the arms, and drew her flush with his body, hugging her close. "Hush," he whispered. "Don't cry, my sweet, please don't."

"You should have been with us." She was sobbing into his shirt, and his heart was breaking with her every sound. How could he have suspected that she'd fallen for Eric's charm? He knew the answer, the unreasonable jealousy based on his unfortunate past experience.

"I'm sorry," he crooned against her hair as she sobbed. "I'm so sorry, I am an idiot. Please forgive me."

All the words stopped for a while as she cried. He took her into his arms and placed her gingerly on the bed. She wiped her tears and regarded him with a wary gaze.

"Julie—"

"Tell me what happened between you and Eric," she whispered almost inaudibly.

Robert closed his eyes briefly, remembering the night before his wedding when he left his bachelor party because he was too eager to see his lovely bride.

"He seduced my fiancée," he finally said. "I found them in bed together the night before our wedding, but I assume it wasn't their first interlude."

Julie frowned for a moment before nodding slightly. "I need to rest, Robert," she finally whispered, dismissing him.

"Julie—"

"Please." She didn't look at him as she pleaded for him to leave.

Robert nodded, placed a kiss on her forehead, and left the room. He closed the door and leaned against it.

That was well done, idiot.

* * *

The next morning, Robert came to breakfast fresh and rested. He was resolute not to let the past stand between him and his wife anymore. He could mistrust her and be jealous of her his entire life, and it wouldn't bring him either happiness or peace.

It was time to let go of the hurt and the bitterness and try to live freely and openly.

Nobody was at the table when he got to the dining room. He put a selection of food onto his plate and sat at his usual place, perusing the paper. He turned the page, and his eyes widened as he saw the article written in bold font with his family's caricature. He shot off the chair as his wife entered the room.

"What's wrong?" she asked, looking at his stricken face.

"I need to—" He battled with whether to tell her the truth now or to weigh the damage first, but he remembered his earlier resolution.

No holding back. No matter how pure his intent, things never seemed to go right when he withheld something from his wife. So, he slowly extended his hand and handed her the paper.

"You might want to sit down before you read this," he said carefully.

Julie took the paper from him and did as he asked. She sat in the chair held out by a footman and read the article. Her eyes widened with every word she read.

He knew what she was reading and wanted to shield her from it, but she needed to know to fight it later. It was an unflattering recital of what had happened to Mary during the asylum days. It was not kind to the asylum, but it was equally unkind to Mary.

"That's… That's… What is it?" Julie asked when she finally raised her head.

"Somebody must have gotten hold of the letter I prepared per Tule's instruction. They've twisted what I've written and posted it to the papers. That is the only explanation I can

think of. I shall have to figure out what has happened, but—"
He paused as he saw a strange expression on his wife's face.

She stood from the table, turned, and left the room without
another word. He followed her out and into her room. She
walked into her dressing room and rummaged through the
pockets of her gowns before she finally found what she was
looking for. She slowly turned to him and extended an
envelope.

Robert took it into his hand and took a deep breath. He
recognized his seal at once. "It is the letter," he said, his voice
hoarse. "Where did you get it?"

Julie grimaced before turning away from him. "I met your
mistress at the modiste's yesterday. She handed this letter to
me as proof that you'd spent the night with her." She paused.
"I haven't opened it. I forgot about it until just now."

"I didn't lie to you—" Robert started, but she waved her
hand, stopping him.

"It doesn't matter. She wouldn't have posted it in the papers
if you were still together, would she?" she said quietly.

"I went to her that night to break off our arrangement. I fell
ill after freezing at the marina and spent nights senseless and
with a high fever. I swear to you, I have never been unfaithful
to you."

Julie kept silent.

Robert raked his hand through his hair. "We don't have
to talk about this now, but I promise we can talk about
everything later. It is better if neither you nor Mary goes
out today. And probably not for the next several days," Robert
added after a pause of uncertainty.

"Or weeks," Julie finished his thought. "This is outrageous.
The way they presented this. It's as if she is to blame for being

born the way she was. And more importantly, as if all the hurt she's been through was her fault too."

Julie raised pleading eyes to him. His heart nearly broke for the sorrow in them. And it was all his fault.

"We should have sent the letter earlier. We should have—" She shook her head. "What are we to do now?"

"Nothing. I shall try to minimize Mary's damage, but the cat is out of the bag. We have to proceed with our allegations toward the York Asylum. I shall have to go to Doncaster and discuss the strategy with Mr. Tule. We'll come back to London to present our case to the guardians' committee, but you and Mary should probably leave the city. I have an estate close by, in Bromley, about five hours' drive from London. You can go there, so you don't have to suffer the long travel."

He paused, waiting for her reaction. Still, she lowered her gaze to the paper and was staring at it with a glass-like look, clearly not listening to him anymore.

"Everything will be well," he said not convincingly.

"All I wanted was for her to have a season in London," she said meekly.

"She did," he said quietly. He laid his hand on her shoulder lightly as he walked past her on the way out of her room.

* * *

Robert entered the house a little after supper, tired and winded. The day had been long and difficult. Things were much worse than he'd anticipated, and he needed to leave for Doncaster first thing in the morning.

He was surprised to see a visitor in the hall having an argument with his butler. Robert moved closer to the young man as he took off his hat and gloves.

"I need to see Lady Julie Weston. It is urgent," the young man said emphatically.

"There's no one by that name here," came the butler's even reply.

Lady Julie Weston. Robert knew exactly who the young man had been referring to.

Julie Weston was his wife's maiden name. Robert took a few steps until he was facing the guest.

He was a young man of middle height, about Julie's age. His light brown hair was mussed, his features troubled. He kept folding his hat in his hands as he talked to the butler. Despite his anxious façade, he held himself with grace and apparent aristocratic poise, but his stance was that of a war-weary soldier. Robert immediately realized who'd stumbled into his townhouse.

"You can go, Hudgins," Robert said with all the authority he could muster. "I can take it from here."

The butler bowed slowly and walked out of the hall.

Robert turned back to the young man in question. "Julie Weston is my *wife's* maiden name." Robert placed a significant emphasis on the word wife. He watched in bittersweet satisfaction as his young guest flinched at the word. "You are requesting a rather late audience with Lady Clydesdale," he said in the same harsh tone.

"John," Julie's soft voice full of wonder sounded behind Robert before the man could respond.

He saw his guest's eyes as he beheld Julie's figure on the top stairs. The gentleman's features lightened, and a smile appeared, taking years off the young man's face. His eyes shone with tears.

Robert felt as if a heavy rock had been placed upon his shoulders. He almost didn't want to turn and look at his wife's face, for fear of seeing her answering gaze full of yearning. He backed a few steps toward the stairs before turning toward Julie.

Julie took a few steps before slowly sinking down.

Chapter 23

J ohn had come back.

Julie closed her eyes to make sure it wasn't her imagination playing tricks on her. When she opened them again, John was still standing in the hallway, her husband in front of him. No, she had not made this up. Fate had just decided to indulge her with another hit.

Not only was he back, but he was also here. In her house, in her hallway. The world darkened for a moment, and the next thing she knew, she was no longer standing but sitting on the stairs.

Both men leaped to catch her. Robert reached her first since he was closer. His hands closed on her arms, and by the look of it, he caught her just before she hit the floor, gingerly setting her down on the stairs.

She looked at him briefly before peeking over his shoulder at John's beloved face.

He was road weary and appeared disheveled. His hair was mussed, his dear hazel eyes troubled, his face etched with worry lines he'd probably gained during the war. But he was still the same.

Julie struggled to get up, then walked past Robert and into John's arms. He hugged her tightly before she could regain her senses and remember herself.

Julie pulled away from John and looked at her husband. He still stood on the stairs where he'd helped her up, not quite looking at them, his hands clenched in fists at his sides, his lips pressed into a thin line. He seemed so tense and forlorn that she wanted to go to him, soothe him, and hug him tightly as well.

She opted for introductions instead. "Robert, Mr. John Godfrey. John, my husband, Lord Clydesdale." Both men bowed and regarded each other steadily from head to toe.

Robert broke eye contact first. He turned to Julie with stony features. "I shall leave you to it then."

With that, he turned on his heel and stalked away.

Julie was so astonished that he'd left her alone with a man, and not just any man, but with her first love, that she went mute for several long moments.

"Let's proceed to the drawing room, shall we?" she said a bit shakily when she finally collected herself. They walked into the room in silence, the atmosphere between them crackling with tension. "I apologize. I am in a bit of a shock," she said while settling into a chair in front of the fire and smoothing her skirts.

"I understand." John smiled softly at her. The smile was so familiar and dear that she almost turned into a puddle.

"I've missed you so much," she said emphatically. "How are you? I mean… Are you well? Are you here for long?"

"I've come to stay." He furrowed his brow before smiling

again. "For you. Obviously."

All Julie could do was just blink.

"I know you are married, but it was arranged against your will. I am sure we can annul it and—" He stopped as Julie turned away and bit her lip. "We don't have to talk about it just yet. We haven't seen each other for a long time."

Julie smiled at that. "Indeed." Then her eyes widened as she remembered one thing they could discuss freely. "Do you want to see Mary?" she asked brightly. "She is here."

"Absolutely." John shot to his feet. "Do you... do you think she remembers me?"

"She does. In fact, we talked about you recently. You won't believe what has come to pass in the last several months. But come, let me reintroduce you to her."

They went to see Mary, and the reunion was filled with hugs and smiles and a bit of reminiscence.

They were already breaking etiquette by allowing John to visit them so late, and Julie didn't want even more talk surrounding their family. So, they agreed that he'd visit them at an appropriate time tomorrow, and they would go for a ride in a barouche with Mary.

The moment John left, Julie felt a cloud settle over her head. She wanted to cry and laugh and rage; she was so confused about her emotions. Several months ago, she would have killed to see John one more time. Now that he was here, she did not know what to feel. He didn't press or demand anything of her tonight, but it was clear by his longing gaze, his gentle smile, that he expected her to make a choice between him and Robert. The latter, on the other hand, seemed to take himself out of the running.

Julie made her way to her room and sat on the edge of

the bed, scrubbing her temples. She was relieved when the connecting door opened, and Robert entered the room. He didn't go farther into the room, just stood awkwardly by the threshold.

"You must be overjoyed," he said evenly.

"I am." Julie bit her lip, wondering if he was expecting a different answer. There was an awkward pause.

"I am guessing he expects you to leave me for him."

That didn't sound like a question. Julie looked at Robert's composed features, trying to gauge his mood.

"I can't do that; we're married—"

"I want you to think on it," he interrupted.

"What?" Julie looked at him, not quite believing she'd heard him right. "You want me to think on *what*?"

"Annulment," he said shortly.

Julie was so stunned she didn't know how to respond. "We can't get an annulment. Nobody would sanction it. We—"

"Don't worry about that," he said calmly. Too calmly for her peace of mind. "I shall take care of that. Since we don't have a child together, it won't be as difficult to obtain. I promise you it won't reflect upon you in any way. Or at least not more than anything already has up to this point," he added after a brief, thoughtful pause. "If Mr. John Godfrey doesn't mind a bit of scandal, and if that's what you want…" He paused as if expecting her to respond.

Julie was ready to fall into a fit; her emotions were in such turmoil.

"If that's what you want," he continued. "Then I am willing to grant you that. You deserve to be happy, and so does Mr. Godfrey."

"And you?" was all Julie could push through past her dry

throat.

"And me too," he whispered. He stood in silence for several moments before turning to the door. "I am leaving tomorrow for Doncaster," he said, staring at the doorknob. "I shall come back as soon as I finish my business regarding the asylum there. It will give you about a fortnight to consider things with your soldier. I hope you can come to a decision by the time I come back."

A colder recital of her options about the potential estrangement she couldn't even imagine. Robert talked of their annulment as if discussing whether to have fish or poultry for supper. After everything they'd been through, couldn't he have scrounged up a bit of emotion? To at least pretend he'd be hurt if she left him?

Julie shot from the bed and paced her room back and forth. Perhaps he was tired of her. He'd had her in his bed, was probably bored with her, and now saw a golden opportunity to get rid of her.

No. Julie shook her head. She needed to be level-headed about this, just like him, and remove emotion from this decision. Robert was practical; he needed an heir, preferably several. He wouldn't give her up so easily just because she was boring. Not unless he'd found a replacement. Her hands hurt, so tightly fisted they were at her sides. She relaxed her stance and took several deep breaths.

Open communication. That's what they needed. She'd talk to him and ask him exactly why he valued her so little, and he'd tell her exactly what was on his mind. She stepped toward the door and froze in indecision.

She was overreacting. He wasn't proposing annulment; he was just willing to go through with it if she wished. And he was giving her time to think it through. True, if his former lover came to this townhouse claiming any rights to him, Julie would bash her over the head. Maybe him too. Then tie him to the bed, so he'd never walk out on her. She wouldn't be amiably discussing an annulment.

Julie laughed nervously at her bitter thoughts. She took a few steps and plopped onto the bed. Since when had she become so possessive of him? Was it truly because she had developed deep feelings toward him, or was she just angry he didn't have those feelings for her?

He had saved her from her tyrant of a father, sheltered Mary, and had given her a sense of peace, of having a home, a safe haven. Perhaps she was feeling grateful. Moreover, she felt safe with him and dependent upon him. He had always made things better for her, taken charge, and solved all her problems.

Now that John was back, he needed the same. He needed an anchor, something to tether himself to. His own safe haven. And he was looking for that in her, his oldest friend.

Robert was right. Julie needed time to consider everything.

John was back. And no matter her feelings toward Robert, she had loved John most of her life. Since she was four years old. She owed it to him to at least consider getting back with him. She owed it to Robert to be sure she didn't still have feelings toward John. Julie closed her eyes and drifted off to sleep.

* * *

Over the next several days, Julie spent time with John and Mary. They went out riding in the park, walking by the

296

Serpentine and along Bond Street. John had even come for dinner several times.

Julie had missed him dearly. They'd talked a lot about their past, remembering all the mischief they'd gotten up to, all the hard times and fun times they'd spent together. It was as if time had turned back, and she was back at Bedford. John had run away from his family, she and Mary from theirs, and they hid away by spending time in their own little world. Everything felt the same.

And yet it wasn't.

John was different, Julie was different, and even Mary, as eternal a child as she was, had changed. They were not neighborhood children running away from their family problems.

Julie had a family of her own. A husband. Robert had been there for her during the most difficult times of her life. And she wanted him to be there for the best as well.

And John... After years of war, nothing was really left of the boy she once knew. He'd become harsher, but at the same time, haunted and troubled.

Julie noted he jumped at every loud noise and looked around suspiciously at every passerby. He tended to zone out of the conversation or just stare blankly at a distance as if seeing something that was not there.

His eyes were even different, haunted, surrounded by lines of fatigue and worry. He needed to be healed, pieced back together. And he could only be healed by love. Not friendship, not reminiscences, not held by the unstable anchor that was Julie's regard for him, but the pure and present love that would pull him out of his current foggy state. And Julie could not provide that. Not with the feelings she had for her husband.

Three days before Robert's arrival from Doncaster, Julie and John had finally gone out for a walk just the two of them, leaving Mary behind. They talked about their past again, laughing at how Julie was afraid to fall through the ice the first time John had taught her to skate.

An image came to Julie's mind unbidden. Robert gliding alongside her and taunting her to move swifter. Holding Mary gently above the ice after he saved her when she fell through. Robert's hot hands as he kissed her, made love to her.

"I've lost you, haven't I?" John's voice broke her out of the reverie.

"My apologies," she said, smiling. "I am afraid I lost track of my own thoughts. I didn't realize the silence had grown so long."

"That's not what I mean," he replied softly.

Julie knew what he meant, but she didn't want to talk about that. Not yet. "You don't talk about the war much. It must have been hard. Would you like to talk to me about it?"

John took a deep breath. "It is hard, Julie. But you truly don't want the answers to the questions you are asking. I don't want to dwell on it. Especially since I am going to go back in several days."

"You are going back?" Julie stopped and spun on him. "I thought you were selling your commission."

"I was going to. If I had something to come home to."

He looked at her then, an expression of deep sorrow and hope mixed in his eyes. He'd hoped she'd be that something. That she'd still ask him to stay. For her.

Julie looked away in misery.

"Don't be sorry you are happy," he breathed. "You are happy, aren't you?"

Julie let out a humorless laugh. "It is a complicated question, isn't it?" She swallowed hard. "Mary is sick, my social life is in ruins, my best friend is going back to war because I haven't kept my promise to wait for him, and my husband—" Julie closed her eyes and shook her head slightly. *And my husband is willing to give me an annulment without a second thought.*

There was another thing keeping her preoccupied. Another thing she didn't know whether to feel happy about or to cry in horror. That seemed to be her life now, jumping from one extreme emotion to another.

"Mary has a happy life, especially the last several months from what she's said. I am good at being a soldier. Besides, if you'd waited for me, Mary would still be in the asylum. And your husband—" He paused and tilted her head up, so she met his eyes. "You love him, don't you?" he asked gently.

Tears sprang to Julie's eyes. She bit her lip and nodded.

She couldn't speak. If she did, she'd bawl her eyes out right there on the crowded path.

"That's all that matters," he whispered.

Chapter 24

Robert arrived late at night. All the lights in the townhouse were out; everyone was sleeping. He came into Mary's room for a quick peek. He'd missed the girl a lot in the past fortnight. He came closer to the bed and placed a soft kiss on her forehead. She stirred and peered from beneath her lashes.

"Rob back," she whispered.

"Yes, darling, I am back. Now, go back to sleep. We'll talk on the morrow." He gave her a wink but illuminated by a single candle, he wasn't sure she'd seen it. Either way, she mumbled something under her breath, turned on her side, and promptly fell asleep.

Robert passed his wife's quarters, but the light was off, so he went straight into his room. He wanted to see Julie. He couldn't believe how much he'd missed her in the two weeks he'd been gone. There was also dread mixed in with the anticipation. What if she'd chosen John over him? That was the primary reason he didn't go into her room as he did

Mary's. She might not be as happy to see him as he was her.

Just as he was thinking it, the connecting door to their suites opened, and Julie entered the room. She was dressed in her nightgown, her hair loose, although she always had it covered by her nightcap when she went to sleep unless they were making love. His eyes devoured her form, her slim neck, her pale hands, and her face. The rest was covered by her monstrous nightgown, which he itched to remove.

"You're back," she whispered.

Robert smiled slowly. He liked to imagine that she'd actually waited for him because she missed him too. He was too afraid to ask and find out whether that was the reason she was still awake, but he did so anyway.

"Did you miss me?" The words slipped out as if without his consent.

"Did you?" She smiled back at him.

Robert made a couple of steps toward her and took her by her hands, which were extremely cold, like blocks of ice. He noticed she was shaking too. By the candlelight, he couldn't see her face clearly, but she seemed paler than usual.

He peered intently at her, trying to confirm his suspicions, but she ducked her head, made another step toward him, and hugged him. Robert was so astonished, he froze for a moment before putting his arms around her. He hugged her cold form tightly to him and kissed the top of her head.

"You are cold. Did the fire go out in your room?" he asked worriedly. Julie shook her head. "Are you unwell?"

She stepped back far enough to look him in the eyes. "I need to talk to you," she said, her voice frail.

Robert started to worry that he'd misread her gestures of affection. Perhaps it was not a greeting of reuniting lovers but a goodbye.

"Of course," he said, frowning. "Have a seat." He gestured to a seat, but she started pacing by the fire instead.

"You must be tired from the trip." She frowned up at him as she paused. "Do you want me to come back in the morning? It's just that I've waited for you all day—"

"No," he interrupted briskly. He wouldn't be able to sleep if he didn't hear whatever she'd decided to tell him in the middle of the night. Her revelation that she'd waited for him all day for this got him even more anxious. "Please continue. What did you want to tell me?"

Julie took a deep breath. "The annulment," she said succinctly. "Would you really grant me an annulment if I said I wanted to be with John?"

Robert was struck speechless for a horrifying moment. She was leaving him. His throat was so dry he had to clear it and lick his lips before speaking. "Yes," he finally pushed out.

"And you would be fine with it?" She was still frowning.

"I would respect your wish. And your right to happiness."

"And if I wanted to stay?" Julie lowered her eyes. "With you."

The dim hope lit up in his soul against his better judgment. He closed his eyes against the traitorous feeling. "I would be honored," he said hoarsely.

"But would you be happy?" Her voice was so small; it was barely audible.

"Yes," he said simply. He was too tired to play games with her. A simple truth would have to do.

Julie finally raised her gaze to his and smiled. "Good," was all she said.

Robert stood there, staring at her before he realized what

she meant. But he would not settle for 'good.' He needed to hear her say it. He needed to be sure.

"You mean you are staying?"

Julie bit her lip and nodded.

"That's not good enough." Robert made a few steps until he stood flash against her. "I need to hear you say it," he said, placing his hands on her waist.

Julie's eyes roamed his face before settling on his eyes. Then a slow smile lit her face. "I want to stay with you. I want to be your wife, always—"

She was going to say something else, but her last words undid him. He lowered his head and captured her mouth in a rough and greedy kiss. Robert felt her tremulous laugh before it turned into a passionate moan under his mouth. She was suddenly as greedy as he, her hands roaming his body, her pelvis rubbing against him.

She slid her hands in his hair, and he groaned into her mouth. He was about to pick her up and toss her onto the bed when she suddenly pulled away. He tried to hold on to her, but she disengaged herself and hastily exited his room.

Robert stood another moment, staring at the place she'd occupied a moment ago, before following her to the dressing room. He stopped cold at the threshold. There were sounds of her being ill. Then the splashing of water and heavy breathing.

That was the reason for her paleness. Her hands had been cold; she'd been trembling. It wasn't her unsuppressed desires as he'd like to believe; she would heat up instead if that was the case. She'd been ill, or else—

"You are with child," he said tonelessly as Julie re-entered his room.

Julie put the backs of her fingers of one hand against her

mouth, while her other hand covered her abdomen as she nodded. Robert closed his eyes against the mixture of feelings that assailed him. The pride, the joy, the anticipation—

And the realization that she hadn't chosen him. He had won by default. Because she was carrying his child, his heir.

"You need to rest," he said on the exhale.

"I am fine. I promise, this... this is normal." She took a tentative step toward him, and he made a step in retreat.

"Then I need to rest." He scrubbed his face with his hand. "It's been a long day and too much news." He waved his hand toward her abdomen.

"Are you... Are you not happy about this?" Julie's face was stricken with horror at the prospect. She might have chosen him by default, but she was carrying his child. He didn't want to distress her.

"Of course, I am." He tried for a smile. "I am just too tired. And I think my emotions are a bit dulled right now."

Julie nodded, with something akin to relief on her face.

Robert stepped toward her, placed a hand against her cold, clammy cheek, and kissed her on the forehead. "Rest," he said with a tender smile. "If you need anything, you know where to find me."

He saw disappointment cross Julie's face. He didn't understand what she was reacting to, but he realized he wasn't lying about needing rest. Several days' journey and several minutes filled with emotional revelations had taken their toll on his well-being.

"We'll talk more tomorrow?" she said with a questioning lilt in her voice.

He nodded and smiled slightly. "Absolutely."

* * *

Robert was perusing his morning paper when his wife joined him at the table. They exchanged polite greetings, and he set the paper away.

"How did you sleep?" he asked cautiously.

"Not very well, I'm afraid." She put some toast and eggs on her plate and sat down with the help of the footman. "I have had trouble sleeping ever since—" She shook her head, staring at her plate. "I think it's normal as well. Together with the constant sickness, the appetite changes, and fatigue."

"Sounds—" Robert cleared his throat, searching for the right word to use. "Bothersome."

A small laugh escaped Julie. "You could say that," she agreed.

"The London air, the smoke, and smells probably do not help," he said thoughtfully.

"Yes, many women choose to go into confinement in the country, but that's months away."

"If you'd be more comfortable there, there is no reason to wait. You and Mary were going to move to the Bromley residence anyway, weren't you? It's not like we are planning to attend any more *ton* events," he said around a bite of toast, then washed it down with a sip of tea.

"You still want us to go?" she said without looking at him.

"I can't see a reason for you to stay here unless you want to," he said carefully. "I shall be occupied with business most of the time, probably moving between London and Doncaster now that the asylum case has moved along."

"You want us to stay there alone, with you moving between London and Doncaster?" Julie raised her puzzled gaze.

"Doncaster is too far for either of you to go to right now. I don't want you traveling that distance. The best scenario is you going to Bromley."

One side of Julie's mouth raised in a half-smile. "Just as we bargained."

Robert took a breath to say something reassuring. He wanted to let her know he wanted only what was best for her, Mary, and the babe. He cared about them all too much to risk any of them. And he had business to attend to. He'd visit them as much as he could; he'd do everything for them to be comfortable, but he had to stay in London.

He was just about to say all that and more when Mary burst into the room, all exuberant delight and a picture of good humor. A complete opposite to the spirit that hung over the breakfast table.

"Mary, I have some good news," Julie said with a strained smile, trying to look cheerful. "We shall go to a new house tomorrow. Remember, we planned to travel to a new place and paint the walls there?"

Mary smiled as she looked from Robert to Julie.

Robert cleared his throat. "And your pony is going to travel there with you. So, you will be able to start your riding lessons with a stable master."

Mary's eyes lit up in pure joy. "Horsie! I shall ride!" she exclaimed and clapped her hands in delight.

Julie's smile softened at her sister's obvious happiness. "We shall start packing your new things after breakfast. Will you help?"

"No!" Mary admonished. "I pack my things; you pack your things."

Julie laughed and stood from the table. "Fair enough, we shall each pack our own things."

Chapter 24

Robert looked at his two favorite girls as they chatted away and laughed. He would miss their laughter and presence in his empty townhouse, he thought with a sigh.

Chapter 25

The next several weeks seemed to fly by and proceed in a slow crawl simultaneously. Julie got acquainted with the new estate staff, got familiar with the house and the estate grounds, and met the tenants.

It was a beautiful place with several walking routes, which Julie perused every morning. She loved the country air, and the doctor was right: She felt better. She was still sluggish and occasionally got abdominal pains, but she suspected they would pass as well.

Most importantly, however, Mary was happy there. She was learning to ride her pony, walked in the meadow to collect her first snowdrops, and made bouquets to decorate the house. She picked a room close to Julie's for her own, but the artist was currently decorating the walls there, so she had to sleep in the nursery on the third floor for a while. After her room was done, however, Julie wanted to commission the painter to decorate the nursery. She wanted everything to be perfect for the arrival of her babe.

She suspected they would live on this estate for a while, and a dull ache in her heart always appeared when she thought about how easily Robert had dismissed them and left them behind.

Of course, he wrote letters, but they were businesslike, with reports on the progress with the asylum. It seemed that the article in the paper had stirred quite a bit of trouble and gave way to adding more governing members to the board, which included Benjamin Tule.

That alone was not enough to reform the asylum, but it was a good step forward. Robert had not mentioned the scandal and how the paper affected his standing in Parliament. There was no mention of any gossip that most definitely surrounded the Clydesdale name. And most importantly, there was not a single warm epithet, not a single affectionate word among the lengthy letters. He worried about her, and Mary, yes, asked about their well-being, but the letters of a lovelorn husband they were not.

As the days went by and her stomach finally started showing, she tried to concentrate on the joy of soon having a babe in her arms, but her fears only intensified. The images of a long-forgotten past made themselves known; the nightmares became more frequent. She found herself putting her hands on her stomach quite often, hoping against hope to feel the first tremors that would indicate her impending motherhood.

* * *

Julie awoke from the sound of a thunderstorm. The wind was howling outside, and hail was beating down the windows. Inside the house, there was some frantic activity, servants yelling and running around. Julie had a terrible feeling that just wouldn't go away. Everything was eerily familiar.

She heard a loud guttural scream. Julie climbed out of bed and ventured outside. Something was extremely wrong. She was not in her house. Another scream pierced the air. Then another one, and another. She closed her ears with her arms and plastered herself to the wall. She froze for a second. What was going on? And then the realization occurred. It was her mother screaming. That thought gave her the strength to peel herself from the wall and move. She ran inside her mother's room and froze in horror.

Her mother was lying on the bed in a pool of her own blood. Blood soaked all the sheets and was dripping down the bedpost. Her legs were bloody, and there was something black between them. Her mother's sweat-stricken ashen face was hovering a little off the bed, and she was screaming in agony. Somebody noticed Julie at that moment and pulled her away from the room.

"No!" Julie struggled against the restraints. "Mother, no!"

Julie woke up with a start, breathing heavily. She was soaked in a cold sweat and something else. She looked down and saw a dark liquid covering the sheets and her legs. She placed a hand against it as if in a daze, then brought her hand closer to her face. The putrid smell of blood hit her hard.

Blood.

She was soaked in blood, and it wasn't a nightmare anymore.

* * *

"You are a complete idiot!"

Robert looked up at the sharp words spoken to him. The Dowager Duchess of Rutland was standing in front of him, dressed in her traveling gown, a turban on her head, her fancy walking stick in her hand.

"Are you going somewhere?" he asked calmly, placing his hands on the table and intertwining his fingers, ready for a tirade, as the dowager took a few steps and sat gracefully into a chair opposite him.

"I am leaving for the dowager's home at Clydesdale Hall," she said nonchalantly. "It's been weeks since Mary and Julie left. You have no need of me in London anymore."

"I always have need of you, Grandmother," Robert said with a slow smile.

He wondered if the dowager felt unappreciated lately. After Julie and Mary had left for Bromley, she had stayed in his London townhouse, keeping to London to weather the scandal. But he suspected she missed Mary and Julie almost as much as he did. He hadn't seen the dowager much himself either, as he'd traveled to Doncaster and stayed there for a good part of a fortnight and arrived home just the night before.

"Don't you try to flatter me," she said a bit too harshly. She had rarely used that tone with him, with anybody, come to think of it. "The person who has need of *you* is stuck in a country home," she said accusingly. "Your wife, your family, is in Bromley. And you're here, doing what exactly?"

Robert threw up his hands. "I was under the impression that I was working."

The dowager just scoffed. "Julie is carrying your child. What can be more important than that?"

"I am not exactly sure that she wants me there," Robert said carefully.

"Like I said. Idiot." The dowager raised a brow. " When

you married Julie, I was not happy about it." She looked at Robert, who had pressed his lips together. *Yes, she was not happy indeed.* "When I confronted you about it, you made me a deal, remember?"

The dowager waited for Robert to nod before continuing.

"Well, I am going to hold you to that deal, now. You promised to listen to my advice, so listen well." The dowager rearranged her skirts in a gesture so unlike her prim and proper façade. She was obviously uncomfortable with this conversation.

"When I was young," she started without looking at him, "there was a young man I loved very much."

Robert blinked at the change of the subject, but she continued.

"I was foolish. I listened to old matrons, to my family members, who believed that breeding was more important than love." She turned to him then. "It isn't. But like many things one does wrong in the name of bloodlines, one can do even more wrong in the name of love. You think you are keeping her calm away from London. You think she is happier without you—"

Robert opened his mouth to protest, but the dowager raised a staying hand.

"I said no interruptions, Clydesdale. She loves you. You don't see it because you are blind to it. You weren't here to see her interactions with that John fellow. You weren't here to see her sulk without you. And you are not there with her now. She's lonely and scared when she needs support from the one person she relies on most—you. I wasn't going to intervene, but I don't see you making any wise decisions, so here I am," she said, getting up.

"You think that by keeping her away, you are holding on to your pride, and maybe you are. But pride doesn't keep one warm at night. And I'd rather you hold on to your love. So, go to her. No matter the hour or day of the week. No matter if she's stubborn or unreceptive. Go to her and tell her how you feel. Tell her she's stuck with you, whether she likes it or not."

Tell her because that's what I should have said. The unspoken words hung between them. The dowager made a few steps to the door. She paused with her hand on the handle and looked over her shoulder. Then she turned back and left the room without another word.

A few hours later, Robert was sitting in his carriage, tapping his walking stick impatiently against his thigh. He'd left his London residence a few minutes after his conversation with the dowager. It wasn't because he'd made a deal with her to listen to her advice; it was more that he was tired of living with this weight in his chest. The dowager was right. He needed to say those things to Julie. He needed her to know all the information. He needed to know that she wasn't sacrificing her love for her soldier just because of the babe. He needed to convince her they could be happy together.

* * *

The carriage drew to a halt, and Robert leaped out of it without the help of a groom. He entered the house and froze.

The household was in an uproar. Footmen running back and forth with buckets of water, maids with lengths of linen. Some were carrying soiled clothes. Soiled, if he'd seen it correctly, with blood.

Robert was jolted out of his stupor by the sight of it and ran upstairs, taking the steps two or three at a time. His most horrifying fears had come true. The maids were bustling in and out of Julie's room.

Robert ran inside and saw a woman, who looked like a nurse, washing his wife's unmoving body with a length of cloth. Julie was sprawled on the bed, covered with a sheet from her thighs to her throat. Her legs were uncovered for cleaning.

"What's going on?" Robert's voice came out in a croak.

The woman stood up and curtsied. "My lord," she said solemnly.

"Tell me what is going on, damn it!" Robert swore and strode to his wife's side. Her face was covered in a sheen of sweat. He ran his hand over her face. It was cold, but not lifeless. He felt her breath on his hand and let out a breath of his own.

"She lost the babe, sir." The woman—the nurse, whose existence he'd already forgotten about, completely absorbed with his wife—pronounced the most gut-wrenching words he could have ever heard.

"How?" His voice was barely a whisper.

"She woke up to a pool of blood," the nurse said quietly. "These things happen sometimes."

Robert fell to his knees next to the bed. His wife, his love, had woken up to this nightmare, and she was completely alone. Because he was an idiot. The dowager was right as always.

Robert spent the entire night by his wife's bed. He sat in a chair, holding her hand, praying for her to wake up. She was pale and cold, but she was breathing, and that was a good sign, or at least that was what the nurse said. He'd sent for a doctor, but he had arrived only in the morning, and he said nothing more than the nurse did. He said that whether she lived was in the hands of God, but the longer she didn't wake, the less chance there was that she ever would.

Robert spent most of his day talking to her, praying, and begging her to wake up. He spoke to Mary when she woke up and told her that Julie was feeling sluggish and needed rest. He didn't want to terrify the poor child, but Mary was more aware than he thought. Apparently, Julie had not been feeling well for days.

Robert felt guilt and anger rise to the surface. If he'd been here, he'd know this. If he'd stayed with her instead of leaving them alone at his remote estate, he'd have been here when she needed him. But the recriminations didn't help Julie.

He instructed the housekeeper to write notes to the dowager and Lady Eabha and keep them apprised of Julie's condition and told Alice not to leave Mary's side.

He also refused to leave Julie's side. He slept by her bed, ate—very little—by her bed, and the rest of the time he talked to her.

"You know," Robert said to his sleeping wife when he was tired of cajoling her to wake up, when there was nothing else to say. "I used to be a great romantic," he said with a small self-deprecating laugh. "You don't know this because you didn't know me back then. You were very young then, as was I. I dreamed of having a family of my own. A wife I loved, a houseful of children." Robert paused and shook his head at the memories. "After all of my dreams were shattered, I admonished myself for being a complete fool. For being as naïve as I was, blind as I'd been. Well, I might not be as naïve

315

as I once was, but I am still blind and a complete fool."

He took her hand in his and raised it to his face. He pressed her hand against his cheek as he continued. "There are things I need to tell you, Julie. And I need you to be awake to hear them. I want you to know. I need you to hear me, and then, you can make your own decisions on what to do next. Just… wake up."

He moved her hand against his forehead and held it pressed like that in both his hands for what seemed like hours. He was drifting off to sleep when he felt something stir against his forehead. He opened his eyes and felt it again as if someone had moved a lock of his hair away from his face. He raised his head and saw Julie watching him.

"Thank God." He moved her hand that was still clasped in both of his to his mouth and kissed her icy fingers. "Thank God, Julie," he said, his voice hoarse.

Tears rolled down her face and her shoulders convulsed in sobs.

"No, don't cry." Robert sat on the bed beside her and pressed her body against his, placing her head against his shoulder. "Please, don't cry," he coaxed, kissing the top of her head, her forehead. She sobbed for several minutes as he crooned soothing nonsense into her ears and ran his hands in circles over her back.

She finally raised her head and regarded him with tear-filled eyes. "The babe," she said on a hiccup, and more tears fell down her cheeks.

Robert closed his eyes in agony as she renewed her sobbing. "I'm sorry, sweet," he said as he pressed her against him once again. "I am so sorry."

Julie quieted down a few minutes later. Robert sent for a

pot of tea and a piece of toast and sat by Julie's side, holding her in his arms.

"It's my fault," she mumbled.

"What is?" he asked, placing a chaste kiss on her forehead.

"The babe," she said emotionlessly. "My father was right; I can't do anything right. Not even carry a babe to term."

Robert turned to her and regarded her quizzically. "Your father is an arse. And why would you say it is your fault?"

"I—I was afraid." She closed her eyes as if speaking gave her too much pain. "I didn't want to be with child because I was afraid. My mother, she died in childbirth," she continued in her solemn voice. "I was there. I saw it happen. The blood-drenched sheets, the screaming, the lifeless body of a babe. I never wanted it to happen to me."

"Why didn't you tell me this?" Robert said against her hair as he hugged her tighter to him, but he already knew the answer. The deal. She'd sacrificed herself to this marriage and pushed down her fears for Mary. He wasn't exactly the most open person to have a conversation with.

"At first, it was the bargain," she confirmed his own deductions. "Then, I was too afraid. I was afraid you'd think less of me."

"What?" Robert pulled away to look at her face. "I would never—"

"You wanted an heir. What kind of wife—"

"I don't care about an heir. Let Eric hold the title! I don't care if I shan't be allowed to bed you again, I need you alive, do you hear me? I don't give a damn about our bloody deal. It's off. All I want is you!" Robert was almost huffing with the outrage. "I love you," he said fiercely, angrily, and won himself a look of pure surprise. "Yes, I love you, and I am an idiot for not saying it earlier. I want you. As my wife, as my love, as my lifelong companion. I love you. I don't care if you don't—"

Julie huffed a breath and turned away from him.

"I don't care that you don't love me," he continued quietly. "I love you enough for the both of us."

Chapter 26

One month later

Julie walked along the meadow path, which was all too familiar to her now. She'd been walking along the same path every day. Last month had been so unbearable that she'd thought she'd never get back to normal.

She was barely eating; she wasn't hungry, but she kept being ill all day long. That was not as daunting as the constant worry and weariness in the eyes of her husband. Robert was always trying to feed her something. He kept sending and even bringing her food that she hadn't the stomach to even look at, much less eat or even smell.

Mary kept coming into her room, inquiring if she needed anything or for her to read something. Not being able to cheer up her own sister nagged even more on Julie's guilt.

The constant worry and solicitousness in the voices of people she cared about suffocated her. She wanted nothing, and the last thing she needed was for them to worry over her. She wanted to be left alone. She didn't need to feel guilty that she didn't feel better. She just existed. And she needed to exist in this bubble of despair. Why wouldn't they leave her alone to grieve?

So, she started each morning walking alone around the estate.

Today had been different, though. She had a lot to think about, so she turned down an unknown little trail leading into the woods.

It is a common tragedy.

The doctor's words rang in her head. This morning the doctor had come for her check-up and given her a clean bill of health.

Yes, it was common. She'd heard of other women losing their children, holding them in their arms, some babes who died too young. Even her own mother had lost a child and her own life in one tragic day. But how does one prepare for it? She thought the most frightening day of her life would be the day she gave birth. As it turned out, the most terrifying day was the day she didn't.

She hadn't even been that far along. She hadn't even told Mary that she was with child. Mary would be a splendid aunt. She'd be so happy to welcome the little one into the world. Julie raised her head and looked at the clear sky through the tree branches. Was it so common as to happen twice to the same woman? Was she brave enough to have another babe?

She walked and contemplated her life, all the things she and Mary had been through. Everything good and everything bad. Life was a gamble. One never knew what tomorrow would bring. That shouldn't make her afraid to live, though.

Chapter 26

Julie scoffed to herself. She wished she were more like Mary. Easy to forgive, easy with a smile. She was open with her emotions and got through them rather quickly. Julie heaved a sigh and walked on.

* * *

Robert was stalking the length of his study like a caged beast. Julie had gone for a walk several hours ago, and she still wasn't back yet. After the night she'd lost their babe, she had become so withdrawn and detached that he didn't know what to do. He tried to feed her, jest with her, and talk to her. Anything to coax any emotion out of her, but she wasn't receptive.

Today, the doctor had come and told Robert that they were free to resume their attempts at having an heir. Robert almost scoffed in the man's face. He hadn't lied to Julie when he said he would not even try to bed her again if she didn't wish it. He needed her alive, and if it meant he would never share his passion with her again, well, it wouldn't be easy, but he'd manage.

And now she'd just disappeared.

At that moment, he heard the front door opening and quiet footsteps.

Robert shot out of his study and into the hall. He encountered his wayward wife just as she was about to ascend the stairs. He grabbed her by the arms and brought her flush with his body, holding her tightly. Julie let out a tiny squeal and looked at him in wide-eyed innocence.

"Where the devil have you been?" he growled, looking her over. Julie's appearance was disheveled, her clothing dirty, her hair mussed, and she had some leaves in her untidy coiffure.

She looked winded as if she'd run for several miles.

"I—" She faltered and wiggled in his hold. Robert realized he was holding her too tightly and probably hurting her, so he relaxed his grip. "I went for a walk, you know that." Julie placed her palms on the lapels of his coat as if to placate him.

All the heat and emotions started rising to the surface: the anger of worrying over his wife, the grief she didn't let him share with her, the unspent passion. He grabbed her once again and placed a hard kiss on her mouth. Instead of drawing away, Julie softened under his onslaught. Her hands were in his hair, stroking him, not in seduction, but in comfort. The comfort he had no idea he needed.

Robert growled and set her gently aside. "You've been out for hours. I've been worried sick! I've sent footmen to look for you all over the estate!"

"I know, and I am sorry." Julie placed her hand against his cheek, stroking it gently with her thumb; Robert couldn't help but lean into her touch. God, how he'd missed her touch. "I am better now," she said quietly.

Robert huffed a breath of disbelief. "Let me call off the search party for you. Go to your room and… change. Your gown is wet to its knees. Where in the blazes were you walking?"

Julie looked down at her clothing and let out a short laugh as if she'd just noticed the extent of her disheveled state. Robert caught himself staring. He hadn't heard her laugh for weeks.

"I'll be in my rooms," she said and ventured up the steps.

Robert almost didn't want to let her go. What if by the time he got to her room, she was back to her gloomy self?

Several minutes later, Robert found himself dragging his feet to her bedchamber. He was about to enter her room, but he paused as he heard voices coming from the inside. He hovered uncertainly outside the room when the door opened, and Alice nearly ran into him.

"Pardon, my lord." The girl curtsied and hurried away from him, giggling.

Robert frowned at the maid before entering the room. What he saw made him halt at once.

Julie, his wife, the same wife who'd locked herself away for over a month, was now standing in front of a looking glass wearing a dark blue evening gown.

"You look beautiful," he said. His breath caught in his lungs.

"Thank you." Julie threw him a timid smile. She turned and sat on the edge of the bed.

"Come," she said and patted a seat beside her.

Robert obeyed, never taking his eyes off his wife.

"Does that mean you'll be joining us for dinner tonight?" he asked.

Julie nodded.

"What happened to you?" he asked.

Julie laughed lightly. "Nothing." She shook her head. "Nothing profound. I just woke up today, and the fog of grief had lifted. I guess it's true what people say; time heals."

"You are not upset with me? Or angry?" Robert frowned, drawing away and looking into her eyes.

"For what?" Julie gently moved a lock of hair off his forehead.

Robert caught the movement and placed a kiss on the inside of her wrist. "For not being here when you needed me, for leaving you here—"

Julie interrupted him, placing two fingers against his lips. "Robert, is that what you think? That I've been angry with you this whole time?"

Robert grimaced and looked away.

"I was grieving, just like you. But I was never angry with you. It wasn't your fault; you couldn't have known." She placed her palm against his face, forcing him to look at her. "I thought about it all day. About what you said after it happened."

"What did I say?" Robert searched Julie's face, hoping to uncover any hidden messages in her features.

"You said that our deal is off," she said quietly, and Robert's heart caught in his throat.

Julie stood and paced in front of him. "I think it's only right. I don't want to be with you because of our deal. I don't want to give you heirs." She paused and swallowed. "I want to give you children. All the things we've been through, all the good and the bad and—" She paused and bit on her lower lip. "And I want to try again."

Robert frowned in confusion. "What?"

"Not now. Perhaps, not even soon. But when the doctor said that we could start trying again, my heart was ready to sing. I realized that I do want a babe. Maybe several."

"Julie." Robert groaned and scrubbed his palms against his face. "I can't. I can't watch you go through that. Not again."

"I know, and I have been so afraid of it myself, most of my life. But having experienced what could have been—" She shook her head again. "This grief and despair I was in, it wasn't because my biggest fears have realized, it was because I've never wanted anything more than to hold that babe in my arms. Our babe. And I still want that."

Robert stood and walked closer to her. He took her hands in both of his and regarded her intently. "Julie, you've just recovered. It's the first day you've said more than a couple of words to me in a month. How about we talk about it in a few weeks?"

Julie nodded. "Of course."

"Don't pout at me," Robert said with a smile. "I want to give you anything, you know that. I would give you the world if I could. I love you." He looked at her beautiful face, praying that he never had to see her grieving again, never see her in pain.

"I do know that." Julie smiled at him, her radiant smile, the one that lit up her entire face. "But do you know I love you too?"

Robert blinked in surprise. For all the things he'd expected her to say, that was nowhere on his list.

She loved him. It felt unreal.

Julie laughed then, and he realized how much he'd missed this lively, laughing Julie and that he'd be willing to do anything to keep her thus. He hugged her and whirled her around once as she continued laughing.

"Good," he said, looking into her eyes. "Because I am never letting you go."

He lowered his head and took her mouth in a slow and sweet kiss. It wasn't an erotic kiss. It was soft and full of love and reassurance. This kiss was meant to soothe their battered souls and give them hope for a brighter future. He finally raised his head and ran a thumb over her lower lip.

Julie leaned into his touch.

"Come," he said with a smile. "Our family is waiting for us for dinner."

"We are probably already late," Julie said with a slight grimace.

Robert took out his watch from his pocket and checked the

time. "No." He shook his head. "According to my superior watch, we are right on time."

Epilogue

November 15, 1817

J ulie sat on the carpet in the drawing room. The 'drawing room' finally had an apt name, since Jared, their three-year-old son, was drawing with his new pencils a few feet away from her. Little Victoria was sitting in her lap, sucking on her tiny fist.

The nanny disapproved of how they were raising their children—spending most of their time amongst adults. Still, Julie could not help it after the difficulties they'd gone through. She'd been scared and nervous during both of her pregnancies, and she wanted to be close to the little humans they'd produced. And Robert was the same way. He hated being away from his children for too long.

She heard familiar steps outside the door and leaped to her feet just as Robert strode into the room. He reached her in three long strides and placed a hungry kiss on her lips.

"Ew," their son intoned in disgust.

"Ew?" Robert raised his head, his eyes dancing with laughter. "Does that mean you don't want a kiss too?"

"No, I'm no babe," Jared said proudly.

"Aren't you?" Robert winked conspiratorially at his wife and ran toward his son, scooping him up in his arms. He placed tiny kisses all over his head and face as the boy shrieked in laughter.

The nanny walked into the room at that moment, wearing her disapproving expression as always. "The children need to be fed, my lord," she said with a curtsy.

"Of course." Robert placed Jared in the nanny's arms.

She settled him on the floor immediately and reached her arms toward Julie. "Ma'am?" She looked at her as if saying, *you know you have to give her to me.* Julie unwillingly placed the babe into the stern nanny's hands, and the latter strode off with Jared trailing after her.

Julie immediately walked into her husband's arms. "How is the asylum?" she asked into his shirt.

"A lot better. It is still prospering under Tule's management."

"And Mary?" Julie smiled.

Mary had started working as a nanny for small children in the asylum. She loved being there, loved playing with small babes, and was learning to assert her independence as well as becoming more and more confident each day. Despite that knowledge, Julie still worried about her.

"Mary is perfect, as she always is. You know she loves it there. Besides, she is there only every other fortnight; she will be back soon enough." He smiled gently at Julie and placed a kiss on her cheek.

"I know, but it's my job to worry." Julie raised her head,

and he ran his thumb over her forehead as if smoothing her frown.

"Yes." Robert nodded. "You have the worst job of all of us."

"Mmm, worrying over all of you," Julie agreed quietly, kissing her husband on the neck. The only bare part of him she could reach. "And I have so many people to worry over," she said absently and kissed him again.

"Not too many, I hope?" he asked with a smirk.

"Mhmm," Julie answered distractedly, as she pulled on his cravat and kissed his chin, his cheek.

Robert let out a muffled laugh before capturing her mouth with his. Julie immediately folded her body to his, running her hands through his hair. Robert groaned as he let his hands wander over her body, his hungry kisses dulling all her other senses.

"Perhaps we can make some more people for you to worry over," he whispered, and Julie couldn't help but laugh.

Suddenly, she was pressed against the wall; her skirts were being lifted. She sucked on Robert's earlobe as he undid his breaches and pressed his hot arousal against her thigh.

"I've missed you," she whispered, then licked the outer crescent of his ear.

Robert groaned and entered her in one swift thrust.

"How much?" he whispered against her lips.

Julie nipped on his lower lip, then soothed it with her tongue. "Very," she said before gasping as he started moving in an erotic rhythm, again and again, bringing them both to new heights of fulfillment.

* * *

"Oh, I almost forgot," Julie said several minutes later, as they were adjusting their clothing. "John is coming in"—she peered at the clock standing in the corner of the room—"twenty minutes."

"Glad you remembered that before I decided to have you again." Robert came closer to her and placed a soft kiss on her mouth. "When did he come to London?"

"Several months ago, he tells me." Julie shrugged a little. "I guess he wasn't ready to see me yet," she said with a sad smile.

"But he is now?" Robert raised his brow at his wife.

"Apparently." Julie smiled into his eyes. "He says he needs my help."

"With what?"

Julie looked up at him with a crooked smile. "He is seeking a bride."

THE END

Thank you for reading!

Loved the book? Sign-up for my newsletter to get a bonus novelette:
https://sendfox.com/sadiebosque
By signing up, you'll also get new release alerts and bonus content such as extra epilogues, deleted scenes, and more.

Curious if John gets his Happily Ever After? Loved Evie? Read more from *Necessary Arrangements* series on Amazon.

Keep reading for a deleted scene.

There's Something About Mary

Hey, dear reader! In case you were wondering, Mary in this novel has Down syndrome.

Her character was created by collecting traits from people with Down syndrome this author knows personally. Sadie loved exploring Mary's character and tried to make adjustments due to the times this novel is set in and Mary's circumstances.

People with Down syndrome are different. Some will be similar to Mary, and some will be absolutely different, depending on their character and upbringing. Keep in mind that Mary had also spent five years in an asylum, which stifled her progress.

Both the York Asylum and the York Retreat mentioned in the text were real places around the time this novel is set. The information on differences between the two places and the treatment of their inmates was taken from this source:

Changes in the Asylum: The Case of York, 1777-1815

Benjamin Tule was inspired by real-life activist and reformist Samuel Tuke.

If you'd love to learn more about people with Down syndrome and donate to organizations helping people with Down syndrome in your country, check out this site:

https://www.ds-int.org/

Deleted Scene

Summer 1808

Robert sat in a smoke-filled room. Giggles and sultry whispers of half—or perhaps already fully—naked women surrounded him. His friends were somewhere in the room too. He heard their occasional laughter and drunken murmurs. But he couldn't see anything through the thick fog.

Robert wasn't much of a drinker or a smoker, and since he met Annie, he wasn't much for cheap whores either. Gabriel would be offended by this insinuation, of course. He would say that he'd have never brought cheap whores to his best friend's bachelor party. They were the most expensive ones. Robert's lips twitched in a smile. Expensive or not, whores did not interest him anymore. No woman did. Except for Annie.

He thought about his golden-haired bride, her coy looks, and shy advances, and decided he'd had enough of this place.

Robert stood, but before he could take a step, a hand reached out from the fog and clasped his arm.

"Oh, no, you don't," came the slurred voice of his best friend. "I go through all this trouble for you. Find you the best"—a hiccup interrupted his tirade—"the best"—another hiccup—"the best whisky in town, the best whores, the best cigars." He waved his hand dramatically at the surroundings, "And you're leaving?"

"Disrespect!" shouted one of the other fops.

Robert peered through the smoke but could not make out the identity of the offending voice's owner. Instead, he turned back to his best friend and leaned in to see him clearer. What he saw made him chuckle. One of the *ladies* was straddling his friend's lap and licking at his neck. Robert shook his head, finding the image pathetic. Now that he was getting married, nights like this seemed meaningless.

"Listen, Gabe, I appreciate what you've done. Really, I do. But women, spirits…" He gestured with his hands to the grand room filled with vice. "This is your thing. I am getting married on the morrow."

"The best reason to have fun while you can," Gabriel slurred again.

Robert made a few steps toward the door and called over his shoulder, "I will have fun when I'm married."

Gabriel waved the lady away, gingerly stood from his chair, and followed Robert.

Robert paused, waiting for his friend to catch up to him, studying him all the while. Gabriel's eyes were red-rimmed, and he was sporting two days of stubble. His shamefully wrinkled clothing indicated that this was not the first party he had attended in the last several days without changing or even stopping by his townhouse.

Many women found Gabriel irresistible with his golden

good looks and stately figure. He looked like one of those Greek gods or a fallen angel. He could get anyone he wanted with only a wink and a smile. If only they could see him now.

"Marriage is boring. I bet you two hundred pounds, *your Annie*," he said in a mocking tone, "cannot do half the things these ladies are capable of."

Robert huffed. "Of course, she can't. That's the point. She is innocent."

Now it was Gabriel's turn to huff. "Please," he drawled. "No woman is innocent. She is just not as skilled."

"I'm not discussing Annie's *skills* with you." Rob patted his friend on his shoulder.

"Of course not." Gabriel took on a serious expression. "You'll also not argue that she is far from innocent."

Robert narrowed his eyes on his friend. "Tread lightly now."

"You should have let me seduce her. You'd see her for who she truly is. Like every one of them." Gabriel waved his hand about the room. "Women are easy. They are good for only one thing: tup and move on."

"You are drunk." Robert squeezed Gabriel's shoulder. "And you are my best friend. These are the only reasons I am not bloodying your face right now." He patted Gabriel good-naturedly on his back, although his patience was quickly waning.

Gabriel put up his arms in mock self-defense. "Fine, fine. No need to get violent. My face is my only asset."

Robert shook his head. Sometimes he thought Gabriel actually believed that. That all he had, and all he was, was just his pretty face.

Robert had known Gabriel, Viscount St. Clare, from the first time Gabriel stepped into Eton. He was eight, and Robert was ten. They ran into each other on the steps and had been friends ever since.

Gabriel was a fragile boy with sad blue eyes, and Robert wanted to watch out for him. But as they grew, they started looking out for each other. Robert was hard-working and serious. Gabriel was cynical, yet still charming. He had a face every woman in London swooned over.

Everyone except for Annie.

That's what Robert loved about her most. She wasn't led by a pretty face or the fanciest title. She hadn't even known Robert was a duke's heir when they met.

Robert moved toward the door. "Thank you for the grand party!" he yelled as he waved and left the room to the jeering of men and women.

Robert hopped into his carriage and banged on the carriage roof with his walking stick. He was going to see Annie, he decided. No matter what he'd promised. Robert leaned against the seat and thought about his betrothed, a smile pulling at the corners of his lips. He could not wait until tomorrow to marry her. It was ridiculous, her insistence not to see him tonight. They'd already anticipated the wedding vows, so he saw no reason they shouldn't make love the night before their marriage.

Gabriel was right; Annie had not been a virgin when they met, but she wasn't skilled either. Not that it mattered to him in the least. Her past was her own; the future, however, was theirs. He loved her, and he was not interested in anyone else. At the moment, all he wanted to do was spend the night in her arms.

As the carriage halted at her residence, he opened the door and jumped out of it eagerly. Like so many times before, he entered by the back door and shuffled quietly up the stairs, shaking off his coat on the way. No need to waste time on disrobing in her room. He trailed the familiar corridor, smiling to himself and anticipating her surprised look when she saw him.

He finally reached the door and paused with a hand on the knob. He heard strange noises coming from inside the room. Strange grunting sounds and whimpers... A struggle?

He pushed the door open with a crash and rushed in. What he saw made his blood run cold. He stopped dead in the middle of the room, his heart freezing over at the sight before him. His Annie, his beautiful, innocent Annie, was crouching on all fours, naked, on top of a man and sucking on his cock. She was doing it skillfully and whimpering in arousal. The man was twisting her hair in his hands and urging her on. She hadn't stopped right away when he entered. Instead, as she saw him, she slowly withdrew the cock from her mouth. Too slowly, as if for show. As if enjoying every last taste of the man she was servicing and wanting Robert to see. Then she sat up, licked her lips, and looked at him defiantly.

"I told you not to come tonight," she said with all her dignity. She sat there with her golden blond hair tumbling down her shoulders in a tangled mess, her cheeks rosy, her blue eyes bright, her mouth swollen. A woman recently and thoroughly fucked.

"Yes," he sneered, "that's the problem, isn't it?" With every word, he felt his heart covering more and more with ice and his soul filling with disgust for the woman he had thought himself in love with only moments ago. He expected to be angry, to want to rage and howl at the moon, to throw things like a madman, but somehow, he couldn't be bothered to scrounge up enough emotion to care.

"You can't refuse to marry me now." She threw her hair off her forehead, thrusting her full breasts to their full advantage. "You'll only bring scandal onto your family."

"As opposed to marrying a whore?" Robert scoffed.

"Oh, I won't be a whore." She stood from the bed in all her naked glory. Her hips swayed and her breasts bobbed. "I will be a duchess."

"Really? Is that what you think?" He looked at her and realized that everything that had happened between them had been an act. She had never been this confident and defiant, with hatred clearly present in her eyes. She was truly ugly at this moment.

"You are bound by honor to marry me. You bedded me. You announced our engagement. And only a lady can cry off the engagement."

"You think I care about that? More than I care about that," he indicated in disgust with his chin to the bed, "that weasel in your bed?"

At that moment, the *weasel* finally sat up and made himself known. Robert almost choked on his surprise. It was his cousin, Eric, the one who had introduced Annie to him.

"Surprised, cuz?" Eric asked from the bed.

"I guess I shouldn't be," Robert spat. He knew Eric had been infatuated with Annie when Robert started courting her. Still, he had been under the impression that she didn't return the feelings. Now that he thought about it, he realized he didn't know Annie at all. "But if what you wanted was to be with her, then you've got her." Robert turned to leave, bile rising in his throat.

"What, no threat of a duel? You will not defend her *honor*?"

Eric sneered the last word.

Robert huffed a bitter laugh. "Honor?" He looked over at his naked former lover, trying to understand what had prompted him to want to spend the rest of his life with her in the first place. "She has no honor."

Robert made a few steps toward the door before throwing over his shoulder, "Besides, she is not worth your life."

"You'll marry me, Clydesdale!" Annie hissed behind him as he shut the door.

A few minutes later, Robert was back at the club. He sauntered toward the private room Gabriel had rented for their party. The smoke had cleared a little, so he could see several men were out cold on the floor. Gabriel was playing Vingt-Un with the whores. That was a sight for the ages. Robert almost chuckled.

He walked further into the room and took a seat beside his friend. Gabriel was silent as Robert poured himself a drink and took a sip. He was still silent when Robert lit a cigar. He dealt him in and raised a brow.

Robert looked at his hand and cleared his throat. "You were right," he said, pushing the chips in the middle of the table. "Women are good for just one thing. And that isn't marriage."

Gabriel didn't press any further. He didn't gloat either. He simply turned his gaze toward his own hand of cards. "I'm sorry, brother," was all he said.

Loved the book? Sign-up for my newsletter to get a bonus novelette:
https://sendfox.com/sadiebosque
Unsubscribe anytime. No spam, just books.

Also by Sadie Bosque

Necessary Arrangements Series

Prequel Novella
To Fall for a Duke by Christmas
Main Series
A Deal with the Earl
An Agreement with the Soldier
A Bargain with the Rake
An Offer from the Marquess
An Affair with the Viscount
A Wager with the Gentleman

The Shadows Series
Return of the Wicked Earl
Secrets of the Wicked Viscount
Curse of the Wicked Scoundrel
Ravishing His Wicked Lady
Taming His Wicked Duchess
More coming soon…

Made in the USA
Las Vegas, NV
26 July 2023